Slowly her eyes adjusted. What she saw made her heart pound so loudly she could hear it. "Jesus," she whispered. She kept blinking and staring. There it was — standing right there bigger than life. She was gasping. The golden statue! The Winged Dancer! No doubt about it; it looked just like the pictures she'd seen.

The statue was partially draped in black cloth, the head and center part of the body covered, but Randy could see outstretched arms and part of a feather cape. It was entirely gold.

She whistled through her teeth. It's actually here and I found it, she thought, knowing how delighted Marinda would be. She ran inside to tell the others.

As soon as Randy got into the kitchen she knew something was wrong. Before she had the chance to have another thought, someone grabbed her arms. Two women held her and pushed her toward the front of the house . . .

# S·L·I·C·K

## CAMARIN GRAE

The Naiad Press, Inc.
1990

Copyright © 1990 by Camarin Grae

Printed in the United States of America
First Edition

Edited by Ann Klauda
Cover design by Pat Tong and Bonnie Liss
   (Phoenix Graphics)
Typeset by Sandi Stancil


**Library of Congress Cataloging-in-Publication Data**

Grae, Camarin.
   Slick / by Camarin Grae.
      p.      cm.
   ISBN 0-941483-74-6
   I. Title
PS3557.R125S58   1990
813'.54--dc20                                              90-6098
                                                              CIP

## Books by Camarin Grae

*Winged Dancer*
*Paz*
*Soul Snatcher*
*The Secret in the Bird*
*Edgewise*
*Slick*

# Chapter 1

Marce Flasch slid her Trans Am into a parking place between a pickup truck and a station wagon. She walked briskly around to the front of the museum, past the two ten-foot totem poles, to the entrance. The other women were in the lobby.

Marce greeted the group — Elizabeth, Sue, and Carla, all members of the host committee, Meredith, a Chicago filmmaker, and Amagyne, from Colorado, a representative from the planning committee. Marce greeted Amagyne especially warmly.

Elizabeth introduced Mr. Hefferman, the museum

curator. He led the women through the main corridor, past small display rooms, to an area sectioned off with curtains. "This is where the Winged Dancer will be displayed," he said, pulling back the cloth. A wooden ramp led up to a two-foot-high platform in front of a large, plate glass window. "Setup is scheduled for tomorrow."

Marce stood back a few feet from the others, her eyes fixed on Amagyne. In profile she looks partly Asian, Marce thought, wondering if her skin would feel as soft as it looked.

"I haven't been here in years." Sue's voice echoed through the halls. "Last time was with this Mexican woman who used to come here all the time. She knew every painting and every pot. Her favorite stuff was Brazilian but she liked the Mexican things too. She was a real art lover. I like it but I can't say I'm that crazy about museums. Her name was Elena."

Carla seemed to be half-listening to Sue's banter. Meredith was playing her camera between the art work, Hefferman, and the women.

"When did you get in?" Marce asked Amagyne.

"Last night."

"You going to hang around awhile this time?"

"A few days," Amagyne said.

"Always on the move, huh? Well, while you're here, maybe we could —"

"Look at that!" Sue's voice cut the quiet like an outboard motor. "A couple of dykes," she said more softly.

Marce looked at the painting of two women gazing at each other. "Could be," she said.

Hefferman led the women to a back stairway and down to the basement level. "This floor contains the washroom, snack bar, administrative offices, and the shipping and storage area." He took them along the corridor to an unmarked door, unlocked it and ushered them in. "All arrivals and departures come through here for inventory. In the room on the right, we store works waiting for restoration and others which we rotate in and out of display. On the left is our supply room and straight ahead is the receiving and shipping section."

"Big," Sue said.

Hefferman unlocked the door to the storage room and beckoned the women to enter. There were shelves and racks full of paintings, and boxes containing sundry *objets d'art*. Next they went to the room directly across the hall.

Hefferman opened the door which had not been locked. "We store supplies in here, as you can see," he said.

It was a very large, L-shaped room, full of plywood and two-by-fours, plasterboard, several mannequins, numerous boxes, tools, paint cans, light fixtures. Marce walked inside, Sue at her heels. When they rounded the corner of the L, they saw more boards and cans of paint and a pile of drop cloths.

Hefferman next took the women to the shipping and receiving section. A small portion of the area was set off as an office. "You can sit here, ladies," Hefferman said, looking at his watch. "The chief security guard, Felix Sampson, should be here any minute. While you wait for the statue to arrive, he'll explain our security procedures. You can be assured that the Winged Dancer will be in good hands during its stay with us. Ah, there's Felix."

A stocky uniformed man approached the group and nodded as Hefferman introduced him. "They're all yours, Felix," Hefferman said.

Carla looked at her watch. "It's due at eleven, right? I have to be in the Castro by noon for a job." She rested her slender chocolate-brown hands on her paint-spattered jeans.

"Doing the mauve and cobalt trim on one of the boys' houses?" Elizabeth asked.

"Peach, maroon and burgundy," Carla said, chuckling. "It's *très* gorgeous, dahling."

Marce watched a workman stacking boxes on the other

side of the room. Near him, in the corner, was a bright yellow forklift truck.

"There is a security guard on duty at all times," Felix began, "day shift, seven to three, evening, three to eleven, and night. The day guard makes his rounds, opens up, then oversees the general security of the building until three when the evening guard comes on. The evening guard handles closing which takes place at four-thirty. When everyone is gone, he checks the basement — the washrooms and snack bar, and the storage and receiving area, then the display areas and the offices on the main floor and second floor."

"What does the checking consist of?" Elizabeth asked. It had been her suggestion for some of the committee members to be present for the arrival of the statue. She'd told them she couldn't get over the feeling that the invaluable work was in jeopardy.

"Entering the rooms, visually surveying each area, checking the locks. In this section, for instance," Felix explained, "the guard enters the front door just like you did. He checks the supply room and the storage room, comes back here and checks the office and the padlock on the back door, then exits where he came in, securing the lock. In the washrooms, we check each stall."

A bell sounded. "That must be a shipment," Felix said, standing.

The women rose also. They watched a museum workman go to the small side door and look through its tiny window.

"The driver's showing Tony the shipping order," Felix explained. "You have to have a shipping order or that door doesn't get opened."

Tony undid the padlock, turned the metal pipe that was sunk into a metal plate on the cement floor, then raised the pipe to clear the floor. He pushed a button on the wall and the huge metal door rose. Outside a truck came into view; it was backed up against the receiving dock. Behind the truck, cars were parked along the street. Marce spotted her Trans Am.

The truck driver opened the back door of the truck and a large wooden crate could be seen within. "I didn't know it would be in a box," Sue said.

"Ah, there's Essie and — mm-m, my, who is *that?*" Carla's tongue tip touched her upper lip.

Two women had gotten out of the truck's cab and climbed the ladder onto the shipping dock. "Hi folks," one of them called.

"Everything go OK, Essie?" Elizabeth asked.

"Totally smooth," Essie said. She was as tall as a basketball player, with wide hips and a sweet cherubic face. "It was really neat watching them unload it from the ship. Hey, everybody, this is Marinda Sartoria."

Marinda was tall and statuesque, tawny skinned, with hair as black as Amagyne's although not quite as wavy. She looked the group over.

"Marinda, meet some of the others on the host committee," Essie said. "Elizabeth, Marce, Sue, and Carla. And this is Amagyne; she's from the planning committee. The one over there hiding behind the camera is Meredith. You'll get to know them all soon enough."

"So it's in a box," Sue said.

Tony drove the forklift out onto the platform.

"You seem very relaxed," Amagyne said to Marinda. "The voyage was a smooth one, I take it."

"It was. I got spoiled and slept very late most mornings." Marinda's deep voice had a distinct Spanish accent.

Tony and the truck driver untied the ropes securing the crate within the truck.

"No seasickness?" Marce inquired.

Marinda was staring at Amagyne.

"Earth to Marinda," Marce said.

"I'm sorry, you . . ." She turned her black eyes on Marce. There seemed an edge of annoyance in them.

"I asked if you got seasick." Marce's voice also had an edge.

"No, no, not at all. Your name was . . .?"

"Marce Flasch. So you'll be staying in the States the whole time the statue is here?"

"Yes, that's right." Marinda's eyes drifted to Amagyne again.

Amagyne was watching the workman lower the lift and slip the tongs under the nine-foot-high crate.

"The statue must weigh a ton," Sue said. "I wonder if that thing is strong enough to lift it."

Meredith filmed the movement of the forklift, then the tying of the crate with rope to the lift.

"Here she comes!" Sue said.

Laden with its cargo, the forklift truck backed up slowly along the platform. When it was fully within the receiving area, Tony drove forward and then to the left, transporting the huge crate to the wall next to the office. Slowly he eased the crate down onto the floor, then jumped from the lift and untied the ropes. Back in the driver's seat, he backed away, leaving the crate sitting solidly on the cement floor.

"He sure makes it look easy," Carla said.

"Is that where it will stay until tomorrow?" Elizabeth asked Felix.

"That's right. Tomorrow the setup crew will move it from here to the freight elevator and up to the main floor."

"And you're sure it's safe here?"

"Absolutely."

Marinda asked Felix numerous specific questions about the security procedures. He answered in great detail.

Elizabeth looked at the huge metal door which was now closed and padlocked again. "But what if someone broke through that door?" she asked.

"They'd have to have an armored tank," Felix replied. "Don't you worry about it, miss. The statue's safe and sound here."

"I thought we'd be able to see it," Sue said.

"Tomorrow," Elizabeth replied.

Accompanied by Felix, the women left the receiving area through the door they had entered. Marinda examined everything carefully. A few yards down the hall a bucket and mop sat on the floor next to a dull green door. Felix stopped, opened the door and put the bucket inside the closet. "I hate clutter," he said.

Marce walked outside with Marinda and Amagyne. "Anyone need a lift?" she asked, looking at Amagyne.

Sue was walking behind them. "I do."

"How about you, Amagyne?" Marce inquired.

"Thanks, but I'm going with Elizabeth and Marinda to the dock to get Marinda's luggage."

"Where're you parked?" Sue asked Marce.

"Will you be here tomorrow for the unveiling?" Marinda asked Marce pleasantly. "Perhaps we'll meet again then."

"Perhaps." Marce gave her a cold look, then walked away in the opposite direction.

# Chapter 2

Randy Van Fleet took her sandwich to Golden Gate Park. She had called Marce that morning and invited her to join her for a picnic, but Marce had said she was going to the Indian Museum for the arrival of the statue. "How about dinner?" Randy had asked.

"I'm going to Marin tonight," Marce had said.

Randy had felt that twisty jealous feeling again. She knew it was foolish to get attached to Marce. They did end up making plans to get together the following night.

Randy lay back in the grass feeling kind of blue. She kept thinking about Marce and she didn't want to. Then she started thinking about Jay which was even worse. A flashback came of that horrible moment five months ago. She had gotten home from work as usual at about five-twenty . . .

* * * * *

The moment Randy walked in the door she realized something was wrong. She checked the house. All of Jay's things were gone; there was a note on the bed. *Dear Randy: I feel like I'm in a big hole and I just have to get away for a while and sort things out. I know I should have given you some warning but you always said I'm impulsive and I guess you're right. I'll contact you soon. Jay.*

Randy couldn't believe it. She immediately went and checked the office Jay rented in the Sunset District. It had been completely stripped. The computer and typewriter were gone and all the office supplies, even the desk and chairs.

Randy racked her brain, trying to make sense of it. She knew that Jay had been somewhat emotionally distant lately, preoccupied and a bit edgy, but Randy had attributed that to the slump in her business and assumed it was temporary. Jay said she was sure she could get things moving again. She had come up with new ways to attract people to the tours, gimmicks like live trumpet performances in the van and free miniature American flags. "Business will boom again," she'd declared. Was the business worse off than Jay had let me know, Randy wondered, or was there another reason Jay had left? Was she dissatisfied with our relationship? Had she met someone else?

They had known each other for two years. Most of that time they'd lived together at Randy's house. Randy thought she knew Jay. She had trusted her. She'd even put up her house for collateral for the loan Jay had gotten from Marce Flasch to start the tour business.

9

"How could she do this?"

"Paucity of moral character," said Randy's friend, Jess Daniels.

Maybe so, Randy thought, remembering some of the stories Jay had told her about her life in Chicago before she moved to San Francisco. She used to manipulate and use people, she'd told Randy, but that was part of her past, she'd stated. She'd gotten therapy; she was a different person. Randy had believed her.

She was very much in love with Jay. Before they met, Randy had suffered through enough failed romances to have become a bit sour about love. Jay had changed all that. Randy found her warmth and high energy, her raunchy playfulness, and her loving affection completely irresistible. She thought herself very lucky to have this exciting woman in her life. What a charmer she was: an extrovert who seemed to know everybody in San Francisco despite being relatively new to the city. Some of her friends were a bit weird, in Randy's opinion, but they were definitely interesting. Whenever Jay was around, things were lively. Their sex life was definitely exciting. Jay had even gotten them into a *ménage à trois* once, something Randy would never have initiated.

Ten days after Jay's departure, Randy got a postcard from her, from Canada. She talked about the beautiful mountains and how she was beginning to feel a new sense of freedom. She said she hoped Randy was doing okay. She mentioned something about *re-thinking her career options.* As a P.S., she said, *Don't worry about that loan. I'll straighten things out with Marce.* That was all she said in the postcard. She didn't even send an address or phone number.

When the May loan payment didn't arrive, Marce phoned. Randy put her off, saying she'd be hearing from Jay soon. A few days after that, Randy got a rambling letter from Jay, again postmarked Canada. She apologized for leaving so abruptly, and talked about *going through so many changes. Maybe I'm just a loser,* she wrote. *For now you have to go on without me.* Randy felt deeply hurt and angry, and also like a fool for thinking she knew Jay, for loving and trusting her.

A week after that, Marce called again. "I had a sense that Ms. Jay Horne might be heavy on the build-up and light on the follow-through," she said after Randy told her the story. "The tour business could have been a success if she'd stuck with it. It's a shame she left you stuck with her debt."

Randy didn't respond.

"Luckily for you, we're not talking about a huge sum of money," Marce said casually.

"It's huge to me."

"Well, I assume you'll manage it," Marce replied. "I'll be watching my mail."

Randy knew Marce was very hard-assed about money matters. She could be a real pain in other ways too sometimes, but Randy liked her anyway. She found Marce's arrogance and sarcasm more amusing than annoying. She also thought Marce was physically attractive. She was a big woman. Formidable, Randy often thought. She had first met Marce a year ago when she and Jay went to Marce's real estate office on Market Street to get the loan. Marce had sat behind her big gray slate desk with Randy and Jay on leather chairs in front of her. Marce definitely had run the show.

Randy hadn't been worried about the loan. Jay had told her she'd operated two businesses in Chicago. She knew what she was doing. The tour agency seemed like a solid venture — showing the sights to Japanese tourists in a twelve-seater van. Jay had researched the project well. She also had a contact at a travel agency that catered exclusively to Japanese, a gay man named Toshi. He would send her a stream of customers. In addition, Jay had

11

assured Randy that if there were any problems with the loan payments, her parents would back her.

For the first month after Jay's departure, Randy had frequent fantasies about her return — the apologies and explanations, the anger and forgiveness. But the more time that went by, the more she began to think that maybe Jay really hadn't changed at all from those days in Chicago when she'd deceived her lovers and ripped people off, that maybe she *was* a loser. Then she began to wonder if Jay had ever really loved her. Had she been taken in by Jay's charm? Was Jay an irresponsible, manipulative bullshitter as she apparently used to be and as Jess said she still was? Damn Jay, Randy thought.

When more time passed with no further word, Randy finally called Jay's mother in Michigan and explained the situation. Mrs. Horne said she felt terrible but said she and her husband couldn't help, and how odd it was that Jay assumed they had any money to spare. She had no idea what Jay's address was in Canada, she told Randy.

The next time Marce called, she told Randy they needed to have a talk. "Let's do it over dinner," she said.

They met the following night at The Patio on Castro Street. Marce amused Randy with witty stories and light conversation, making no mention of Jay or the money during their meal. Randy couldn't deny the attraction she felt for Marce. She always had felt it, since their first meeting. After finishing her own dessert and the rest of Randy's, Marce leaned back in her chair. "Two payments are now due," she said. "Four hundred and fifty dollars."

The sudden change took Randy by surprise. "I don't have much more than that in my checking account," she said.

Marce didn't respond.

"Doesn't it seem a bit unfair," Randy said, "to hold me responsible for money that Jay owes you?"

"Randy, you *are* responsible," Marce responded, as if

12

talking to a child. She took some bills from her wallet and laid them on the table, enough for both their dinners. "Get the money to me, kiddo," she said. "It would be a shame to lose your house for a mere six thousand dollars."

Randy was aghast. "Lose my house? Come on, Marce, you go too far." Randy had bought the house five years ago with money inherited from an aunt. She loved every window, board, and creak of the place. "That's really bringing out the big guns, wouldn't you say?"

"Don't make me use them," Marce responded matter-of-factly. Then her face became softer and her tone changed. "The whole thing with Jay was a bad investment," she said gently. "You have to absorb the loss and move on, Randy. The quicker the better." She stood and gave Randy a warm smile. "Call me sometime if you need company."

Randy contacted everyone she knew who knew Jay to see if they had any idea where Jay was or how to get in touch with her. She showed a lawyer a copy of the contract she'd signed. The lawyer said the terms were clear: if Jay defaulted, Randy was responsible for the payments, and if Randy defaulted, her house could be taken. It had been a mistake to sign the contract, the lawyer told her. That Randy already knew.

She sent Marce a check for four hundred and fifty dollars. Afterwards she sat at her kitchen table poring over numbers — her expenses, her income, her minuscule savings. There was no way she could manage an extra two twenty-five a month on her research assistant's salary. She'd have to get an extra job, she concluded, feeling intense disgust toward Jay.

In mid-June, Marce called and asked Randy to go out with her. Randy was only slightly surprised. She agreed to go despite some apprehension about what she might be getting herself into, sure she should avoid anything that smacked of romance.

Marce picked her up and they went to a movie. During the film Randy was very aware of the closeness of Marce's body to her own. Occasionally their arms touched and Randy felt tingling sensations along her spine. The fact that she felt slightly intimidated by Marce added an extra edge of excitement, she realized.

Randy couldn't say she didn't want what happened to happen. After the movie they went to Marce's house "for a glass of wine." Not surprisingly, Marce turned out to be an aggressive lover. When she kissed Randy that first time, it was deep and hard and she did it like she had every right to and like Randy was wanting it and eager for it. Randy supposed she was. Her body certainly responded enthusiastically.

They started seeing each other regularly after that. Marce told Randy from the start that she had another girlfriend in Marin. Randy got the picture — no strings. This romance is destined to go nowhere just like all the rest, she'd thought. Nonetheless, she enjoyed her time with Marce, especially when she slept overnight with her sometimes, held in Marce's big powerful arms.

Jess thought Marce was dangerous. "You really can pick them," she told Randy. Jess tended to get protective of Randy sometimes. She had seen Randy through her breakup with Katherine three years earlier, which had almost done Randy in, and she was the one who'd listened to Randy's anger and pain about Jay. She thought Randy would end up hurt by Marce too. Randy told her she'd be careful, that she wouldn't let herself get too invested.

A few months after Randy and Marce started their romance, during a walk at Strawberry Hill in Golden Gate Park, Marce mentioned a conference that was going to take place in San Francisco. "It's called Other Ways," she said. "Marian Jordan got me involved in it. I'm on the host committee. You know Jordan, don't you?"

Randy curled her lip. "She's a friend of Jay's," she said.

They rarely mentioned Jay. Nor did they talk about the debt. Randy had made four payments at that point and another would be due in a week, the first of September. She had done what she could to cut down on her spending, including canceling her cable TV subscription. That hadn't been enough so she'd started working from time to time for Jess at her window washing business. She loathed the work but the pay was better than she could have gotten at any other part-time job.

"The conference is about alternative communities," Marce told her. "You know, little utopias where everyone goes around acting humanely." She chuckled. "I suppose that's laudable if you're into that kind of thing."

Randy had heard of experimental communities like Skinner's Walden II and Twin Oaks, but hadn't known there were any presently in existence. Marce told her there were. She said many of the people who lived in them would be coming to San Francisco for the conference in November.

"It reminds me of something I heard a few years back," Randy said, "about women suddenly packing up and going off to some place in Brazil and a lot of them never returning. Supposedly it was some kind of women's utopia."

"I've heard those rumors too," Marce said. "I don't believe them."

They walked to the top of Strawberry Hill and sat in what looked like an old amphitheater. Marce pulled Randy to her and kissed her. That was the end of that conversation.

That night, at Marce's house, Randy read some of the Other Ways literature. Over a thousand people had attended the previous year's conference in Denver, she learned. The communities varied in size from a dozen or so members to several hundred. Some had charters and bylaws, while others operated without much formal structure. Some were based on communist economics, others were capitalist, and some were in between. A number of them were religious, but most were not. All claimed to be non-sexist. Randy wondered if that was really true. Most of the communities had men and women, some just women, and some were made up entirely of lesbians.

The conference was to be held at the Embarcadero Convention Center. The participants would discuss such topics as how their communities were organized, their problems, who they allowed in. They were supposed to learn from each other and come up with new ideas to take back to their communities with them. Another purpose was to start new communities. The more she learned, the more interested Randy became.

"Maybe I'll join one," she told Marce. But she knew she never would. She would never leave San Francisco. Her city was far from a utopia, but she'd adjusted to living in a less than perfect society. Besides, she was sure that life in a collective would be restrictive, that she'd feel cramped by it.

She read about a gold statue called the Winged Dancer that was being shipped in for the conference from somewhere in South America. It would be displayed at the Indian Museum for a month, then placed in the main lobby at the convention center. The statue was the symbol of the conference, the literature said. Part of Marce's job was to make sure everything went smoothly with the shipping of the statue and setting it up.

Over the next few weeks, Marce became increasingly involved in Other Ways. Randy suspected she was more interested in one of the committee members — a woman named Amagyne — than in the work the committee was doing.

One evening Randy picked Marce up after one of the meetings, hoping to get a look at Amagyne, but Amagyne wasn't there. Marce introduced Randy to several people including a woman named Meredith Landor who was making a documentary film about Other Ways. Meredith lived in Chicago and had received a grant to make the film. She told Randy she'd been to all the Other Ways conferences and had visited some of the communities. Randy enjoyed the conversation with Meredith and suggested they get together sometime. They made plans to meet the following evening for a drink.

Marce was in one of her irritable moods that night and had little to say on the drive home. Randy made a quick stop at a corner grocery store on Twenty-first and picked up some coffee, which Marce was out of, and a yellow tulip for her. The tulip brought a smile.

When they got to Marce's house, they had some ice cream and talked a little about the conference. Then Marce said she was tired and that she'd give Randy a call the next day. Although Randy had expected to spend the night, she wasn't particularly disappointed by the brush-off since Marce was in one of her lousy moods.

The next evening Randy met Meredith at Wild Blue Yonder. She liked how at ease and comfortable with herself Meredith seemed. After having a drink, they decided to go for dinner together at a place Meredith knew about on Haight Street. Meredith had been to San Francisco before and seemed to know her way around.

Randy enjoyed the evening. Usually she didn't confide in people quickly or easily, but for some reason with Meredith it had felt very comfortable. She ended up telling her about Jay and about how unlucky she always seemed to be in love relationships.

"Loneliness is the worst pain," Meredith said, looking as if she were about to cry. Obviously Randy had touched a nerve. She was trying to think of something to say, but Meredith suddenly snapped out of it.

Before they parted, Meredith invited Randy to a party

that a friend of hers was having Saturday night. Randy wrote down the address and promised to be there. She thought about all the parties she'd gone to with Jay. They always had a great time. She'd had many great times with Jay.

* * * * *

Randy picked up the scraps of her sandwich and put them in her bag. Her eyes roamed the park. She and Jay had come for a picnic at this same spot once, she recalled. Jay had done a joke-athon, telling joke after joke, each one raunchier than the one before. Randy had rolled in the grass laughing. As much as she despised Jay, she found she still got nostalgic about her at times.

She watched the ducks in the pond preening and flapping their wings and thought about how simple animals' lives were. No egos, no complicated romances, no betrayals. She picked up her blanket and lunch bag. It was time to go back to the lab and assay some more rat enzymes.

# Chapter 3

Marce took the steep hills on Divisadero Street with minimal use of her brakes. Sue had both hands on the dashboard.

"That Marinda's some number, isn't she?" Sue said. "Yum. She could put her boots under my bed anytime. Heh-heh-heh. I don't know, there's something about Latinas. I had a Cuban girlfriend once only she was . . . I don't now, confused, you know, about her identity. Last I heard, she was pregnant. Oh well. Wow, this is like a roller coaster. I love it."

Marce was barely aware that anyone was in the car with her.

"Amagyne's not bad either. I love her eyes and those high cheekbones. What nationality is she, anyway?"

"Your place is on Stanyan, right?"

"Yeah, just south of the park. She's into some weird religion, you know. It's not Christian or Jewish or Buddhist or Pagan Goddess or anything you ever heard of. She sort of fascinates me. Does she have a girlfriend in Colorado, do you know?"

"She's not your type, Susie."

Sue laughed. "Oh, well, aim high, I always say."

Marce took Haight to Stanyan and turned left.

"It's a few blocks up, on Grattan. I really appreciate the ride, Marce. I get so sick of buses. Someday I'm going to get a car. Of course, it'll be a bitch to park."

Marce turned left onto Grattan.

"It's in the middle of the block," Sue said. "Oh, there's the U-Haul." A sixteen-foot U-Haul truck was parked in the driveway, half-way into the garage. "It's a big one, isn't it? Barb ought to be able to fit all her stuff in that all right. This is the place, Marce, you can stop here."

Marce stopped in front of the two-story frame building with lavender, gray, and blue trim.

"My roommate's moving out tomorrow. Going to Canada. That's what the U-Haul's for. I have a new roommate moving in next week. Barb's lover, Jay, lives there now — in Canada, someplace near Banff. It's in the Canadian Rockies. Maybe I'll go visit them someday." Sue was fumbling for the door handle. "I love to go to new places. I'm really into traveling."

Marce's eyes had narrowed to slits. "Stay a minute."

"Sure." Sue sat back, looking quizzically at Marce. "You want to come in? Barb and Jay are probably there. I think you'd like them. Barb is a pain sometimes, kind of temperamental, you might say, but I know I'm going to

20

miss her. I used to always tell her I wish she'd move to Alaska, but now that she's really going away, I feel kind of sad."

"How did she meet a Canadian?"

"Oh, Jay's not Canadian. She used to live here, in San Francisco. I don't know where they met. They were going together for a while. Well, sort of. Actually, Jay had another girlfriend at the time. She was living with her. So she had to sneak to meet Barb. She ended up splitting for Canada and not telling her girlfriend where she was or anything. She's been in town a few days but she stays in the apartment because I guess her old girlfriend is a real bitch and would make a lot of trouble if she knew Jay was in town. Jay's such a nut. She puts on this stupid pair of sunglasses upside down, you know, and says, *I'm traveling impetigo.* You know, incognito."

Sue looked at Marce for a reaction. Marce was not smiling.

"Anyway, after Jay went to Canada she kept in touch with Barb. Barb visited her there once. And now she's moving there. Jay's got a business there, something to do with chauffeuring people around in the mountains. She owns this twelve-seater van. I guess she's doing okay. You ought to meet her, she's a trip. She cracks me up."

"She sounds like a real trip."

"You okay? You look upset or something. Are you okay?"

Marce nodded.

"A regular wheeler-dealer, too, Jay is. She got this woman, Gerry, to help with the rental cost on the U-Haul. Gerry needed a truck or van or something to help her move. She was moving from this crummy place she had on Valencia to an apartment on Cole. It's supposed to be a much nicer place. She needed a truck and Jay said she'd rent the U-Haul a day early and Gerry could use it and chip in something for it. I'm sure Jay made out like a bandit on the deal. So Barb and Jay went and got the truck real early this morning. I know they were trying to be quiet but they woke me up anyway. I assume Gerry's all finished moving since the truck is here. Jay said she'd help Gerry with the moving but she had to remain *impetigo,* you know, inco —"

"Right, incognito."

"Right. So would you like to come in for a few minutes? Have a beer or something?"

Marce considered it. "No," she said. "I'm enjoying our conversation. I think I'd rather just stay here and talk a little longer."

Sue smiled broadly. "Well, great. Yeah, I'm enjoying it too. For some reason I thought you never were particularly crazy about me."

"I'm crazy about you, Susie. You always have so much to say."

"Yeah, I know, I'm a real talker. Some people seem to get annoyed by it."

"Really?"

"My mother's the same way." Sue sighed. "I'm going there tonight, to my mom's. Every Tuesday night. Like clockwork. 'Someday you'll be bringing a husband with you on Tuesdays,' she always says. Little does she know."

Marce nodded.

"Barb's going to the Mission District to say goodbye to some friends there today and to eat at the Athena Cafe and then she's going to Baybrick tonight. For the strip show. I've never been."

"Never on Tuesdays," Marce said.

"Right, they always go on Tuesdays, strip night, and I have to go to my mom's."

"So Barb and Jay and some other people are going out tonight to be decadent and you —"

"Not Jay. She's staying home alone. All afternoon and all evening. She's pissed about it, that Barb's going out with friends all day and night even though she can't. Barb says to Jay, 'You'll survive.' She says she wants to say goodbye to the Athena Cafe and then to Clementina's — that's what they call Baybrick for some reason — she wants to go even though Jay can't go because of being afraid to risk being seen."

"Her impetigo."

Sue laughed. "She pouts about it, about Barb deserting her. She can be a real baby sometimes."

"Hm-m."

"She says to Barb, *You really shouldn't stay out late, you know. We have to leave early in the morning.* What a laugh. There's no way they'll leave before noon. They have to be in Banff by Saturday because early Sunday morning they're off on this camping trip with some friends of Jay's. Barb's sister's coming over tomorrow morning to say goodbye. She's not coming until ten."

"I see."

"I have to work tomorrow, so I guess I'll say my goodbyes this afternoon before I go to my mom's. I thought I'd get to see that statue today. By the time I do get to see it everyone will have seen it already. I get a kick out of being the first to do things. Oh, well."

"So it goes. I'm going to leave now, Sue."

"Oh, gotta go, huh?"

"Right."

"I enjoyed talking to you."

"It was mutual, Sue. I'll be seeing you."

"Yeah, see you at the next meeting. At Elizabeth's, right?" Sue found the handle and opened the door. "Thanks a lot for the ride, Marce. Be cool."

Marce had soared halfway down the block before Sue reached the door of her building. Music was coming from the apartment. Sue found the others in the back — Barb, Jay, and a woman Sue had met only once, Carolyn, who Sue didn't especially like. "Greetings, sports fans," Sue said.

23

"Hi, brat. So, did you see it?" Barb was stretched out on the sofa, her legs resting on a cardboard box. She was thin with blonde hair and a gaunt face.

"Shit outta luck."

"You're kidding. What happened?"

"It was in a big box. We couldn't see a thing, just the box."

"Bummer."

"I got to watch them unload it, though. That was kind of interesting. They use this little car with prongs like big fingers and that's how they moved the thing."

"A forklift."

"Yeah, right."

Jay yawned and took a hit of the joint Barb passed her. She held it out to Carolyn, but Carolyn declined.

"They're keeping it in the storage garage of the museum, down in the basement. You probably always wondered what it's like behind the scenes of a museum."

"It's on my mind constantly," Barb said.

"I'm going to treat you to a blow-by-blow account." Sue sat on one of the cardboard boxes in the middle of the room. "Say you're a security guard there. Here's what you do. Say it's after closing time and you're making your rounds. You go to each of the rooms, looking around . . ." Sue put her hand on her forehead like a sailor checking the horizon. ". . . checking for anything unusual."

"Like fornicating Peruvian goddesses." Barb made an obscene gesture.

Jay chuckled. Wearing a pair of white coveralls, she was slumped in the fat easy chair. Her heavy-lidded, gray eyes were topped by thick brown eyebrows. Carolyn sat on a footstool next to Barb, listening to Sue, saying nothing.

"In the basement where they ship things and store things like the Winged Dancer and other priceless treasures, you open the door with one of your hundreds of keys. You go into the corridor and check the junk room on the left.

24

That's the place with all the paint and big sheets of plasterboard and boxes of who-know's-what. That room isn't locked, I guess because there's no real treasures in there unless you think plywood and plasterboard are treasures. You check it out carefully. Who knows what could be lurking in there?"

"The abominable snowperson?" Barb said.

"It would melt. Then you go to the storage room across from the junk room, unlock it and check it out very carefully."

"Is that where they keep the Indians?" Jay said.

"Then you lock that door and go to the shipping and receiving room. You make sure the padlock on the big garage door is secure. After you check out the shipping section real carefully, you go out the door you came in, by the storage area, and you walk down the hall, to the janitor's closet. You look inside. Then you go to the johns. You look in each stall for stowaways."

"Then you sit down on a commode and do yourself." Barb made another obscene gesture.

"Are you still horny?" Jay asked.

"Again." She winked at Jay.

"Did you know I used to want to be a security guard?" Sue said. "It seemed kind of exciting, but actually I bet it's pretty boring."

"Speaking of boring," Barb said, "I think I'm going to miss you."

"Yeah, I know, like you miss your last yeast infection."

Jay roared.

# Chapter 4

3:35 p.m. September 29, 1992.

Wearing running shoes, navy blue slacks, an oversized gray jacket, a heavily made-up woman in a brown wig enters the San Francisco Indian Museum. Concealed beneath her jacket is a shoulder bag full of tools.

The woman strolls past exhibits to the rear stairway and down to the lower level. When the corridor is empty she puts on thin leather gloves and sneaks inside the janitor's closet.

* * * * *

At 4:40 p.m. the last museum worker leaves. "Good night, Glen," she says to the security guard.

"See you tomorrow, Lily," he says.

The guard locks the door and begins his rounds, starting with the basement level.

* * * * *

It is close to 4:30 p.m. when the woman hears the footsteps. She stands behind hanging coveralls, her back pressed against the back wall of the closet. The footsteps become louder. Clack, clack, with a slight echo. They stop. She stops breathing. The closet door opens. She holds her breath until finally the door closes again. Exhaling silently through clenched teeth, she listens to the footsteps. They go about a dozen paces. Keys jangle. After counting ten seconds she opens the closet door.

Creeping in her sneakers, she moves to the open doorway of the next room, looks in at the short wide hallway. The door on the left is open. She moves back into the corridor and stands flush against the wall, listening. A door closes. Footsteps. Keys. A door opens. In a flash she enters the inner hallway and then the room on the left, closing the door behind her. It's pitch dark. Taking a flashlight from her pocket, she guides herself to the back of the L-shaped room, past paint cans, a pile of two-by-fours, sheets of plasterboard. She waits until she hears the sound of the hallway door closing and being locked, then leaves the supply room for the shipping area. It's dimly lit but bright enough to see without her flashlight. She heads straight for the forklift. The keys are in the ignition. Next she goes to the metal garage door, removes a hacksaw from her bag, and begins sawing the padlock.

* * * * *

His rounds completed, the security guard goes to the office next to the souvenir counter, opens a small metal door and begins flipping switches. Throughout the museum, lights go out, in sequential order, until only the dim night lights remain.

\* \* \* \* \*

It takes her fifteen minutes to saw through the lock. When she's done, she takes off her gloves, flexes her fingers and rubs them together. Then she puts the gloves back on, removes the lock, turns the metal latch and pulls up the bolt. She goes to the hand crank at the side of the door and slowly begins to turn it. The heavy door lifts inch by inch. She takes it up a half a foot then lowers it again.

\* \* \* \* \*

Still in the office next to the souvenir counter, the security guard is sitting in the easy chair. His portable TV is on. He's eating a submarine sandwich, watching the evening news.

\* \* \* \* \*

She drives the forklift slowly toward the large crate on the other side of the room, the crate whose shipping label says it came from Marigua, South America.

# Chapter 5

Xavier draped a dampened cloth over her sculpture, then brought their drinks out onto the balcony. She took the padded redwood chair next to Marce. "I'm surprised you don't confront her while you have the chance."

"I considered it," Marce said. She sipped her Bloody Mary and looked out over the lights of Sausalito and the Bay.

"I think you should sue her."

"Not worth the trouble," Marce said. "She'd declare bankruptcy. Besides, I'm getting my money."

"Right. Speaking of Randy Van Fleet, don't you think she should know Jay's in town?"

"I imagine she'd like to know," Marce replied.

"But you're not going to tell her."

"Nope."

"I bet she'd like a crack at Jay."

"Randy shouldn't go anywhere near the woman."

"So you can keep Randy for yourself? Or are you being paternalistic?"

"Don't talk sexist to me."

Xavier grimaced. "Seriously. Randy does a favor for her lover and gets stuck with a six thousand dollar debt. Don't you think she ought to have a chance to confront the woman?"

"It's not my responsibility, Xav."

"That's debatable, Marce."

Marce did not reply.

"Don't you feel any guilt about taking her money? You said yourself she earns peanuts at that lab job and her mortgage payments aren't small."

Marce looked sharply at Xavier. "Hey, what is this?"

"I think you're being rotten to Randy."

"Why all the sympathy for Randy all of a sudden. Last week you called her the little tart."

"Separate issues."

Marce set her drink down on the redwood table with a thud. "This conversation is getting on my nerves."

"Good. You do have a conscience."

"If the payments get to be too much for her, I can be flexible," Marce said. "Maybe I'll let her be my valet or sex slave or something."

"You lowlife."

Marce looked at Xavier from the corners of her eyes. "I'm going to ravage you tonight," she said.

"How about some dinner first? Everything's ready, I just have to shove it in the microwave."

30

"Good, I'm starved," Marce said. She looked at her watch. "It's almost eight o'clock already. Feed me, girl."

* * * * *

The phone woke them early the next morning. "It's for you," Xavier said.

Marce pulled herself to a half sitting position on the king-sized waterbed and took the phone.

"Marce, this is Elizabeth. I'm calling everyone on the committee. There's been a terrible . . . last night the museum was broken into. The Winged Dancer was stolen."

Marce sat up fully, her eyes blinking. "You're kidding!"

"Marinda and I have been with the police for the last hour. It was stolen sometime last night. The security guard reported it at about midnight."

"How could it have happened? I can't believe it." Marce ran her fingers through her disheveled hair.

"We're getting together, everyone on the committee who can possibly make it. At my place. At ten-thirty this morning. Can you come?"

"Well, I'll have to cancel some appointments and . . . sure, yes, I'll be there."

* * * * *

An hour later Marce walked into a room full of nervous energy and the sound of many voices speaking simultaneously. Everyone was sitting except Marinda who paced anxiously.

"Okay," Elizabeth said. "Everyone's here who's coming. Sue can't make it and we weren't able to reach Jordan. Let me tell you exactly what I know."

"Do you have any coffee?" Marce asked. She sat on the sofa next to Amagyne. Marinda took a seat on Amagyne's other side. Marce shot her an angry glance.

"I'd like a cup myself," Carla said. Elizabeth went to get the pot.

"So, Marinda," Marce said, stretching her arm over the back of the sofa. "What do you think of America? A land of felons just like our reputation, eh?"

"The thief may not have been a North American," Marinda answered.

"Oh, the Iranians, maybe?"

Marinda looked at her disdainfully.

The doorbell rang. It was Jordan. A strikingly attractive woman in her early thirties, she was dressed in a tan pants suit and heels. "I got the message. Hi, everyone. Hi, Marinda, are you okay? I got here as quickly as I could. Was it really stolen?"

Marinda nodded. Amagyne laid a hand consolingly on Marinda's knee.

Elizabeth returned with the coffee and a tray of cups. "Help yourselves." She sat on an upright chair brought from the dining room. "All right, here's what we got from the police. At a little past midnight last night, the security guard made his routine check of the shipping and receiving area. Next to the office he saw two mannequins arranged in what he called *obscene positions.*"

Carla chuckled. "You mean they were doing it?"

"Two naked female mannequins," Elizabeth said, "one going down on the other."

Carla laughed heartily. "Ooh, ooh."

"Apparently in the dim light, the poor guy thought they were real people at first. He pointed his gun at them and said something."

"Stop or I'll come," Carla said, guffawing.

"So then he realized they were mannequins. He thought one of the shipping guys was being funny. Then he discovered that the padlock on the garage door had been sawed off. He phoned the police immediately. While he was waiting for them to come, he checked the locked storage room, the room where they keep a lot of art works. Nothing seemed disturbed. He was still looking around in the receiving area when the police arrived and it was at that moment that he realized there was no big crate where Glen — that's the evening shift guard — had told him it was. Over by the wall, you know, where he saw them put it. The mannequins were there instead. The guard — his name is Murphy — he and the cops searched the whole museum but they found nothing. Nothing else was missing. There was no sign of forced entry anywhere. The police are figuring the burglar had a key."

"An employee?" Jordan asked.

"They're questioning everybody now. All the security guards and the people who work in shipping. They're going to question everyone who works at the museum."

"How could anyone get it out of there? That thing is huge. That box was about ten feet high," Essie said.

"Nine feet, three inches," Elizabeth said. "They probably got it out the same way it was brought in. They put it in a truck. They moved it with the forklift."

"Didn't anybody see anything?" Carla asked. "Outside, I mean. Didn't anyone see a truck or anything?"

"It's being checked," Elizabeth said. "The police are questioning people who live or work nearby. Directly behind the museum there are some businesses. A printing press, I think, and a place that makes machine parts. None of them work night shifts, but the police are checking."

"What's this stuff about the burglar not being a North American?" Marce asked Marinda.

Marinda looked at everyone but Marce as she replied. "One of the reasons I came myself on this trip, to accompany the Dancer, was because two years ago someone attempted to steal the statue from its place in the village square. It happened in the middle of the night. It was just by chance that a policeman was in the area. The would-be thieves had a truck with a crane. The policeman gave chase but the thieves got away. One of them was a woman and I'm fairly sure I know who she was."

"Oh?" Marce said. "A friend of yours?"

Marinda ignored her. "After that, the statue was secured to its base, underneath, by steel bars and locks."

"You think it was the same people?" Elizabeth asked.

"I think it's very possible." Marinda was leaning forward as she spoke, her leg flush against Amagyne's. "The woman's name is Andrea Herrara. She is the sister of a convicted murderer — a real swine, that man. He caused a great deal of trouble for some friends of mine when he once tried to get the statue. He's in prison now, but his sister —"

"Now you think she's trying to get it." Essie seemed excited by the intrigue.

"Do you know the history of the Winged Dancer?" Marinda asked.

"I don't," Meredith said. "I'd like to hear." She had her video camera set up on a tripod and was taping the conversation.

"So would I," Carla seconded.

"I know the story as we tell it, among my people," Amagyne said. "The Dancer had been missing for years and only recently was found, by some heroic women in your country, Marinda. I would very much like to hear you speak of it."

Marce spoke to Elizabeth. "Is there any more information you have to give us on the burglary?"

Elizabeth set down her coffee cup. "Just that the detective — his name is Ben Turillo — said that he'll be in touch with all of you. I gave him all your names. Marinda, did I leave anything out?"

"They mentioned using lie detector tests on the security guards," Marinda said.

"Did you tell the cops your theory about that guy's sister?" Jordan asked Marinda.

"Yes. They're checking to see if she left Marigua, if she's here in the States. I will do some checking on her myself. I know she was still in Postero at the time I left Marigua. She could have come here since, or she could have hired others to steal the statue."

"That thing must be worth a fortune," Essie said.

"The statue's true value is not material," Amagyne said.

"Well, I know *Other Ways* was sure eager to have it at the conference," Carla said. "They say it stands for justice and peace and love and all those kinds of good things. You were going to tell us abut its history, Marinda."

Marinda pushed strands of black hair back from her angular face. "The statue itself is breathtakingly beautiful," she began. "A dancer with its arms spread and the head back, wearing a huge cape of feathers. The entire statue is gold, brilliant gold. When you look at it, it seems to be moving, flying almost." Marinda's face was glowing. "You get a strong sense of vitality from it. But also of a calmness, strength, nobility, joy. It's a magnificent piece — visually, aesthetically. And yet the Dancer's main importance, as Amagyne has suggested, is a symbol. To me it represents the best that human beings are capable of." Marinda's hands were clutched at her chest; her eyes had a faraway look.

"Who actually made it?" Meredith asked. "Some native Indians, wasn't it?"

"The Bowesos," Marinda replied. She relaxed and leaned back on the sofa. "They were a very unusual people, very special. For centuries they lived in Marigua, long before the Europeans came. They were gentle, truly enlightened human beings. Their way of life was loving and sharing and completely classless and non-sexist. Amazingly unusual then as it is now." She looked from face to face. "They no longer exist."

"We do have *Other Ways*," Elizabeth said.

35

Marinda nodded. "Yes, and as you know, *Other Ways* has adopted the Winged Dancer as their symbol."

"Like on the logo," Jordan said.

"Mm-hm."

"Who owns it?" Essie asked.

"No one really owns it," Marinda said. "The people of Marigua. It's considered one of our national treasures."

Jordan shook her head. "Son of a bitch. A fucking national treasure — gone."

"We will get it back," Marinda said.

"The police think the thief will melt it down for the gold," Elizabeth said.

Marinda's jaw was set. "We cannot let that happen." Her black eyes were narrowed and fierce. "If Andrea Herrara is the thief as I suspect, I do not think she'll risk trying to ship the statue out of this country. I'm sure she has no appreciation of it as a work of art or as a symbol. She wants money to try to free her brother from prison. She will try to sell it or melt it down for the gold, I suspect, or perhaps try to extort money for its return."

"How much is it worth?" Jordan asked.

"It is priceless," Marinda replied crisply.

"Yeah, I know, but I mean —"

"The statue's insured for nine hundred and fifty thousand dollars," Elizabeth said.

"Jesus," Jordan whistled through her teeth.

"Is it solid gold?" Carla asked.

"Gold with some copper," said Marinda. "Mostly gold."

"I wonder what it would be worth melted down," Carla said.

"Two to three hundred thousand American dollars," Marinda said, "according to the Mariguan appraisals."

"I'd like to hear more about the Bowesos," Meredith said. She had the video camera aimed at Marinda.

Marinda looked off into the distance. "To the Bowesos the Dancer represented their success at evading a very aggressive tribe called the Omilato, and the success of their settlement and culture. Centuries ago, the Bowesos fled from the vicious Omilato, migrating until they found a safe place to settle. Their settlement had mountains on one side and the Suga River on the other. It was impenetrable. From the river, they got the gold, from the gold they made the statue. Then every year, on the anniversary of the beginning of their new settlement, they would bring the statue out of the cave where they kept it, and for a month they'd display it and celebrate."

Amagyne was nodding as Marinda spoke. "What you say is true," she said, "but there is more to the Bowesos than you may know."

Marinda looked at her with what seemed a mix of curiosity and desire. "Oh? What is that?"

"Kwo-am — who many call God — has revealed to us that she came centuries past to the people you speak of, the Bowesos. They were Kwo-amians, that Indian people, inspired by Kwo-am."

"I never heard this," Marinda said.

"It is so. It was revealed to us through our Sage. The Winged Dancer is a very important spiritual symbol for the Kwo-amians. We have many depictions of it at our community."

"At Circle Edge?" Carla said.

"Yes."

"What's Circle Edge?" Jordan asked.

"Amagyne's home," Meredith said. "It's one of the utopias. I'll be visiting it one of these days. It'll be in the film."

"And your people believe the Bowesos shared your . . ." Marinda was gesturing, searching for the word.

"They were Kwo-amians, yes. The Omilato could not destroy them, but the more insidious forces of Zetka did so in the centuries that followed. Yet the statue survived as an inspiration and symbol."

37

"I never heard any of this," Marinda said.

"It is so," said Amagyne.

"Who's Zetka?" Carla asked.

"He is Kwo-am's counterpart," Amagyne said. "The dark side, the force of pain, destruction, and death."

"What a bunch of crap," Marce said. "Mystical mumbo-jumbo."

Amagyne hummed quietly. She had turned her head and was looking at Marce, her dark eyes softly seeking Marce's. Marce was drawn to the eyes but then quickly turned away.

"Is this the first time the statue was ever outside of Marigua?" Carla asked.

Marinda nodded sadly. "It makes me sick to think I was one of the people in favor of loaning the Dancer to the museum here and allowing it to be part of the *Other Ways* Conference."

"You had no way of knowing," Elizabeth said comfortingly.

"There's a group in Arcedia — that's the region where I live — called the *Arcedia Landmark Council*. I am a member. We had many arguments about allowing the statue to come here. Unfortunately, I and my supporters prevailed. This wasn't the first request we've had. Dozens of museums have tried to borrow it. Because of my involvement with *Other Ways,* I supported this request. I'm sure it would not have been difficult for Andrea Herrara to discover where it was being sent."

"We'll get it back," Carla said. "We'll all work together. Between us and the police, we'll do it."

Marinda nodded. "We must."

"If your compatriot took it," Marce said, "and her motives are what you say, I wouldn't be surprised if it's being melted down right now." She watched Marinda as she spoke.

"How could that be done?" Jordan asked. "I mean, how do they do that? How do you melt a statue?"

"At a foundry," Meredith said. "Hey, you know, we should find out if there are any foundries around here and contact them."

"The insurance company is already doing that," Marinda said. "I called them as soon as I heard about the theft. They're getting in touch with every facility within hundreds of miles of here that would be capable of extracting the gold. The man I talked to, Frank Redman, seemed to know just what to do. He said he'd call me as soon as he hears anything."

"So they're working on it. That's great." Jordan put her hands behind her head. "I'm hungry. It sounds like everything that can be done is being done. Anyone interested in an early lunch?"

"But what if the thief manages to get the statue out of the area, or even out of the country?" Carla said.

Marinda got to her feet and began pacing again. "That is a possibility. If that happens, then we have lost."

"What about road blocks? What about notifying the different ports?" Carla now as on her feet also.

"Too late for that," Marce said. "If they left the area last night, they'd be miles away from here by now."

"It could have been anybody," Essie said, "anybody who knew the statue was going to be here. I guess a lot of people knew."

"The police are checking everyone," Elizabeth said. "I think we should do some checking ourselves." She looked at Marinda. "The woman you suspect may be the thief and she may not."

"It could have been somebody who was opposed to the conference," Jordan said. "Some rightist religious group maybe, or some homophobics."

"The biggest danger as I see it," Carla said, "is if the thieves have already gotten the statue someplace where it's being melted down. Once that happens, then that's it, right? The insurance will be paid off, but the statue will be

39

history. Then finding out who took it becomes much less important. All that would be left for us after that would be revenge."

Nobody spoke for a while.

"It doesn't seem too hopeful," Jordan said at last. "But, who knows, maybe we'll get lucky. I'm going to get something to eat, then get back to work before I get fired. Is there anything I can do to help?" She was looking from Elizabeth to Marinda.

"Not that I can think of," Elizabeth said. "Not now, at least. I suggest we wait until the police get back to me. I'm supposed to hear from Detective Turillo by sometime this evening. I'll keep you posted."

# Chapter 6

Randy went to Marce's office on Wednesday night to pick her up for their dinner date. Marce put her feet up on her desk, leaned back, and told Randy the Winged Dancer had been stolen. "Someone copped it right out of the museum shipping room," she said.

Randy thought this was pretty upsetting news but Marce seemed completely calm, even a little pleased. She had a strange little smile on her face as she told Randy what had happened and how distressed the Mariguan woman, Marinda, was. Randy got the strong impression that Marce really disliked the Mariguan for some reason.

Although Randy wanted to hear more about the theft, Marce seemed bored with the topic after a few minutes. She turned away from Randy and started looking through the papers on her desk. Randy had been thinking lately that she really should stop seeing Marce, but then Marce would make her laugh or give her one of her rare compliments, and make love with her, and then Randy would like her again.

They stopped at a chicken place and brought the food to Randy's house. They were still eating when Marce got a phone call by way of call-forwarding. Randy figured it was Amagyne even before Marce said her name because of the flirty, seductive way Marce talked to her. Randy tried to think about other things while Marce was on the phone, trying not to let the call bother her. When Marce hung up, she told Randy the call was about the stolen statue, that Amagyne and Elizabeth were calling everybody on the committee to fill them in. "The cops have been busy," she said.

Randy waited. Knowing Marce, she might say more or she might not. Showing curiosity would probably make her not tell, so Randy didn't say anything.

"Yep, great detective work. They found out that one of the security guards uses marijuana."

Randy tossed a chicken bone into the bag. "So what does that have to do with anything?"

"They're probably going to fire him."

"That figures."

"That's all they found from the lie detector tests. They tested all the guards and all the people who work in shipping and, I guess, everyone who has access to museum keys. No one seems involved in the theft."

"It doesn't sound like that statue was very well protected," Randy said, shoving a french fry into her mouth, "given how valuable it's supposed to be."

"That's good hindsight, Randy." Marce wiped her

fingers with a wet paper towel. "They lifted fingerprints," she said, "from the garage door, from the padlock. Other places too, the forklift, doorways. Nothing so far. Oh, yeah, and Marimba got a call from the insurance company."

"Who? I thought her name was Marinda."

"Whatever."

"What's your problem with her?" Randy asked. "What do you have against the women?"

"Hey, she's a gem." Marce chuckled in the nasty way she did sometimes. "No foundries were asked to melt down any statues. The insurance people have put up a nice reward for any information. To keep the foundries honest, I'd guess."

"How many people knew where the statue was being stored?" Randy asked. "I think the cops should check that out. Whoever took it obviously knew exactly where it was. Maybe it's somebody on your committee." Randy chuckled the same way Marce often did. She can bring out the worst in me, she thought. "Someone who wants to make her own private utopia," she added.

"Randy, you cynic." Marce was smiling as if she was proud of Randy. "Maybe so," she said. "A couple of the committee girls are going to the museum Friday to check things out, see if they can figure out how it was done."

"Look for clues, huh?" Randy let Marce's use of the word *girls* pass, knowing she'd said it just to irritate her. "Is Meredith going?"

"No, just Amagyne and the South American wonder. I think I might go myself. Want to come along?"

"I have to work," Randy said.

"They're going at noon. I'll pick you up if you want to go."

The invitation pleased Randy. "All right. Sure," she said. "I have to be back by one-thirty at the latest, though."

"No problem."

43

Marce's pleasantness made Randy feel warmly toward her. She moved closer to her and started rubbing her neck. Marce pulled Randy to her and gave her a kiss that tingled Randy's knee caps and gave her wet underpants.

They made love right there in the living room, on the sofa and on the floor. Randy felt like a shooting star. Afterwards she was lying on the floor with her eyes closed, just gliding through the universe, her legs entwined with Marce's when Marce suddenly said she had to get going. Marce frequently did things like that. Just when Randy was feeling close and cozy and intimate, she'd up and leave. Randy knew she didn't quite have Marce figured out yet, but she had some ideas.

After Marce left, Randy cleaned up the mess from the chicken and went out in the back yard to look at the sky and the Bay. She and Jay used to sit out here often. Jay would regale Randy with stories of her adventures in Chicago and get her laughing until her belly ached. I really loved that woman, Randy thought sadly. Maybe I still do, as stupid as that seemed. She decided she loved the parts of Jay that were funny and warm and loving, and despised the irresponsible, inconsiderate, piece-of-shit parts of her.

\* \* \* \* \*

At 11:45 a.m. on Friday Marce picked Randy up outside the hospital where she worked and they drove to the museum.

She drives like a maniac, Randy thought. No, that wasn't true, she conceded. She drove very fast and would weave in and out of traffic but she was always in control. Every second.

Randy was eager to finally meet Amagyne. "What's she like?" she asked Marce, not really expecting a serious answer.

"Otherworldly," Marce said.

This didn't sound like Marce at all. "What do you mean?" Randy asked as they zoomed up Van Ness Street.

"You'll see," Marce said. "She's very unusual."

Maybe she was, but when Randy was introduced she hardly paid any attention to Amagyne at all. Marinda Sartoria totally mesmerized her. Talk about unusual. Never had Randy had a reaction like that to anyone. She felt completely blown away. She stammered and was shy and felt funny in her stomach and absolutely overwhelmed by the woman. Marinda was magnificent. Randy couldn't explain her reaction. She felt awed . . . overtaken. She just wanted to look at Marinda, follow her around, listen to the beautiful sounds that came out of her beautiful throat. Everything Marinda said seemed profound. And she was gorgeous. She was probably only about an inch or two taller than Randy, but seemed like a giant. She had luxuriant black hair and black, black eyes. Her skin was a rich brown and she talked with a wonderfully charming Spanish accent.

Marce told Randy later that she'd acted like a star struck groupie. Randy replied that she wasn't interested in Marce's opinion.

Marinda didn't pay much attention to Randy, or to Marce either for that matter. She was very interested in Amagyne, though. Marce mostly talked to Amagyne, ignoring Marinda. Amagyne was nice to everyone. She was very nice to Randy. By the end of the hour, Randy felt as if she'd known Amagyne for years. Marinda was cordial to Randy, but obviously Randy's reaction to her was unilateral. That didn't surprise Randy and it didn't hurt her either. She wouldn't have expected anything else. After all, Marinda was a goddess and Randy just a mortal. She knew that was a ridiculous analogy, but it was how she felt.

The five women sat at a table in the museum cafeteria. Elizabeth broke the news that she'd received an extortion note from the thief. To Randy, the whole situation was becoming increasingly interesting, capturing her attention even though she spent much of the time staring at Marinda.

Elizabeth had gotten the letter that morning. Amagyne had a copy of it with her and she read it aloud. *I've changed my mind. I was going to turn the dancer into liquid and see how many ingots it would make. I've decided to let her/him/it survive if you do your part. Your part: The statue belongs in San Francisco, along the Bay somewhere. It will be the West Coast's statue of Liberty, or is it libertine? I want a mere $400,000 for my magnanimity. My finger is on your pulse — if Turillo or his friends learn of my contact with you, the left foot goes. A differently-abled dancer. Or maybe I'll just chisel the whole thing to pieces. You have two weeks to come up with the money. Contact me by an ad to Slick in the SF Chronicle personals. Sincerely yours, Slick.*

"It puzzles me," Amagyne said when she finished reading. "It just doesn't make sense, unless Marinda is right."

"It's worth a lot more than four hundred thou'," Marce said.

"Right about what?" Randy asked. She wanted to look at Marinda while she spoke but couldn't seem to maintain eye contact with her.

"That the letter may not be from the thief," Marinda said, only she said *frome* the thief. Randy loved the accent. "Anyone who knew about the theft could have written that note to Elizabeth."

"That's true," Marce said. Randy wondered if it was hard for Marce to give Marinda credit for this. "We need proof," Marce added.

"Are you going to tell the police?" Randy asked.

"No!" Marinda looked at Randy as she spoke. Randy was afraid she blushed. She hadn't done that since adolescence.

"We've already decided that's too risky," Amagyne said.

46

Randy was beginning to notice Amagyne a little more. She had a smooth, soothing way of talking that Randy liked.

Marce nodded. "Good decision." She smiled warmly at Amagyne.

"I think the first thing we should do is demand that this *Slick* person give us verification that she or he has the statue," Marinda said.

"*She,*" Marce said.

"What makes you so sure it's a woman?" Randy asked.

"She's not only a woman, she's a dyke," Marce said. "*Differently-abled,* come on."

"That's no proof," Randy said disdainfully. "I can say, *Jesus Loves You,* and I'm no Christian."

"Good point," said Marinda. That made Randy feel good.

"No, I do not think it was the thief who wrote that note," Amagyne said in her velvety voice.

Marinda was watching her closely. "There's something you aren't telling us, isn't there?" She was looking at Amagyne very tenderly. Randy wished she'd look at her that way.

"You are very perceptive. Yes, there is something. It's difficult to say because I don't want to believe it's true." Amagyne looked off into space. "I had a premonition," she said. "A feeling. An itch at first but then it grew as the time came closer for the statue to arrive in this country."

"What was it?" Randy asked.

"That the statue would disappear."

"Hm-mm." Randy was thinking that Amagyne was kind of weird. A mystical kind of weird.

"Say more, please," Marinda said.

If Marinda said that to me that way, Randy thought, I would tell her anything she wanted to hear.

"There are those of us who have experienced a truth that most do not know," Amagyne said.

Oh boy, Randy thought.

"We call this truth *Kwo-am* and it means something like what others call God. We who know this truth are still few, and, sadly, we are divided among ourselves. A new prophet is claimed by a faction who were of us but have moved away. They are mostly here, in California, some in San Francisco. It was revealed to them, the claim from Kwo-am, that the Winged Dancer is coming home to them. I fear they may believe it was theirs to take."

"What a crock," Marce said contemptuously. Randy shot her an angry glare.

"But it's strange that they would offer to return it in exchange for money," Amagyne said.

"You're really convinced they took it?" Randy asked.

"I wish it were not so."

"Maybe they wrote the note to get you off their track," Randy suggested. "Or maybe they want the money as a bonus and still plan to keep the statue."

"I have similar thoughts," Marinda said. "Except I still suspect it is Andrea Herrara who is behind it."

Randy was about to ask who Andrea Herrara was, but Marce spoke first. "So you think the thieves are some religious nuts," she said, looking at Amagyne, "and this one thinks it's some murderer's sister." She gestured toward Marinda without looking at her. "Carla thinks the thieves are racist homophobics, did you know that? And how about you, Randy? Do you have a favorite enemy? Who do you think did it?"

I shrugged.

"Elizabeth thinks it might have been an anti-gay group too," Marinda said.

"Jordan thinks it was Felix," Amagyne added.

"Who's Felix?" Randy asked.

Marce looked at her watch. "Hey, if we're going to get out of here by one-fifteen we better find him and take a look around."

The women left the cafeteria and went to the office

48

down the hall where they had Felix the guard paged. They were following him to the shipping area when Amagyne stopped in front of a green door in the corridor. "Just a second," she said, opening the door. It was a janitor's closet. Amagyne looked as if she were drifting away somewhere. Randy wondered if she was having a vision.

"What is it?" Marinda asked. She put her hand on Amagyne's shoulder. Randy got a vicarious thrill. Felix was waiting a few yards down the hall near another door.

"When you do your rounds," Amagyne said to Felix, "you come down this hall, open that door where you are now, the door to the shipping and storage area, and you leave it open while you check the area. Is that correct?"

Felix nodded. "That's right, ma'am."

"Do you check this closet as well?" Amagyne asked.

Felix seemed a little uneasy. "Of course," he said.

"Is there a light in here?" Amagyne felt along the wall near the door jamb.

"No," Felix said.

"It's quite dark back there where the coveralls are. I wonder . . ."

"I suppose it's possible," Felix said. His voice was scratchy.

"Ah," Randy said. "You mean the thief might have hidden in this closet and then when the security guard opened the shipping room door, she snuck in."

"Could that be?" Amagyne asked Felix.

Felix had an odd look on his face and didn't say anything.

"Sure," Marce said. "I bet that's exactly what happened. She hid in here until she heard the guard go by and open the shipping room door, then she slipped into the storage area and hid somewhere until the guard left."

"What exactly is the routine?" Marinda asked Felix. "Will you show us?"

Felix's jaw was working nervously as he unlocked the

49

door. He went into the room on the left, turned on the light, checked the room very quickly, then closed the door. Then he went to the door directly across the hall from the first room. This one was locked. He unlocked it, turned on the light, and checked it out. While he was checking the second room, Marinda slipped into the first room and closed the door behind her. Felix then went to the shipping area, a big open space with a small office and a big garage door.

Marinda came out of the room she'd entered. "And you do not recheck this room, I assume," she said.

Felix shook his head.

"That is how it was done," Marinda declared.

"I think you're right," Amagyne seconded. "The thief entered the museum during its open hours, through the front door like any visitor. She hid in the closet until the guard came by and then she did just what Marinda did. She would not need a key at all."

"Good detective work," Randy said heartily. "The thief would have had to know the system here though, where all the rooms are, how the guards do their inspections."

"A lot of people knew," Marce said. "I knew. Amagyne knew. Elizabeth. Carla and Essie and Sue knew. You knew too, didn't you, Marinda?"

"I didn't know," Randy said playfully.

"Everybody knew except Randy. Who else?" Marce asked Felix. "Have you told the details of your security procedures to half the city?"

"I was told to fill you people in on them," he said defensively. "I was supposed to tell you anything you wanted to know about how we'd protect your damned statue."

"I bet your wife knows, too," Marce said, "and your brother and cousins and the other guards' cousins and nieces and nephews and . . ."

"Marce, lay off," Randy said angrily.

Felix glared at Marce. "Do you want to look around?"

50

he said sharply. "The police already went over the place with a fine-tooth comb, and so did I. You're not going to find anything."

"Where are the mannequins?" Marce asked.

Felix blushed. It made Randy laugh inside. Marce had told her about what the thief had done with the mannequins. The thief has a sense of humor, Randy thought. She was reminded of Jay.

"Is that something your Kwo-amians would do?" Marce asked Amagyne. "The mannequin scene?"

Amagyne shrugged.

"Or your Andrea?" Marce said to Marinda.

"As a diversion," Marinda said. "It is possible."

"The mannequins are in the junk room," Felix interjected. "Do you want to see them?"

"Are they still . . . ?" Marce let the tip of her tongue protrude ever so slightly. She's such an evil tease, Randy thought. Felix turned his back to Marce.

The group went into the junk room and looked at the mannequins which were standing primly side by side against the wall.

"They look worn out," Marce said.

There was nothing else of interest in the junk room so they went to take a look at the shipping area. The garage door had a new padlock on it.

"This wasn't here before," Marinda said. She was pointing to a thin wire on the garage door.

"It's part of the new electronic security system," Felix said. "It was just installed this morning."

"Great," Marce said. "Close the barn door after the cows are in the next county."

"We've never before been burglarized," Felix protested. "You people come into the museum and the next thing you know, there's a major theft."

"Ah, yes, blame the victims," Marce said.

Randy wondered what it was about Marce that she

51

thought she liked. "I have to get going," she said to Marce. "It's almost one-fifteen."

"Here." Marce handed Randy her keys. "Take my car. I'm not ready to leave. Call and tell me where you parked it. I'll pick it up later."

Randy figured she wasn't about to leave Amagyne and Marinda alone if she could help it. Maybe I'll accidentally smash a few of her fenders, she thought.

"I'll take a cab back to my office," Marce said.

"We can give you a ride, Marce," Amagyne said.

Amagyne's nice to everybody, Randy thought. Randy gave Marinda a warm handshake and told her she hoped to see her again. She felt all melty when she touched Marinda's hand. She shook Amagyne's hand too but the feeling wasn't the same at all, even though Amagyne seemed quite a likable person despite being weird about the Kwo-am business.

My life is getting very interesting again, Randy thought as she drove toward the medical center. Who needs Jay, anyway?

# Chapter 7

Randy was near the stereo talking with Meredith when Marce arrived. Marce was not a classically beautiful woman by any means but sometimes Randy found her immensely handsome. This was one of those times. Marce hadn't mentioned that she was invited to Meredith's friend's party. She seemed a little surprised to see Randy, and Randy realized she herself hadn't mentioned the party either. After greeting Randy with a big kiss on the lips, Marce moved on to greet other people.

Besides Meredith and Marce, the only people Randy knew at the party were Amagyne and Marinda Sartoria.

Even though she only spent about three minutes talking one-to-one with Marinda, that turned out to be the high point of the evening. Randy was wearing her rope and bead bracelet and it caught Marinda's eye. Marinda seemed intrigued by it, as if it had some special meaning. She looked at Randy in a very unusual way after noticing the bracelet, gave her a penetrating look, as if she knew something Randy didn't know, or as if they shared some important secret. Randy felt goosebumpy the whole time Marinda was talking with her. Then she had a fantasy — that Marinda took her by the wrist and led her out of the party and away with her somewhere.

Late in the party when many of the people had left, a group formed into a little circle and talked about the Winged Dancer.

"At least we know it hasn't been melted," Sue said. "That's a relief. It gives us some hope, at least."

"We don't know that," Marinda responded.

Randy stared at Marinda's fiery eyes. She seems to exude so much energy, Randy thought. She's so dynamic. She wondered if other people noticed this.

"But the note . . ."

"We don't even know that the note came from the thief," Elizabeth said.

"Oh-hh, I never thought of that." Sue cocked her head, nodding thoughtfully.

"Anybody could have written it," Elizabeth said.

"Anybody who knew the Dancer was stolen," a woman named Lou Bonnig said. Lou was from Wisconsin where she was part of a collective farming group, Randy learned. She had come to San Francisco when she heard about the burglary.

"Why not demand that they prove they have the statue?" Carla said. "*Dear Slick,* we can write, *No proof, no loot.*"

"How many people knew about the burglary?" Carla asked.

"Many," Marce said. "By the day after, word probably had gotten around half the women's community. I agree that our next step should be a message to Slick requiring some verification that she's the crook."

"I already did it," Elizabeth said.

"Did what? Wrote the ad?" Carla glared at Elizabeth through her wire-rim glasses.

"Yes, and called it in. Marinda and I did it. We were going to check with everyone but we didn't think there was time."

"Hey, I thought we were a committee," Carla said. "We're supposed to make decisions like that collectively."

"There wasn't time," Marinda said matter-of-factly.

There was no apology or defensiveness in Marinda's voice, Randy noticed. It didn't surprise her. She was sure Marinda wasn't particularly susceptible to peer pressure.

"I disagree," Carla said. "We have to coordinate this. We can't all be going off in our own directions."

"Yeah," Essie said, "we could end up working against each other." Essie was sitting on a low chair and her legs seemed to stretch halfway across the room.

"I agree . . . in a way," Elizabeth said. "But time is a factor, too. The stakes are high here and if we wait to get everybody's input on everything —"

"We need a system," Carla cut in, "a method of handling the decision-making."

"Maybe we should just let Elizabeth be in charge," Sue said. "She's the chairperson."

"No," Carla said. "The host committee is non-hierarchical. Elizabeth volunteered to be the coordinator but that doesn't mean it's an autocratic operation."

Randy was watching Marinda, trying to figure out whether she was amused or irritated by the conversation.

"Look," Essie said, "there are six of us on the host committee. That's not so many. I think we should all be involved in all the decisions. It wouldn't be that hard to do. Elizabeth has an answering machine."

"I can be reached at my office, too," Elizabeth offered.

"All right, I say we use Elizabeth as the hub and we all call in frequently to see what's happening."

"What about Marinda?" Carla asked.

"She's not on the committee," Marce said sharply.

"Yes, but she's as involved as any of us."

"Of course she is," Elizabeth said, looking at Marinda. "More so." Marinda said nothing. "You definitely have to be part of the decision-making," Elizabeth said to her.

"How about Meredith?" Sue asked.

Meredith was sitting on the floor leaning against the wall. "Hey," she said, "I'm just here to document the action. If you want to consult me I'm full of opinions, but I don't need a vote."

"All right," Elizabeth said. "I think if Amagyne or Lou or anyone else from the planning committee is in town during this, that they should be consulted."

"That's fine," Lou said.

"Where's Amagyne?" Sue asked.

"Last I saw her she was in the bedroom with a group of other women," Carla responded.

"Oh?"

"Talking about goddesses or something."

"She should be here now since we seem to be having a meeting," Elizabeth said.

"Should I leave?" said Karen, an Asian woman. Karen was not connected with Other Ways.

"No," Elizabeth said. She looked at Randy and then back at Karen. "I don't think that's necessary."

Carla spoke to Karen. "Listen, nothing against you, Karen, or you, uh . . ."

"Randy," Randy said.

"Yeah, Randy. Nothing against you two but I think the fewer people who know about all this, the better. I think we should keep it within the organization."

Karen stood up. Randy was feeling pissed and a little hurt.

"Hold on," Elizabeth said. Karen sat again. "I've already told Karen everything that's been happening from day one."

Karen shrugged. "I'm not a spy," she said.

"And I suppose you told her," Carla said to Marce, referring to Randy.

"As a matter of fact . . ." Marce was smiling sardonically.

"All right, let them stay," Carla said, "but how about we try to keep things a little quieter from now on."

"You don't trust our sisters?" Sue said.

Carla glared at her. "Sisters-schmisters," she said. "I've been fucked over by more *sisters* than I'd care to tell you."

"You two understand that this has to be quiet," Elizabeth said to Randy and Karen. "The thing I'm most worried about right now is the police finding out about the note."

"I never talk to cops if I can help it," Karen said.

Randy put her finger on her lips. "I understand."

"Can we get back to the ad?" Essie asked. "I'd like to hear what Elizabeth wrote."

Everyone looked at Elizabeth. Randy was also watching Marinda out of the corner of her eye.

"*Dear Slick,*" Elizabeth said. "*Anyone can write a letter. Please provide proof that you have the Dancer.* I signed it *Elizabeth.*"

"To the point," Randy said.

"And you put it in the *Chronicle?*"

"It'll be in Monday."

The talk continued, about the Winged Dancer and then about the conference. Randy only partially listened; mostly she was concentrating on Marinda. After a while the conversation shifted to other topics and soon after that Marinda and Amagyne left the party. Randy felt a real loss, but suspected Marce felt even worse. "You have the hots for the Colorado Amazon," she whispered in Marce's ear. "You're so obvious," she added.

"Stifle yourself, Van Fleet."

Randy chuckled. She had admitted to Marce that she had a crush on Marinda. Not that Marce didn't already know it, she thought, aware that her feelings for Marinda were quite apparent.

"I don't know about your taste, Randy," Marce said.

"Well, I've got a crush on you, too," Randy retorted, laughing.

"You're a study in contrasts."

"I think the two of you have a lot in common."

"Yeah, we both have two feet."

Randy laughed.

"But I have ten toes," Marce added.

"Have you seen Marinda's toes?" Randy asked. "I'm jealous."

"You'd just love to lick her feet, wouldn't you?"

"Mm-mm," Randy said, as if considering it.

"Eat your heart out," Marce spat.

"Yeah, I know. I'm hot for Marinda and you and Marinda are hot for Amagyne and Amagyne's hot for some goddess."

"Did you hear Amagyne talking about that tonight?" Marce asked.

"A little. I left after a few minutes. I'm not into that kind of thing."

"A little religion never hurt anyone."

"Like hell."

"You've got a point," Marce said. She and Randy were sitting in straight-back chairs in the dining room near the window. There was a nice breeze. "This one might be different though."

"What do you mean?" Randy asked.

"This Kwo-amity that she's into. I think I might want to learn more about it."

"Marce, you shock me. Are you that hung up on her?"

"I've got an open mind."

Randy smiled. "You look very sexy tonight," she said.

"I know."

"Do you come here often?"

"I haven't come here yet."

"I could change that," Randy said, batting her eyelashes.

"What would Marinda say?"

"Ah, good, you're jealous."

Marce laughed her big hearty laugh. There was music playing and a few people were dancing. "Want to dance?" she asked Randy.

They danced for a while and then Randy ended up smoking a joint off in a corner with Meredith. Meredith told Randy about her girlfriend, Allison, in Chicago. She thought Randy and Allison would like each other because Allison was a biologist and they'd probably have a lot in common.

"So do you think we'll ever get the Winged Dancer back?" Randy asked at one point.

"I'm having evil thoughts about that," Meredith said.

"Oh-h, say more."

"This is just between me and you."

"OK."

"You know that Marinda?"

Randy nodded, trying to keep her face blank.

"I get bad vibes about her. I think there's more going on with her than she's saying."

Marinda sure made strong impressions on people, Randy thought. "What do you mean?"

59

"I just get this feeling about her. I think she's real devious. I have no evidence to support this, but I think she may be the one who took the statue."

Randy looked at her as if she were crazy.

"I'm just telling you about the vibes I get."

"You're crazy."

"She thinks that statue is a lot more than metal. I think the woman is into power and the statue represents power to her. I think she volunteered to come here with the statue so she could rip it off."

"That's ridiculous!"

"And her story about Andrea what's-her-name is just a cover. Whoever took the statue must have been very familiar with the security set up at the museum. Marinda asked the security guard a thousand questions. The impression I get about Marinda is that she'd just love to have that statue for her very own."

"If I were you, Meredith, I wouldn't tell anyone else about these *vibes* you're having," Randy said. "I think it sucks."

"You're right. I've had too much to drink tonight."

"I'd advise you to keep your theory to yourself."

"Good advice. The cops suspect her too."

"Oh, come on, what are you talking about?"

"They interrogated her this morning."

"Interrogated her? You mean they asked her questions about the statue and all. That doesn't mean they suspect her. They're asking everybody questions."

"They got real pushy with Marinda. They didn't do that to me or anyone else, as far as I know, except Elizabeth."

"Elizabeth? You mean they suspect her too?"

"They found fingerprints on the garage door. Elizabeth's and Marinda's."

"At the museum? Are you sure about this?"

"Elizabeth told me."

"Well, the fingerprints don't mean anything. Marinda

60

and Elizabeth were there that day. So they touched the garage door, so what?"

"They didn't find anybody else's fingerprints there, on the door. None of the other women's. Elizabeth can prove she couldn't have been at the museum Tuesday night. She was home with her lover, Jane. But Marinda's alibi is a joke. Supposedly on Tuesday night, she was out with a friend of a friend. The woman she was supposedly with works for some oil company here in San Francisco. Marinda was with her, she says, on the night in question, but interestingly enough, the woman is now in Kuwait, on business, so Marinda says. Her one witness is out of the country. Interesting, don't you think?"

"And the cops suspect her?"

"They're trying to locate this woman in Kuwait. That should be a challenge."

"Does Elizabeth think Marinda's involved?"

"That she stole the statue, you mean? I doubt it. She didn't say so."

"But you really think so."

"I think it's an interesting theory."

"I think it's a bullshit theory."

Meredith laughed. "You're probably right. I have another theory."

Randy rolled her eyes.

"Your friend, Marce."

Randy shook her head. "I don't want to hear this."

"In her case, I'd say money would be the motive. Supposedly she was with a friend in Marin that night, but she still might have had time to pull off the theft."

"I'm done with this conversation," Randy said, thinking that she really liked Meredith, but she sure had a weird streak to her.

"It crossed my mind that it might have been you," Meredith said. Her eyes were dancing mischievously.

"Very funny."

"Motive . . ."

"Shut up."

"Money to pay off Jay's debt."

Randy snickered. "That would sure be overkill, wouldn't it? I'd have three hundred ninety-some thousand left over."

"You'd find something to do with it."

Randy was starting to feel annoyed. "Where were *you* Tuesday night?" she shot.

Meredith laughed. "I sure wouldn't mind being rich. Did you know there's not a lot of money in documentary filmmaking? At least I haven't found it."

"So how did you do it? Did you hide in the janitor's closet?"

"Hell, no. I've been out of the closet for years."

"You belong in a mental ward," Randy said.

Meredith suddenly looked very upset. There was a total shift. She looked like she was about to cry.

"What is it?" Randy asked. Meredith looked so vulnerable that Randy felt like taking her into her arms.

Meredith shook her head. "Just stuff from the past," she said.

Randy wondered if she'd say more. She didn't want to push her but thought maybe Meredith needed to talk about it.

"Someone I was close to was in a psychiatric hospital once. It was pretty gruesome."

Randy nodded. "I bet."

Meredith relit the weed. "Anyway, for my final theory. You ready?"

"Hit it."

"The Ku Klux Klan."

"No. Phyllis Schlafly," Randy said.

"Jerry Falwell."

"You name-droppers." It was Carla. She joined Randy and Meredith and they had a few more tokes off Meredith's joint. They were laughing and being silly when Marce came and accused them of all being stoned out of their minds.

Then Marce told a couple of stories that had them all rolling on the floor. Marce could be a lot of fun to be with sometimes, Randy thought, and was about to suggest Marce spend the night with her, but then Marce went off and danced with some baby butch and Randy didn't see her again that night.

# Chapter 8

They were making slow sweet love. Lips and tongues, breasts, arms, calves, soft legs and smooth vaginas. Touching, stroking, kissing, caressing. Gentle probing finger-tentacles, entering, arousing.

Never before had it felt like this.

Sexual, sensual, mental, spiritual, physical, encompassing. Skin that was fragrant moss; bodily juices exotic erotic nectar. Floating, diving, soaring, drifting. Colors, the rainbow. Warmth and wetness and softness. Flight. The purity and sweetness of it left Marinda dazed.

Slowly, eyes blinking, she came back. Yes, the room was

real. A living room, Amagyne's friend's apartment. Marinda was on the futon. She sat up. I must have fallen asleep afterwards, she thought. Her head was still fuzzy. Or had it all been a dream? Where was Amagyne? Marinda couldn't remember getting undressed or dressed again. She remembered the stroking, the humming, the soft words.

Amagyne came into the room carrying a tray of wine.

"You're not like anyone I've ever met," Marinda said, accepting the glass.

Amagyne sat next to her on the futon, looking silently into her eyes. "I sense deep pain in you, Marinda. A sharp dagger piercing your core."

Marinda frowned. "Is it so obvious?" She shook her head. "I should be over it by now, or at least be able to hide it better."

"Hidden pain grows," Amagyne said softly. "You need to speak of it."

Marinda stared at the oil painting on the wall, a black woman in a cape of fuschia, mountains in the background.

"It needs healing," Amagyne said.

Marinda looked at her. "Being with you is helping."

Amagyne stroked her arm. "That is not what will do it," she replied. "I think you hold too much inside. I would not be surprised if you have not spoken to anyone about how tortured you are."

"I've told people," Marinda said. "Several friends at home know. It's an old story, and a common one at that. A triangle. Two winners, one loser." She sipped her wine. "I'm the loser."

"I see." Amagyne folded her hands across her flat belly. "Would you tell me about it?"

Marinda sipped more wine. "Her name is Galia."

"A beautiful name."

Marinda's eyes were deeply sad. "I love her and she loves Salvador. She chose him. I was not able to keep her with me."

"That was a painful loss for you, but more than that, I think. It feels like powerlessness for you, a failure, perhaps?"

Marinda looked through the bay window and out at the hilly streets. "Many people love me," she said, "but when it comes to lovers . . ." She looked at Amagyne. "Yes, I am a failure."

Amagyne took her hand. "Tell me more about Galia."

Marinda again looked out the window. "A complex woman. Very determined and hard in some ways, but very soft too. And loving. She is a doctor at the Settlement. She and I were together for six months, her first time with a woman. It was a joyful half year for both of us, but for Galia there was always an inner turmoil. It never felt quite right to her and we would have long talks about it."

Marinda looked at Amagyne's hand, still entwined with her own. "Then she met Salvador. I made the mistake of introducing them. He's an engineer at the oil fields where I work. She says she loves me deeply, but it is not the sort of love she feels for Salvador. Salvador is the best man she has ever known, she says. I cannot dispute Salvador's virtues. He was my friend for many years. The last time I spoke to Galia she said she was very happy. That was a year ago."

"And Salvador?"

"I see him at work. It's difficult. Mostly I avoid him. We are no longer friends."

"So you lost both a lover and a friend."

"That's right. The story of my life," Marinda said. "Marinda, the unintentional matchmaker. The next time I fall in love I should keep her locked in a cabin, never introduce her to any of my friends."

"So you've had other losses."

"Yes." Marinda's eyes were very sad. "But it's Galia I can't get out of my mind."

"It eats away at you."

"Like a dozen foxes gnawing at my guts."

Amagyne stroked Marinda's forehead. "Inside you still have not accepted it," she said. The lines began to smooth out of Marinda's brow.

"I don't have many options," Marinda replied. "I can't seem to let go. You're the first woman I've felt drawn to since Galia left me. I've been with others. I go to the city — Postero — and I spend time with women I know there, some I even make love with, but it isn't really love we make."

"You're too closed to it still. That place in your heart is still filled with Galia."

"I seem to be finding room for you."

Amagyne stroked Marinda's brow. "A refuge," she said.

"Oh, no." Marinda's eyes flashed. "You're much more than that."

"A place to hide and warm yourself. I can tell. There's healing to be done first. Acceptance — that Galia and Salvador are together, and that this does not mean you have failed."

"You know, it's interesting. I've felt better since I came to the States." Marinda emptied her wine glass. "To tell the truth, for a long time I've been thinking of moving here, and the urge gets stronger and stronger."

"It's always tempting to run."

Marinda pulled away from Amagyne, looked at her angrily. "I suppose I should just stay there and be reminded every day, look at Salvador happily enjoying the woman who should have been mine."

"Still so raw," Amagyne said. "That bitterness is unhealthy for you. I even sense that it could lead you to things that would not in the end give you any comfort at all."

Marinda's muscles were tight.

"You're a very strong person," Amagyne said. "Full of power."

67

"I used to think so. I don't feel it anymore. I didn't. Since coming here, I'm starting to feel it again."

"It's part of you and can never be taken away," Amagyne said.

Marinda was silent, deep in thought. "You seem more powerful than any of us," she said at last, "though you are the gentlest woman I've ever known."

Amagyne nodded. "Mine is the power of kwo-ami," she said. "I think you sense this is a more solid kind of power. I think that may be what draws you to me."

"I don't know," Marinda said, shaking her head. Her eyes brightened. "You're beautiful. And very sexy."

Amagyne laughed. "Multi-determinism. You know, Marinda, as your anger and self-blaming fester and grow, your kwo-ami grows too, to counter it. You are in a great struggle now. Bitter about love, doubtful about yourself, yet another part of you is drawn to me, which is the part that wants to love and knows you can."

"We'll see," Marinda said. "I'll have to be careful who I introduce you to." Amagyne started to respond, but Marinda interrupted her. "Tell me about your religion," she said. "You've gotten me curious."

Amagyne closed her eyes. She was nodding. "Yes, I think you should hear." Her voice took on a chanting quality. "Kwo-ami is the force of love, of creativity, the movement to life, to caring for self and others, nurturance and growth."

"Mm-mm. And where does it come from?"

"It has always been. Swirling, flowing, everywhere, emanating from Kwo-am, the creator of all form. Kwo-ami intertwines with every living soul, at birth. We all are filled with it." A frown came to Amagyne's forehead. "But Kwo-am and her energy are not alone," she said sadly. "Kwo-am's counterpart, Zetka, pervades us as well. The two forces battle for control of our spirits."

68

"Hm-mm." Marinda stretched out her long legs.

"The battle is very strong in you."

"I suppose that's one way of putting it."

"I think you are ready to hear of this. I will talk some more with you, soon," Amagyne said. "First I will give you the *Words of Kwo-am* to read. But now I must leave. There are some people I must meet."

Amagyne rose. Marinda began to stand also.

"You may stay here as long as you wish," Amagyne said.

"It's a shame you have to go."

"Would you like the book?"

"I suppose." Marinda stretched her arms. "I should get going too."

Amagyne walked across the room and got a book from a drawer. She handed it to Marinda. "We'll talk soon," she said, giving Marinda a parting embrace.

\* \* \* \* \*

At a little stucco house in Bernal Heights, the others were awaiting Amagyne, a group of six former Kwo-amians who called themselves Kwo-amjamites. For them the new sage, Jamma, was the vehicle of truth.

"We welcome you, Amagyne."

Amagyne gave the sign of Kwo-am, a closed hand against the chest, and the others returned the salutation. "It has been a long time, Doralee, since we've seen each other. I have been hearing of you though, of you all."

"We've found some new ways."

"Yes."

"I want you to meet the others," Doralee said, and introduced Amagyne to Lorloge, Carolyn, Jenny, Flo, and Orwena. The women nodded and smiled at Amagyne.

"We've heard a lot about you," Orwena said. "You are

an important part of our history and I, personally, feel no animosity toward you or any of the pre-enlightenment Kwo-amians."

"We must all try to be understanding," Amagyne said, "accepting of others' ways."

"Of course."

"How can we help you?" Carolyn asked.

Amagyne looked from woman to woman. "I've come about the Winged Dancer."

There were frowns around the circle. "We heard what happened," Flo said.

"It is a great loss to all of us," Jenny said. "Our sage has told us the Dancer belongs amidst the enlightened."

"I know that," Amagyne said. "That is why I've come." She hesitated. "This is difficult for me."

The six Kwo-amjamites waited silently for Amagyne to continue.

"Those who took the statue surely were zetkap-driven though they might not know it."

"Surely," several voices said.

"Does Jamma speak of money in connection with the Dancer?" Amagyne winced as she spoke the words, clearly not enjoying this.

"Surely not," said Lorloge. "What are you getting at?"

"I'm very puzzled," Amagyne said. She looked at the others. "You feel no animosity. We are sisters at the core. Can you tell me anything?"

The women looked back and forth at each other, questioningly, seeming confused. They remained silent.

"I will not stay," Amagyne said. "I will say no more but I will leave my phone number and address here with you." She rose and placed the slip of paper near the telephone. "Tell the other Kwo-amjamites."

"The Dancer belongs to the enlightened," Jenny said.

"If you really think about it," Amagyne replied gently, "letting kwo-ami fully in, I think you will see the Dancer

70

belongs to no one. Her ancestral home is in Marigua, which is where she should remain. I think truly you know that."

Doralee walked her to the door.

# Chapter 9

Meredith filmed a closeup of Elizabeth holding up the pieces of board.

Sue arrived with her beagle, Gertie, who went from woman to woman smelling crotches while Sue talked about the guy on the roller skates who bumped into the kid with the ice cream cone and how Gertie got an unexpected dessert. "What are those?" Sue asked.

"Parts of the crate." Elizabeth laid them on the floor. "They arrived this afternoon, Express Mail."

"You mean the crate the statue was in?"

"No, the crate we're building to send your animal to Jersey City," Marce said.

"She's not an animal. Gertie, sit!"

Gertie went and sniffed somebody's running shoes.

"Yes, they're from the crate the statue was in," Elizabeth said. "Slick sent them."

"And you know for sure they really are from the crate? You can tell?" Sue sat on the floor next to Carla. Gertie sprawled across Sue's legs.

"No doubt about it," Marinda said.

"Do you still think it's that woman from Marigua?" Essie asked Marinda.

Marinda slipped off her maroon jacket and hung it on her chair. "The police found out that Andrea Herrara left Marigua a week ago. Supposedly she went somewhere in Mexico for a holiday. Yes, I still think she might be the one who did it."

"Can I see the note?" Marce asked.

Elizabeth handed Marce the sheet of paper. Marce read aloud, *"Time is ticking and my chisel hand is getting itchy. You have your proof: now I want my payoff. You have until October 16 to raise the money. I will contact you by October 15 with delivery instructions. Sincerely, Slick."*

"That's less than two weeks," Sue said.

Marce tossed the letter on the table. "I love the *sincerely* part." She put her feet up on the table next to the note. "So, shall we pass this on to the insurance company?"

"That's one of the things we have to discuss," Elizabeth said.

"Do you think they'd pay?" Sue asked.

"I think they'd rather pay four hundred thousand than nine hundred fifty," Marce said.

"Anybody in favor of letting the police know about Slick?" Essie asked.

"That would be too risky," Marinda said. "Our thief apparently realizes she could get more money by extortion than by extracting the gold, but if we frighten her with the police, she may choose to get what she can for the gold rather than risk getting caught."

"It reminds me of one of the Perry Mason shows," Sue said, "the one where this woman is being blackmailed and —"

"Later, Sue. We have a lot to talk about tonight." Elizabeth kicked off her shoes and Gertie immediately went for them.

"Well, I was just going to say that the leak turned out to be a clerk who worked at the police station," Sue said.

Elizabeth rescued her shoes and tucked them under her legs. "What about the idea of letting Redman know what's going on?"

"Who's Redman?" Sue asked.

"The insurance investigator," Carla said.

"What's to stop Slick from taking the money and the statue?" Meredith said. "I think we should find out who she is."

"Yeah, but how?" Sue spread her hands. "That's the question."

"By putting our heads together and figuring out everyone who could have learned about the statue from any of us," Essie said, "and then investigating them." She started to light a cigarette, but glanced at Elizabeth and put the pack away.

"Well I still don't think the thief has anything to do with anyone we told," Elizabeth said. "Thanks for not smoking, Ess. I bet the leak is one of the security guards."

"Could be," Marce said.

"I don't think so," said Marinda. "They know they'll be the first questioned when something like this happens."

"You really think it was someone in the women's community? I hate to believe that," Sue said.

"I had my lawn chair stolen at the Michigan festival," Elizabeth said. "I think one of us innocently told someone who told someone who decided to rip off the statue. You know how word spreads. I bet right now, between us, we could name two dozen people who knew about the Winged Dancer coming and the museum security routine, and who now knows about the cops, the note, everything. I told my friend, Karen, and I told Jane. Jane tells her sister everything. She probably told her therapist too."

"I told a few people," Carla said.

"I didn't tell anyone," Essie said.

"Oh?" Carla confronted her. "What about Lucie?"

"Oh, right. I did tell her."

"How about you, Sue?" Elizabeth said. "Did you tell anyone?"

"Me?"

Everyone looked at her.

"I know it has to be secret, about the note. I hardly told anyone about that."

"I see." Elizabeth's frown covered a grin.

"Nobody I don't trust completely."

"Who did you tell?" Elizabeth pressed.

"Besides my new roommate and my ex-roommate, no one else, except this friend of mine, Lana, but she never breaks her word."

"Your ex-roommate?" Marce said. "You mean Barbara? I thought she moved to Canada."

"Yeah, she did. We've been talking by phone. I might have mentioned what was going on to her."

"About the note from Slick?"

Sue looked at the floor. "I believe I did mention that."

"I've told people, too, and so did you, Elizabeth, and probably everyone else here. So don't pick on Sue," Carla said.

"I'm not picking on her. I'm just making a point."

Marce was looking at Sue. "So your ex-roommate called you so soon. Are you two that close?"

"Sure, we're pretty good friends."

"Hm-mm."

"What are you thinking, Marce?" Elizabeth asked.

"I just find it odd," Marce said. "Sue's ex-roommate's lover is someone I know. I just find it curious that they called Sue so soon after leaving."

"I didn't know you knew her," Sue said.

"I agree with Meredith about trying to trace the thief ourselves," Marinda said. "If we all work together, maybe it's possible. For one thing, we can check at the post office to see if the clerk remembers the person who mailed the boards."

Amagyne had been listening silently. "Let us remain open to all possibilities," she said. "The thief may be someone who learned about the statue through one of us, or she may be someone who already knew about the Winged Dancer from other sources. It may or may not be someone connected with the women's community. It may be Andrea Herrara, as Marinda suspects. It maybe a stranger, or it may be someone we know. I think we must remain open to every possibility."

"Really, Marce, why do you think it's so odd that Barbara called me?" Sue said.

"I'm remaining open to every possibility," Marce said.

"Is there any possibility the insurance company would refuse to pay?"

"They'd be fools if they did," Marce said.

"Redman told me that as a last resort, they do pay extortion money," Elizabeth said. "Of course, he'd want to bargain it down."

"So why don't we just offer Slick two hundred thousand then agree on three hundred and let the insurance company pay her off?" Carla leaned back on her easy chair and crossed her arms. "Then we can enjoy the statue."

"Because we might never seen the statue again if we did that," Meredith said. "The thief might take the money and keep the statue too."

"That could be true," Elizabeth said. "We'd be safer if we learned the thief's identity. If she knows we know who she is, then she wouldn't risk trying to keep the statue."

"Yeah, and I'm dying to find out who Slick is," Essie said. "The problem is she'll probably get wind of the fact that we're looking for her. We can't seem to keep anything secret."

"Good point. I say it's time to take the vow of silence." Elizabeth sat forward on her chair. "We should have done it long ago."

"You're assuming the thief's an outsider," Meredith said.

Everyone looked at her.

Meredith looked straight ahead. "Maybe she's one of us. Maybe the thief is somebody right in this room."

"Hey, come on!"

"Let's not get paranoid."

"Be serious."

"Just being open to all the possibilities," Meredith said.

"Well, if it's one of us, we're really fucked," Essie said.

"Come on, let's not start this," Elizabeth said. "If we start suspecting each other, we'll all lose. It's bad enough the cops suspect some of us."

"What?" Sue's eyes were wide. "Who?"

"Me, for one," Elizabeth said. "You didn't know? They found my fingerprints where I guess they thought they shouldn't have been. They asked me a bunch of questions. Luckily Jane could verify that I was with her the night of the theft, but who knows, maybe they think she and I are in it together. They did the same thing to Marinda, only her alibi's in the Middle East so she's in bigger trouble than I am."

"I didn't hear about this," Sue said.

"Good, that means the Canadians don't know yet," Marce said.

"They didn't like where my fingerprints were either," Marinda said. "They're apparently trying to contact Farrel Pembroke, who is presently in Kuwait."

"She's your alibi?" Sue said.

"She and I were together the night the statue was taken. She's a friend of a good friend of mine in Marigua. I brought a gift for her from my friend. Farrel and I had dinner, I gave her the gift, we talked. Then she drove me to Lancy's where I'm staying. That was at about nine-thirty."

"Why do you feel you have to explain all that to us?" Meredith said. "We're not accusing you." She looked around the room at several of the other women. "Are we?"

"I think Elizabeth is right," Marce said. "We have to assume that none of us is involved in the theft. I'm willing to do that. I don't believe it was any of you."

"Of course it wasn't," Essie said. "This is dumb."

"All right, so let's all agree to keep everything between us from now on — the six of us on the committee, plus Lou Bonnig, Amagyne, and you, Meredith. Where's Lou tonight?" Elizabeth asked.

"Otherwise occupied," Marce said. "I'm calling her later to fill her in on what happens."

"And Jordan?"

"Jordan has better things to do. She's got a new love," Carla said.

"Oh, yeah? A new month, a new woman," Essie said.

"She needs to take the vow of silence, too," Carla said. "I'll call her and tell her what we talked about tonight."

"So, agreed then," Essie said, "from now on everything's just between us. No more blabbing." She looked at Sue.

"My lips are sealed," Sue said.

Elizabeth was rubbing her chin. "I think our next step

should be to tell Slick she's convinced us that she's the thief, but we're still not convinced that she hasn't destroyed the statue."

"And she'll tell us to take a flying leap," Marce said.

Elizabeth ignored her. "We'll tell her we won't give her any money without better proof than these boards. And not a photograph. That won't do since photos can be faked. She has to show us the actual statue."

"Right," Marce said, sneering. "Slick will surely go for that. She'll have a party maybe. Invite everyone to her hiding place to dance with the Dancer."

"What she'd do," Carla said, "is figure out some way to show the statue without revealing its location."

"Or her identity," Essie added. "She'd probably blindfold the person who comes to see it. But we could outwit her. We could use a wire, you know, those radio transmitters that you can attach to people. Then whoever goes can tell us where she is, give us clues somehow."

Marce rolled her eyes.

"I don't know," Carla said. "Even in the cops and robbers movies, that's not real reliable. You have to be following in a car, very closely. We don't have the equipment much less the know-how."

"Anybody know any undercover cops?" Meredith asked.

"Carla has a point," Elizabeth said. "I have no idea how those transmitters work."

"So we'll learn how it's done," Sue said. "Go to the library maybe and read up on it."

"How stupid do you people think Slick is?" Marce said, shaking her head. "If you jerk her around too much, she just might start chiseling off chunks of the Dancer, maybe starting with the wings."

"I don't think a chisel would do it," Sue said.

Marce chuckled. "A hacksaw would. She could use the same one she sawed through the padlock with."

"I don't think that would happen," Elizabeth said. "If

that's what Slick wanted, she would have done it by now. For some reason, she obviously prefers that the statue survive."

"Don't be so sure," Marce said. "I think the smartest thing we could do is pay her off. She's got us by the short hairs."

"I never thought you'd be a quitter," Sue said.

"I'm a realist," Marce responded, unruffled. "If we insist she show us the statue, I suspect she'll get so annoyed that we never hear from her again and never see the damned statue again."

"Another possibility is to bring in the cops at this point," Essie said. "Don't look at me like that. If we warn them that Slick will destroy the statue if she knows the cops are onto her, then I would think they could manage to be especially careful about who they let know about it."

"I'm against telling the police," Marinda said.

"Hey, we agree on something," Marce responded.

"I'm against it too," said Carla. "They'd be more interested in catching the thief than getting the statue back. I think we have to take Slick's threat seriously. If she somehow got wind that we told the cops about her, I'm afraid she really would cut up the statue and sell the gold and forget about it surviving in San Francisco."

"Will it really be able to stay in San Francisco if we get it back?" Sue asked.

"Of course not," Marce said, "but we'll promise her anything."

"Lie?" Sue said, scratching her head.

"We should tell her one of us must see the statue," Marinda said. "And I think the radio transmitter idea is excellent. I very much doubt that our thief would suspect we'd do that. That way we may not only find the statue, but also capture the thief."

Marce laughed uproariously.

"What's funny?" Sue asked, looking questioningly at Marce. She shifted her legs under the weight of her dog.

"We'll throw a big net over her and capture her. Is that how they do it in Marigua?" Marce said, looking at Marinda.

Marinda ignored her.

"I wonder if the person who goes to see the statue would be in any danger," Elizabeth said. She was stroking her chin nervously.

"We'll send a butch," Sue said.

"Let Redman do it. It's beginning to sound like boy's work to me," said Carla.

"You know, that's not such a bad idea," Elizabeth said. "Redman might know about radio transmitters." She was drumming her fingers on the coffee table. "He's an investigator, right? Like a private detective. He probably does this kind of thing all the time."

"Yeah, every day," Marce said.

"I don't think it's that complicated to use a radio receiver and a transmitter," Carla said. "They may not sell them at Radio Shack, but I bet we could get one."

"From Redman," Essie said.

"Possibly."

"He'd probably insist on being the one to go."

"So let him go."

"Okay by me," Essie said.

"I'm afraid he'd tell the cops about Slick if we let him in on this," Carla said. "He'd probably have to, legally. Withholding evidence, or something like that."

"You could be right," Elizabeth concurred.

The discussion continued for another hour. In the end, the women agreed, some more enthusiastically than others, that they would notify Slick that they were willing to pay what she demanded, and that they would keep the statue in San Francisco once they knew for sure that it hadn't been destroyed. To buy time in case they ended up needing it, they also decided to say that they were raising the money themselves. They agreed to pass this story on to everyone they had given information to earlier. They also decided not to involve the insurance company, but to figure out on their own how to wire someone with a radio transmitter.

* * * * *

"I have to talk with you," Meredith said to Amagyne as women were preparing to leave the meeting.

Amagyne suggested they go for coffee. They went to a little restaurant on Eighteenth Street. "I think I know who Slick is," Meredith said as soon as they were seated.

"Oh," Amagyne cocked her head.

"Marinda Sartoria."

Amagyne's eyebrows lifted.

"I can't shake the feeling even though I have nothing solid to base it on." They ordered their drinks, coffee for Meredith, tea for Amagyne. "I know it sounds crazy, but I just don't trust her. I think her talk about Andrea Herrara is bullshit. Her cover. I just sense something about her, Amagyne. The way she talked about the statue. I've looked at that piece of film over and over. She talks as if the statue is a person, as if it's alive."

Amagyne listened intently, looking puzzled and concerned.

"I think she's in love with it . . . in a way, in love with what it stands for to her. Power, maybe. Connectedness. Something. I think she wants it for herself. I've been doing a lot of thinking about this, looking at that film, and observing her. She seems like she's in a whole lot of pain, suffering deeply inside. I think she must have lost something very important, some part of herself . . . that it was taken from her, and she believes she can get it back by possessing the statue. It's almost like she believes she

82

can absorb the statue's qualities somehow, take on its . . . its soul."

Amagyne gave Meredith a very penetrating look. Meredith stared at the table. "Interesting," Amagyne said. "Did Marinda speak of this with you? About losing something, about feeling incomplete?"

"No. That's the weird part. It's just something I sense in her."

"Hm-m." Amagyne looked at Meredith in a warm, caring way. "Meredith," she said gently, "did something like this happen to you? Do you perhaps feel as if you've lost part of yourself?"

Meredith squirmed. She fingered her spoon. "I can't talk about that," she said.

Amagyne waited a few moments. "All right."

"But I don't think it's just that." She looked earnestly at Amagyne. "It's the way she talked about the statue. And it's the pain I see in her eyes. I don't think I'm just projecting."

Amagyne nodded.

"What I was hoping," Meredith said, "is that you might . . . I don't know. You two are seeing each other, right?"

"Hoping I might what? Try to find out if she's the thief?"

"Yes."

"It seems very important to you."

"You can't take someone else's soul. It doesn't work that way."

"No, it doesn't."

"I want to help her."

"I see."

The beverages arrived. Meredith sipped silently. "I know it sounds crazy."

"It sounds to me like you identify with Marinda, that you sense her pain and that it stirs up your own. Your own loss must have been extremely painful."

Meredith exhaled loudly. "Yes."

Amagyne waited.

"She was someone very close to me. That's true. And that's why I can tell what's happening with Marinda."

"If you would like to talk about it . . ."

"No."

"About your loss."

"No, I don't want to. That's not the point. The point is that Marinda is the thief. I want you to help me prove this and once we do maybe we can help her."

Amagyne sat quietly for a while, her fingers playing with the napkin. "I know you believe what you sense is true," she said at last, "and clearly your feelings are very strong. But I think you are mistaken about Marinda."

Meredith nodded. "I could be. If I'm right, though, I don't condemn her for it. And I give her credit for being clever, for pretending that she wants money and that she plans to return the statue. And for distracting us with the story about Andrea Herrara. I think the Winged Dancer is already on its way back to Marigua and that Marinda has some special secret place where she plans to keep it."

"There are others who believe the Winged Dancer must be theirs," Amagyne said. "Because of what you feel, you believe it is Marinda who needs the statue. There are some people I know who believe the Winged Dancer belongs with them."

Meredith cocked her head. "Who are they? Have they said this?"

"Very clearly," Amagyne said.

"Women of your religion?"

"Not exactly. They call themselves Kwo-amjamites. They separated from us."

"You think they took the statue?"

"I'm afraid so. But, like you, I could be wrong."

Meredith sighed. "Maybe it's just a common thief," she said, "a professional burglar."

"That, indeed, is possible." Amagyne took a deep breath. "But I don't believe it."

"Neither do I."

"If you want to talk sometime," Amagyne said, looking very caringly at Meredith, "about yourself . . . let me know."

"Thank you." Meredith looked warmly back at Amagyne. "I think if I did want to talk, you'd be the one I'd talk to."

Amagyne smiled.

"Amagyne, don't tell anyone what I said, all right? About Marinda."

"All right."

"I haven't told anyone else, not really. I did mention it to one person, but then I covered it up, pretending I suspected everyone."

"I see."

The two women were silent for a while. "This is going to make quite a film," Meredith said at last.

"I imagine it will. Have you been a filmmaker long?"

"For years." Meredith pushed back a strand of her reddish hair. "Have you been a Kwo-amian long?"

Amagyne laughed. "For years," she said. "All my years."

They stayed talking for another hour and a half. When they left the restaurant they walked arm in arm down Eighteenth Street.

# Chapter 10

Marce took Amagyne's hand and entwined their fingers. "Strong, soft hands," she said. "They melt me." She gave a half-smile. "And I'm not easy to melt."

"That I believe," Amagyne said.

"Oh, yeah?" Marce narrowed her glinting eyes. "And why is that?" She drew out the words, smiling, moving yet closer to Amagyne.

"There's a hard crust encircling you. Your protection, I would guess."

"Oh, I see. And do I need protection from you?" Marce's voice was cooing and seductive.

"I think you do. I think my honesty may hurt you."

"Oh no, you're not going to tell me you have a headache?"

"I think you think you want a physical intimacy with me . . ."

"Mm-mm . . . you are so-o-o perceptive . . ."

". . . But I know that it would not be fulfilling for either of us."

"Hey, speak for yourself." Marce pulled her hand away. "So, what are you saying? You're not interested?"

"Not in our trying to connect through our bodies."

"Connect, shit. How about we just make love?" She trickled her fingertips along Amagyne's neck. "Enjoy ourselves."

"I think you are not being in tune that there are two of us here."

"I'm highly in tune. That's exactly the right number."

"I am not feeling recognized as one apart from you."

"The two of us are one."

"But we are not."

"Oh, I get it. It's Marinda, isn't it? You're saving yourself for her."

"To you, I think, I would be primarily a pillow, a soft nesting place. Or perhaps a conquest, a mountain to climb. I don't feel you can look at me and see me as separate and complete. Our coming together would be empty without that."

"Heavy, heavy." Marce stretched her arms and yawned. "Why are you always so serious, Amagyne? I think it comes from too much religion."

"Our feelings are serious."

"Well, I'm seriously crazy about you. Can't you tell that? I find you absolutely fascinating and luscious." Marce looked deeply into Amagyne's eyes, a hint of a taunting smile on her lips.

"I'm aware of your attraction to me."

"Well, that's a start."

"But I sense it's based on a view I don't share."

Marce pulled her head back. "So what are you saying? That we have to share a common world view and philosophy to enjoy each other's company?"

"The crust I mentioned, does it have any soft spots?" Amagyne asked.

Marce took Amagyne's hand and placed it on her hip. "Feel around and see," she said.

"You are difficult to reach," Amagyne said.

Marce shook her head. "Talk, talk, talk. Is that all you want to do tonight?"

"Yes."

"Hm-m." Marce leaned back. "Okay, then let's talk." She looked challengly at Amagyne. "So, what do you want to talk about? Politics? Movies? We could talk about art. What do you think of that?" Marce gestured toward the painting on the opposite wall, a woman in a bright pink cape. "Is that Kwo-amian art?"

"I would prefer talking about you. About your crust. It's better than playing cat and mouse. So what about it?"

"It saddens me. I think you're lonely in there."

"Oh boy, this is like talking to a shrink."

"Rest your head here." Amagyne took the afghan, folded it and placed it on the arm of the sofa. She stood to give Marce room and Marce stretched out her legs along the cushions. Amagyne pulled a chair up next to her. "At my home," she said gently, "when someone seems to be strangling her own ability to be giving and receiving and connected, we offer guided listening to —"

"You think I'm strangling?"

"Metaphorically, yes. It is what I sense. Am I wrong?"

"Oh, no, I'm sure you're right. You're a wise woman. A guru, of sorts, aren't you? So I'm strangling my capacity to give and get. Go on, you have my attention."

"If I were to do guided listening with you, I would ask

you to close your eyes. I would ask you to imagine the feel of a stream of warm sun shining on one central part of your forehead. Warming your face. Warming your mind, loosening it; warming your body, relaxing it."

Amagyne started humming softly, a low, flowing, chant-like hum, a circular melody with no beginning or end. The lines on Marce's face began to soften. Her eyes were closed. Her arm and leg muscles visibly relaxed. Her breathing became slow and regular.

"And now you are letting yourself make contact with yourself. Feeling the many yous. You can feel that crust you know so well, feeling the hardness of it. Perhaps you can crawl around that barrier until you find a place you can enter . . . yes, going inside, and, being inside, feeling it, feeling what it's like in there, behind the crust." Amagyne paused for nearly half a minute. "And when you are ready, you may want to tell me what you experience in there."

There was silence for a while. "Anger," Marce said.

"Hummm . . . you've been hurt."

"Who hasn't?"

"Yours is very frightening. It makes you build those walls."

Marce opened her eyes. "I don't think I like this."

Amagyne nodded. "Shall we stop?" she inquired gently.

Marce shrugged. She closed her eyes again. "I'm not surprised that you don't want me. It's your loss, though. Heh-heh. But it doesn't surprise me. I'm too much for you to handle, I think. I think you have your own fears."

"You're not surprised . . . hummm . . ."

"No, we're a real mismatch. Personally, I don't think Marinda's your type either. What's the humming supposed to mean?"

Amagyne continued the soft, low, undulating sounds.

"My aunt used to sing to me," Marce said. "It was very soothing. She'd sing to me when she'd come over and my mother was raving drunk and I was in the bedroom huddled up against the wall. I liked it. I like what you're doing."

"Hummm . . . soothing you . . . hummm . . . like your aunt used to do . . ."

Marce said nothing for a while, then, "I must have made love with more than a hundred women over the years . . ."

"Many women . . . hummm . . ."

"Or had sex. I don't know that there was much love involved. I'm not one to get real attached."

"Keeping away . . ."

Marce started to say something but the words caught in her throat. She sat up suddenly, brushed briefly at her eyes. "This is not for me," she said, running her fingers through her hair. "It's interesting, though. So this is the kind of stuff you do at Circle Edge." She tossed the afghan to the other side of the couch. "Tell me more about what goes on there."

Amagyne looked very tenderly at Marce. "We try for understanding, making sense of our thoughts and feelings. We try for that rather than judgmental condemning. It doesn't always come easily."

"I say call a spade a spade. If someone's an asshole, why pretend they're not?"

"We try to go beyond the easy labels to what's underneath. To understanding preceded by what we call *Acceptance of Presence*. When someone's behavior is bothersome to us, different from our own preferences, perhaps reflecting values or beliefs we do not share, then we know we must first accept that that is where she is right now. That is the first step, the acceptance."

"In dealing with assholes."

"In dealing with difference. In the Kwo-amian view, we see some of the differences as only that, differences,

90

reflecting our multiplicity. Some of them, though, we see as zetkap."

"Ah, yes, the evil spirit."

"The negative force, the force of destruction and pain. If it seems that zetkap is present, then we offer what means we have to bring about the *Rising of Awareness* and the emergence of kwo-ami."

"Sounds like a mix of pop psychology and religious magic," Marce said. "But do go on. So if you think the behavior that turns you off is inspired by the evil spirit, then you have a little trouble being so accepting, and you try to get the person to change, is that it?"

"We accept the presence," Amagyne said. "We do not condemn the person. We do not attack. We do not reject."

"Mush."

"We offer guided listening, stretch talks, rituals, therapy. The goal is the *Rising of Awareness* which, hopefully, will subdue the zetkap and free the kwo-ami."

"Insight leading to the superego taking charge and stifling the id."

Amagyne laughed.

"You think zetkap has hold of me?"

"All humans are torn by the battle of Zetka and Kwo-am within them. For you, perhaps, the pain of your childhood gave Zetka a firm grip. When we are vulnerable, he moves in. But Kwo-am is ever there. You are what we call zet-kwo. What you were given at birth and what you experienced in your life combined with the zetkap and kwo-ami within you to create your views of self and others and life and make you zet-kwo. Too much zetkap, too much of your kwo-ami submerged. There are more satisfying ways to be if you can touch your wish to rise."

"Zet-kwo, huh? I get the distinct sense I haven't made a very good impression on you. It's happened before.

91

Occasionally people find me hard to take. I consider it their problem and it doesn't bother me a bit. In your case . . . well . . . I'm really not all that bad, Amagyne."

"No, not all that bad," Amagyne said. She smiled. "Difficult though."

Marce laughed. "I won't argue that. I'd like to learn more about your way of thinking, how you deal with hard-noses like me. You said you were free until nine tonight and it's almost nine. Have you changed your mind? Shall we keep talking?"

"We must stop at nine."

"Do you have a date?"

"A visitor is coming."

"Spiritual or corporeal?"

Amagyne smiled. "A person."

"All right," Marce said, "I'll get out of your way tonight, but why don't you and I take a drive up to Mendocino tomorrow? That will give us a good chance to talk some more. You can tell me all about not being judgmental and how my crust is strangling me and Zetka is doing his dirty work in my soul."

"Yes, there is much more to talk about. I am not free tomorrow, Marce. In the early evening, I'm speaking at the bookstore, *Old Wives' Tales*. Perhaps you will come. I will speak about Kwo-amity — what we have learned from our sage, La, and what it all means for our lives — for your life."

"How about if I pick you up after your talk?"

Amagyne shook her head. "Better that you come and listen."

The doorbell rang.

"Ah, your visitor," Marce said. "So, my time is up, huh?"

Amagyne looked slightly uncomfortable. "She's early."

"I was supposed to be out of here before she came,

wasn't I? Too bad, now I'll have to meet her." Marce smiled mischievously.

"You could go out the back if you like."

"No thanks," Marce said sharply. "I definitely prefer front doors. Don't worry, I'll just say hello and then I'll leave."

Amagyne buzzed the visitor in.

Marce stood, picked up her jacket from the futon and slung it over her shoulder. Amagyne opened the door.

"I know it's not nine-thirty yet." The visitor embraced Amagyne warmly. "I hope you don't mind that I'm early . . . oh, hello, Marce."

Marce stared at Marinda.

"Marce was just leaving," Amagyne said.

"I'm not in a hurry." Marce tossed her jacket back onto the futon. "Come on in, Marinda. We were just talking about zetkap, you know, the bad juices. I imagine you're familiar with all that. In fact, I wouldn't be surprised if you're letting Amagyne think she's converting you? How far would you go, Sartoria? Would you become a Kwo-amian for her? Are there no limits to your perfidy?"

Marinda looked at Marce with a mix of puzzlement and contempt.

"What's the matter? The word not familiar to you? English is tricky for the novice. Perfidy. It means falseness, deceitfulness."

"It means treachery," Marinda said. "Would you like me to come back later?" she asked Amagyne.

"No," Amagyne said. "Come, sit. Marce knew she could only visit with me until nine."

Marce sat herself determinedly in the chair near the sofa. "Is this seduction night, Marinda? Or have you already scored with her?"

Marinda's black eyes narrowed. "You're behaving obnoxiously," she said.

"Shouldn't you be out searching for a statue or something? Really, where's your conscience? You come to our country to protect that piece of metal and it disappears from right under your nose. And what do you do? You just go about your pleasures like a bitch in heat."

"Is she on something?" Marinda asked Amagyne.

Amagyne looked very sad. "You are not happy, I know," she said to Marce. "Let us talk, tomorrow. Come, I will walk you to your car."

"Now what's the politically correct term for that?" Marce said. "You know about such things, don't you, Marinda? You're a staunch feminist, I assume. Would you say Amagyne is *patronizing* me or *matronizing* me? Never mind, it's not important. Have the cops located the mystery woman yet? The one you supposedly had dinner with the *night in question?* Did you score with her or was your score that night the androgynous golden dancer? Come on, you can tell us."

Marinda had folded her arms and was looking down at Marce. "I think you had better leave."

"Mm-m, tough. A true butch. Relax, Marinda. Come on, we can all be friends. Here, sit on the couch next to Amagyne. Amagyne tells me I'm not her type anyway so apparently I'm no threat to you. Relax."

"It's hard for you to accept that Marinda and I are friends," Amagyne said.

"Hey, not at all."

"Somewhat," Amagyne insisted.

"Somewhat, maybe," Marce acknowledged.

"Perhaps you view her as a competitor."

"What's this called now?" Marce asked. "Is this what you call a stretch talk, or is this some other technique? Oh, I know. This is the understanding rather than condemning. Am I right?"

"You are right," Amagyne said. "Is my understanding correct?"

"It doesn't take a psychologist to figure that out. She has the same effect on you, doesn't she, Marinda? You're quite a special woman, Amagyne."

Amagyne was on the sofa. Marinda remained standing until Amagyne gestured for her to sit. She sat on the other end of the sofa.

"I thought you were busy being a star tonight," Marce said to Marinda. "Wasn't Meredith supposed to interview you, get the true story of Winged Dancer's protector?"

"We finished," Marinda said.

"Did it go well?" Amagyne asked.

"Not especially. Meredith seemed edgy. A little hostile toward me, I think. I don't know why. Most of it went well enough, though. She's still there with Lancy. They seemed to like each other."

"Ah, Cupid is everywhere," Marce said.

"Lancy is eighty years old," Marinda said.

"You're never too old," Marce responded. "How old are you, Marinda?"

Marinda looked pointedly at Marce for several seconds, then turned to Amagyne. "Do you have anything to drink? It doesn't really matter what, just so it's wet."

"Just so it's wet," Marce repeated, licking her lips and leering.

"I will get you something. And you, Marce, do you want another?"

"No, thanks Ammy, I'm fine."

Amagyne left the room. "Do you have a hangup about your age?" Marce asked Marinda. "I'm right on the big four-O. Two years older than Amagyne. I'd say you're in the same ballpark."

Marinda stared coldly at Marce, then looked away.

Neither woman spoke for a while. Marce took a deep breath. Then another. Then she sighed. Her expression had changed. "I can be a tad rude sometimes, can't I?" she said, at last. Her face had lost the hard look.

Marinda's eyes went up and held Marce's, but she did not move her head.

"I suppose I should apologize. Amagyne is absolutely right, of course — what she said. It has nothing to do with you personally."

"I see."

"She just swept me off my feet." Marce shook her head. "I can't explain it. I've never reacted this way before. She . . . I feel . . . I don't know, it just feels so good to be near her, with her. She's like . . . like . . ."

"Mother Earth."

Marce smiled. "Maybe. You know, I think I would even convert to that crazy Kwo-amian religion if I thought that would do it."

"Do what?"

Marce pursed her lips. "Good point," she said. She stared at the floor. "This is very hard for me."

"Yes, I think I know how you feel." Marinda's face had softened considerably.

"You're being kinder than I deserve," Marce said. She stood. "I'm going to leave now." She reached for Marinda's hand. "No hard feelings?"

They shook hands. Marinda smiled. "Take care of yourself," she said.

Marce waited at the door until Amagyne returned to the room. "Good night, sweet Amagyne. I'll see you in my dreams."

"Good night, sweet Marce," Amagyne said caringly. "I will see you soon."

# Chapter 11

Amagyne was awake for an hour the next morning before she noticed the envelope lying on the floor near the back door. In it was a note addressed to her. *I would like to talk with you,* it said. *I'll be at Bawd's between 2 and 3 today. Doralee.*

Amagyne smiled. "Dancer, we shall have you back soon," she said aloud.

Several hours later, when she walked into Bawd's, Doralee was seated at a table near the wall. They greeted each other in the Kwo-amian way and Amagyne sat across from her.

"What would you like to drink?" Doralee asked. "Irish coffee?"

Amagyne laughed. "You remember. Yes, that would be fine. I haven't had one for a long time." Smiling nostalgically, she watched Doralee go to the bar. They had been friends at Circle Edge and Amagyne missed her.

Doralee returned and placed the cup in front of Amagyne. "I would have phoned but I was afraid Robyn would answer."

"Does she not treat you well?"

"She's polite, but I know she's angry. She thinks I'm a deserter. She thinks Jamma is a charlatan."

"That's putting it strongly."

"They're her words."

"Said in anger long ago. She speaks kindly of you."

"Mm-m. I've always liked her."

Amagyne nodded. "Bridges can be mended."

"Perhaps. In a sense, that's why I asked to see you." Doralee sipped from her glass of Seven-up. "I believe the Winged Dancer belongs to all people who are guided by kwo-ami energy."

Amagyne nodded. "I believe that too."

"Yet I don't think it is right to take it from the Mariguans."

"Nor I."

"I know when you came to visit us last weekend, you were suspecting that some of the Kwo-amjamites took it."

Amagyne waited.

"I'm afraid you're right."

"Tell me," Amagyne said.

Doralee took a deep breath. "We have several acres of land near the Russian River. We go there for special ceremonies and rituals. There are two cabins and lots of trees and flowers. Behind the cabins is a secluded area surrounded by rocks and boulders and trees."

"It sounds very peaceful."

"Carolyn said the Winged Dancer belongs there."

"I see."

"I agreed it would be nice, but I never thought . . ." Amagyne blew a soft stream of air over her coffee.

"We have a truck. It's Lorloge's, but really it belongs to all of us. We all use it. We find things, discarded objects, furniture, appliances, household things. We fix them up in Lorloge's garage and we sell them. It's one of the ways we survive financially."

"A good way, I think," Amagyne said.

"It's very different here from Circle Edge." Doralee laughed softly. "We live humbly. Some of us, at least. Anyway, we have the truck and everyone uses it. The night the Winged Dancer disappeared, Carolyn used it. She had it overnight. When she came back the next afternoon, the truck was empty."

Amagyne nodded.

"I tried to ask her about it, about where she was, but she evaded, wouldn't be pinned down. I'm sure she believes it was the right thing to do. I don't know how to approach her, Amagyne. I'm afraid she'll think I'm a traitor. All of them — the Kwo-amjamites — if they find out I'm telling you, they'll consider it betrayal."

"Do you not discuss such differences?"

"Like I said, it's very different here from Circle Edge. Jamma says Kwo-am is angry, angry at La, who Jamma says was not truly a sage, and angry at all you unenlightened Kwo-amians who stuck by her. La betrayed the faith, Jamma says. She was chosen, enabled, and she distorted this gift Kwo-am gave her. She gave in to the power of Zetka. Now Kwo-am has become harsher. Now Kwo-am knows that even Kwo-amians need to steel themselves vigorously against Zetka's power. Things are different here. We have lots of rules. Penance, even. Everyone is always feeling guilty. We try to purge the zetkap from our souls in ways that . . ." Doralee shook her

99

head. "I didn't mean to go into all this." She took some more of her drink. "My point is, Amagyne, that I think Carolyn took the statue and I think it was wrong. I want to help you get it back."

"I am glad, Doralee. I think you do well. Do you fear them?"

Doralee did not answer right away. "Not really," she said. "Not fear. I love them, most of them. I don't know if I belong with them though. There are about thirty-five of us here in the Bay area. Jamma says our number soon will begin to swell."

"Because of the Winged Dancer?"

"I think that's what she means. I wasn't sure at first that they took it. I know they keep things from me. I'm not part of the Inner Circle and I probably never will be. I don't feel fully a part of them, not the way I felt at Circle Edge. Anyway, what confirmed my suspicions about Carolyn was when I heard she knew about how the museum is guarded, how the security is done."

"So she knew that."

"Yes. We all knew the statue was coming to the States. I mean, everyone knew that. It was in the newspapers. But I didn't think the Kwo-amjamites took it because I didn't think they could pull it off. Having the motivation and the justification and a truck isn't enough, I thought. How could they get into the museum? How could they avoid getting caught? Of course I knew there had to be security guards. But then, a few days ago, I overheard Carolyn and Val talking. I was in the john; they didn't know I was home. Carolyn was talking about her friend, Barbara, who moved to Canada. Carolyn had gone to say goodbye to her the day the statue disappeared. She was at Barbara's apartment and this woman named Sue who Carolyn described as a *motor mouth* came in and began talking about the Winged Dancer. Carolyn pretended she wasn't all that interested, but she listened to every word. This Sue had been at the

100

museum when the statue arrived from the dock. She described everything that happened and the exact procedures that the security guards followed to guard the museum."

Amagyne was nodding.

"She knew enough to pull it off," Doralee said.

"It sounds like she did."

"What I figured she did was go into the museum during the day, before it closed. And then, she must have somehow gotten to the statue and gotten it into the truck and out of there."

"I think I know how," Amagyne said. "We figured out that the thief probably hid in the janitor's closet until the security guard made his rounds, then sneaked into the area where the statue was. Once inside there, she was free to do what she wanted. Do you think Carolyn did it alone?"

"I doubt it. But she and whoever else was involved are keeping it secret. I imagine they plan to inform us — the rest of the Kwo-amjamites — after everything has quieted down."

"You know they asked for money."

"You mentioned something about that."

"We received a note from the thief demanding four hundred thousand dollars."

Doralee shook her head. "We could sure use it." She was frowning pensively. "I didn't know about the note."

"Would Carolyn do that?"

Doralee thought a moment. "Yes. I think she could justify it to herself."

"The one who wrote the note also demanded that the statue remain in San Francisco, that it be displayed somewhere overlooking the Bay."

"Really? That surprises me. I don't think that would be enough for them — for Carolyn and . . . no, having it near us wouldn't be enough. They believe we have to have it with us, on our land."

101

"At the Russian River?"

"Yes. My guess is that they just said that to throw people off the track. To throw *you* off the track. You're the one they'd be worried about. No, I'm sure the statue is at our land and that's where they plan for it to stay. The note said they'd give it back if they got the money?"

"If they got the money and assurances that the statue will remain in San Francisco."

"They won't return it."

"I don't imagine they intend to."

"It's zetkap, Amagyne. Too much zetkap. They think it's zetkap in me that gives me trouble with their ways, but . . ." Doralee chewed her lip.

"You have been struggling, Doralee." Amagyne placed her large hand over Doralee's smaller one.

"I think about coming back."

"We would welcome you."

Doralee smiled sadly. "You are a very good person, Amagyne." A pool game had begun and the bar was getting noisy. Neither woman said anything for a while.

"Perhaps if I speak to Carolyn," Amagyne said.

"She respects you."

"And to Jamma."

Doralee shook her head. "That might not be such a good idea. One thing I was thinking is that if they know we know, then they might just move the statue, hide it somewhere. I think we need concrete proof before we confront them so if we have to involve the police or anyone . . ." Doralee's eyes filled with tears.

"I know," Amagyne said. "This is difficult for you."

"Plotting against my own people."

"Would you like to stay out of it, Doralee? It could be done without the Kwo-amjamites ever knowing that you were involved."

"No." Doralee shook her head vigorously. "I would never do that."

"I thought not."

"Perhaps this was meant to be," Doralee said, looking into space. "I don't think I belong with them." Another period of silence passed and then Doralee spoke again. "What I think we should do first . . . I mean before we say anything to anyone . . . I think we should go and take a picture of the statue. We could get a shot of it with the cabins in the background. That way they couldn't deny that they have it and then if we have to we can use the photograph as proof to show to . . . well, to whomever . . . the police, if necessary."

"I'm sure that won't be necessary," Amagyne said reassuringly.

"I would go by myself, but . . . would you come with me, Amagyne? Would you do that?"

"Yes, I would do that, Doralee."

"Oh, good. I thought you would. We should do it as soon as possible. Maybe right now. I could go now if you could."

"I must speak tonight at the bookstore," Amagyne said. "Tomorrow morning?"

"Yes, all right. Can you get a car?"

Amagyne nodded.

"Is nine too early?"

"Nine is fine."

"I'll meet you someplace." Doralee thought a moment. "On Mission and Fourteenth. I'll meet you there at nine."

\* \* \* \* \*

When Amagyne arrived at home, she found a message from Robyn. *Meredith called. Said it's important. Wants you to call her as soon as poss. How about brunch tomorrow morning at The Patio? Robyn.*

Amagyne pulled her little yellow address book from her leather pack. She dialed Meredith's number.

"I played detective," Meredith said right after the hellos. "It was gross in a way and I felt shitty while I was doing it, but the end justified the means. I found what I was looking for." She took a deep breath. "Marinda is definitely the thief."

"Marinda." Amagyne's almond-shaped eyes blinked rapidly.

"Yes. I found the proof. I want to confront her, talk with her, but I'm not sure how to do it. I know she needs help. I feel bad for her. I was thinking maybe you and I could talk with her together."

"Tell me about the proof you found, Meredith."

"It's a receipt. I found it in her room. I was at her place last night, at her friend's apartment where she's staying. I was interviewing her for the film and after the interview Marinda left and I was there alone with her friend, Lancy. While Lancy was in the bathroom, I went into Marinda's room and searched it. I found the proof that she took the Winged Dancer. It's a receipt for the shipment of a crate to Marigua. It was sent October third, a few days after the statue was stolen. I just knew it, Amagyne. I knew I was right about her."

"Hmm-m. Does the receipt say what is in the crate?" Amagyne asked

"No. Well, actually it might but I'm not sure because it was written in Spanish. I could read enough of it to know exactly what it meant, though. *Recibo* means *receipt* and *embarque* has to do with shipping. And there were the words, *caja de carton*. Amagyne, it's so obvious. She shipped the Winged Dancer to Marigua. She had to have it. It's just what I thought."

Amagyne kicked off her moccasins and lay back on the futon. "Maybe so, Meredith."

"*Maybe!* What do you mean, *maybe*? This is absolute, concrete proof. I haven't a shred of doubt whatsoever."

"We might ask her about it."

"I think we have to approach it very carefully."

"Yes, I agree. Do you have the receipt?"

"No, I was afraid to take it. I probably should have, though. I wish I had."

"Meredith, there is something I must tell you. I spoke to someone today who is sure *she* knows who the thief is, and it's not Marinda. She has evidence too. She believes she knows where the statue is hidden."

"Impossible. She's wrong. Who is she? Who does she think took it?"

"We are planning to go tomorrow to where the statue is."

"A waste of time," Meredith said. "The statue's in Marigua, or on its way there. I only hope we can get it back in time for the conference."

"I hope so too."

"I think we should approach Marinda gently. Talk about how we understand that she's hurting inside and that she sees the Winged Dancer as a salve for her pain. Partly I feel angry at her, though, so I'm not sure I could do it diplomatically. I'm afraid I might piss her off. That's why I want you with me, Amagyne. I know you could do it right."

"Perhaps before we talk to Marinda we should see if the other possibility is the correct one. I am planning to go tomorrow to find out. Can you wait until then, Meredith?"

"Going where?"

"To see the statue. To photograph it."

"Where? Who? What makes you believe this other person?"

"There is evidence. My friend tells me that the person she believes is the thief knew about the security procedures at the museum."

"So did Marinda."

"And that she used a truck that night."

"Marinda could have gotten a truck with no problem. She could have rented one. That's what I figured she did.

Did you notice how closely she was watching when that guy was driving the fork lift? She was plotting."

"My friend's suspect believes the Winged Dancer belongs with her and the others of her group. This I know is true."

"What group? Those Kwo-amjimmies you talked about?"

"Yes."

"But Amagyne, don't be blinded by your religious ideas here. This is real life. Maybe I should just confront Marinda myself."

"Was Marinda's name on the receipt?"

"Yes. And there was another name, and an address — Rosa something, and the address was in Posteria or Postria or something like that, in Marigua. That's who she's sending it to. The receiver of stolen goods."

"If Marinda is the thief and you accuse her, she most likely will deny it. Your proof may disappear very rapidly."

"I should have taken the receipt."

"Can you wait until tomorrow, Meredith? I will call you as soon as we return."

"Maybe I'll go back and try to get it."

"Wait, though. Let's make a good plan. Wait until I come back tomorrow, perhaps with some photographs."

"You won't come back with any photographs, Amagyne. Not of the Winged Dancer. It won't be there. You'll see."

"I will call you as soon as we return. Tomorrow evening. Will you wait?"

"All right, I'll wait. Then we'll plan how to approach her."

"This is affecting you deeply," Amagyne said.

"It sure is. It makes me cry inside and it makes me angry that she's so ridiculous as to believe that it's possible to absorb the essence of another, especially a statue."

"If she believes that, then surely she is troubled."

"She needs help."

"We'll talk soon. I will contact you tomorrow as soon as possible."

"I'll be waiting."

Amagyne placed the phone on the floor. She lay back and began humming — a gentle, rhythmic tune, a melody with no beginning and no end.

# Chapter 12

On Friday night, Randy went with Jess and her lover, Judy, to the Women's Building for a dance performance by a group called Floral Wall Border. During the intermission, Jess was off talking with an old friend and Judy and Randy were standing in the lobby having a drink of apple cider, Judy talking about the latest developments at the Women's Crisis Line where she volunteered. Suddenly, out of the corner of her eye, Randy caught a glimpse of Marinda Sartoria. She felt herself getting hot and flustered.

"What is it, Randy? You okay?" Judy put her hand on Randy's arm.

Randy was staring past her into the crowd, feeling absurdly jittery. "I just saw someone I know," she said, stammering a bit.

Judy smiled understandingly. "You look like the first stages of love." She laughed warmly.

"Just a crush," Randy said. "I'm merely an admirer from afar."

"Too bad," Judy said. She was scanning the crowd.

"The one in the gray jacket," Randy told her. "The beautiful one with the gorgeous black hair."

Marinda caught Randy's eye and smiled at her. Randy smiled back, feeling her face reddening. Marinda began making her way through the throng of women. She can't be coming here, Randy thought, her heart pounding madly.

In another few seconds Marinda was at her side. "Hello, Randy." She took Randy's hand and examined her wrist. "Where's your bracelet?"

Randy knew she meant the rope and bead one she'd worn to the party the weekend before. "If I offered it to you as a gift, would you accept it?" Randy asked.

"I might." Marinda's smile gave Randy goosebumps.

"This is Judy Orlando," Randy said. "Judy, Marinda Sartoria. She's visiting here from South America." Randy was impressed with herself for managing to seem so calm.

"Welcome to our country," Judy said. "Is this your first visit?"

Randy barely heard the next few minutes of conversation, but then Marinda said something about wishing she had her motorcycle in San Francisco and Randy was brought back to earth. "I have a Honda Three-Fifty," she said. "I could take you for a ride if you'd like."

Marinda cocked her head. "Maybe so," she said.

Randy's palms were sweaty. "How about tomorrow?" she said. "We could go up to Twin Peaks, then drive along the Bay, maybe even go over to Marin County."

"Hm-mm," Marinda said. "It might be fun, but —"

"Right," Randy interrupted. She felt embarrassed by her presumptuousness.

"I'm busy tomorrow."

"I understand. Maybe some other time," she said to let Marinda off the hook.

"How about Sunday?" Marinda suggested.

Randy couldn't believe her ears. "Uh . . . sure, yeah, Sunday would be fine."

Marinda took out a little notebook, wrote something, and handed the paper to Randy. "Here's the address of where I'm staying. Would four o'clock be okay?"

"Yes, sure, four o'clock sounds good. I'll . . . I'll be there."

"Good," Marinda said. "I'll see you then." She said goodbye to Judy and then she was gone in the crowd.

Randy was having trouble breathing. She stared into space, her eyes wide. "I have a date with Marinda Sartoria," she said.

"Maybe the crush is mutual," Judy said.

Randy couldn't concentrate on the performance after that. Don't get your hopes up, she warned herself. It means nothing. Marinda just likes motorcycles, that's all. Nothing will come of it. But she was flying nonetheless.

# Chapter 13

*The one from South America will be allowed to see it. She's to go to the corner of Lombard and Divisadero at 9:30 Saturday morning. She's to go alone. On foot. No vehicles. There's a mailbox there. Taped underneath the mailbox will be a note. She's to follow the instructions in the note exactly. She should bring a map. If the police are involved, I will know, and this will be the last you'll hear of me or the statue. Slick.*

As each woman arrived, she read the letter.

"Are you nervous, Marinda?" Carla asked.

"She can't be nervous," Elizabeth said. "If she sweats,

it will mess up the transmission." Elizabeth was taping the wire to Marinda's chest, just below her right breast. "You ride with Essie," Elizabeth said to Carla. "Jordan, Meredith and I will be in the radio car."

"So where's Essie?"

"She'll be here."

Carla took a banana from the bowl of fruit on Elizabeth's coffee table. "You tested that thing?"

"It works great," Elizabeth said. "A friend of Essie's told us how to do it. It's really very simple."

Carla smiled. "I have a feeling we're going to pull this off. We're going to get the statue back without paying a cent."

"Don't get overconfident," Jordan said. "What time is it?"

"Nine-oh-five," Meredith said. She pointed to the binoculars hanging around Jordan's neck. "What are those for?"

Jordan patted the glasses. "I plan to do a lot of looking today, in the vicinity of Lombard and Divisadero Streets."

"You think Slick will be there?"

"You never know. She might be nearby somewhere making sure Marinda's alone. You never know."

"You really want to do this, huh, Marinda?" Meredith said.

Marinda finished buttoning her blouse. "Of course."

"Anything for a laugh, huh?" Meredith accepted the piece of banana Carla offered her.

"I don't see the humor," Marinda said.

The doorbell rang and Elizabeth buzzed in Essie. After the quick greetings, Essie read the letter. "I bet I know what's going to happen," she said, handing it back to Elizabeth. "The note at the mailbox will tell Marinda to go to some secluded place and there will be a blindfold there, like a black cloth sack or something. And Marinda will have to put it over her head and wait until Slick is sure

Marinda's alone, and then Slick will pick her up in a car and take her to the Dancer that way, blindfolded."

"And we'll be right behind them," Elizabeth said. "I figure it will go something like that too. We've just got to be very careful." She pushed a wisp of blonde hair back behind her ear.

"If she spots us it's all over."

"She won't spot us. But if she does, we'll take her," Carla said. "Capture her."

"We'll take it a step at a time," Elizabeth said. "Watch for our signal. If we need to talk, Jordan will put her hand out the window."

Essie nodded. "Okay. We should get going," she said. When she stood, she towered over the others.

Essie and Carla got in Essie's 1987 Ford, Essie in the driver's seat. In the 1991 white Toyota were Elizabeth, Marinda, Meredith, and Jordan. "Stick with us, partners," Elizabeth called out the window.

"Like glue," Essie called back.

They drove up Divisadero, Essie following behind the Toyota. When they reached Filbert, Elizabeth stopped as planned and Essie stopped behind her. Marinda got out of the car and began walking north. The two blocks to Lombard were a steep downhill walk. She checked her watch: 9:27. She paced herself so she arrived at the mailbox at 9:30 almost to the second. Leaning against the mailbox, she looked up and down the block, then bent and felt beneath the box. When she stood, she held a sealed envelope.

*Walk up Divisadero to Vallejo,* the note said. *Take a right on Vallejo to Baker, then a left to Broadway. There's a phone booth on the south side of Broadway. Be at the phone at 9:40.*

Marinda consulted her map, then her watch. She began walking up the steep Divisadero hill. The white Toyota was parked at the stop sign on Greenwich, a block up the hill, facing Marinda. She passed it without looking at the passengers who seemed to be fully absorbed in the map they had spread out on the dashboard.

Inside the car the women could hear Marinda's heavy breathing coming over the receiver.

"Why doesn't she talk?" Jordan said.

"She will." Elizabeth did a U-turn and parked. They watched Marinda trudging up the hill.

"She seems to be in a hurry," Meredith said.

"Sh-h-h. She's saying something."

The voice was low but audible. ". . . Baker and Broadway . . . and that I'm supposed to be at the phone booth at 9:40 . . . I don't know if I can make it on time . . ."

"The radio works great," Jordan said.

"Shit, that's all uphill," Elizabeth said.

"Should we give her a lift?" Meredith suggested from the back seat.

They watched Marinda fighting gravity, making her way up toward Vallejo. It was a five-block walk. They drove slowly. Parked. Waited. Drove a little more. Parked again. In the rear view mirror, Elizabeth could see Essie and Carla behind them. They watched Marinda arrive at Vallejo Street and turn right. She was out of sight.

"Signal Essie," Elizabeth said.

Jordan stuck her arm out the window.

The Ford that was parked half a block downhill pulled into traffic and continued until it reached the Toyota. It pulled up behind and parked. Carla got out and came to Jordan's window.

"She's going to a phone booth at Baker and Broadway," Elizabeth said. "You follow her. Don't get too close. We'll go ahead and cover the phone booth."

"Is Slick going to phone her?" Carla asked.

"Probably," Elizabeth said, her voice strained. "Get going. Park as far away as you can where you can still see the phone booth." Jordan hunched forward in the front passenger seat as the car started moving. She was clutching the binoculars. Meredith lounged casually in the back. "How far is Broadway and Baker?" Meredith asked.

"Broadway's one block south of Vallejo. Baker's two or three blocks west."

"She'll never make it by nine-forty."

The Toyota reached the corner of Broadway and Baker. After spotting the phone booth, the women drove another three-quarters of a block, then pulled into a driveway, turned around and parked. They listened to the breathing.

"I hope her heart's in good shape," Elizabeth said.

The breathing continued, getting heavier and heavier. Then there were words. "I'm on Baker now. I'm almost there."

"We should be able to see her any second," Jordan said.

The women in the front seat waited tensely. Meredith was stretched out in the back, cleaning the lens of her video camera.

"There she is. God, she's dragging. She looks beat."

"It's already nine-forty-five."

"Slick is a bitch. That walk can't be done in ten minutes."

They watched Marinda. A half block behind her, the Ford pulled into a parking place.

Marinda reached the corner. "All right, she's at the phone," Elizabeth said. "If it rings, we'll hear it."

They heard only the heavy breathing.

"Maybe it's an obscene phone call," Meredith said.

Marinda wiped her face with a handkerchief, speaking as she did. "There's a message written on the wall."

Meredith leaned forward to hear better. "What'd she say?"

"Sh-hh."

"*For Winged Dancer check nearest mailbox,*" Marinda's voice said. "That's what the message says. All right, I'm going to look for the mailbox. Apparently, she's not going to call." Marinda's breathing still sounded quite labored.

Across the street, diagonal from the phone booth, Marinda spotted a mailbox. She moved toward it, looking around as she walked, noticing the different pedestrians, motorists, a woman on a bike. Among the parked cars she saw the white Toyota on Broadway and the Ford on Baker Street. No one appeared to be the least bit interested in what she was doing. She looked at the mailbox. Nothing unusual about it. She bent and reached beneath it and there she found another note.

* * * * *

Amagyne had arrived at the corner of Fourteenth and Mission a few minutes after nine. Doralee was waiting with a thermos in her hand and a knapsack slung over her shoulder.

"Coffee," she said, climbing in next to Amagyne. "Let me know when you want some. Do you know the way?"

"I know we must first cross the Golden Gate Bridge," Amagyne said. "You will direct me after that."

"It's about a seventy-mile trip," Doralee said. "Are you nervous?"

"Excited," Amagyne said. "I have never seen it, you know. Only pictures. In one of our recent paintings, the face looks like that of La."

Doralee laughed. "And we have a painting in which the face looks like Jamma's."

They crossed into Marin County and drove steadily northward along Highway 101. At 9:45 Doralee poured them each a cup of coffee.

* * * * *

116

Marinda downed the water and asked for more. The woman behind the counter frowned, but filled the glass and Marinda drank it all. The restaurant was near Pacific Avenue and Van Ness. She had walked fourteen blocks since the second mailbox note, up and down hills, and she had at least ten more blocks to go before she reached her destination.

*Proceed by foot on Pacific to Hyde, then south to California, then east to Taylor. Go into the john in the basement of the Grace Cathedral,* the note had said.

"She must have gone for something to drink," Jordan said. "I bet she's dying of thirst." They waited in front of a fire hydrant.

A half block down the street, Essie and Carla waited in the Ford. "Hey, look," Carla said. "That woman on the bike. See her?"

Essie glanced at a bicyclist who had stopped and was adjusting something on her bike. "So?" She looked back at the restaurant door. Marinda emerged.

"She was there!" Carla was jumping around on the seat. "That woman was back there where Marinda got the second message. She was at the gas station a couple doors down from the phone booth."

"She was?"

"Look, she's looking at Marinda."

"Hm-m. I imagine a lot of people look at Marinda." Essie stared at the bicycler, squinting. "I don't remember seeing her before."

"I'm sure it's the same one."

"You think she might be Slick?"

"Come on, they're going."

Essie pulled the Ford into traffic. They passed the biker who was still off her bike. She was looking in the direction Marinda had gone, east on Pacific Avenue. From the rearview mirror, Elizabeth saw her mount and begin to ride along Pacific.

"It could be her," Carla said. "She could be making sure Marinda's not being followed. We should tell the others."

"Let's see where she goes." Essie pulled over. "I'm going to let her pass us. If we lose Marinda, we'll just go to the Cathedral."

The biker came at a very leisurely rate.

"She's going about the same speed Marinda is walking," Essie said.

The woman looked directly at them as she passed.

"She spotted us."

"Shit!"

"She's picking up speed. She must know we're following Marinda."

"She probably saw us earlier."

The biker took a left on Larkin.

"She's turning. She's going to leave. Oh, shit. And we'll probably never hear from her again."

"Go after her!" Carla ordered. "Don't let her get away!"

Essie pressed the accelerator.

"She'll destroy the statue."

"Not if I can help it," Essie said.

The woman on the bike was moving very rapidly now. The Ford stayed on her tail. The biker turned left on Broadway. The car stayed with her. She turned right on Polk.

"She knows we're after her. She's trying to ditch us."

"There's no way she can get away."

At the next intersection, the biker took a left. Essie got caught by a red light. The biker continued on, passing cars on the heavily trafficked street. The pursuers were nearly a block behind her now on Polk Street.

"She's going to get away," Essie said. "There's too

118

much traffic, I can't keep up with her." She beeped her horn at a left-turning car. It started to move and she swerved around it on the right.

"She took a right at the next corner," Carla said. "She looked back. She probably saw us. We have to grab her, Essie. It's the only thing we can do. Grab her before she gets away."

Essie sped up, weaving around cars. Then there was a clear section. She gunned it. They came to the biker, rode beside her. The woman slowed. They slowed. She sped up. So did they. Finally the biker pulled to the curb and lifted her bike onto the sidewalk. Essie slammed on the brakes. Carla flew out of the car and ran down the sidewalk. The woman was off her bike. She saw Carla, and started to remount. Carla reached her in time. She grabbed her by the arm.

"Hey, what's your problem?" The woman jerked away.

Carla seized the bike. Then Essie was there. She twisted the woman's arm into an armlock. Carla leaned her face close and hissed into her ear. "I've got a knife. Now cool out and just walk with us."

"Why are you doing this? What's the matter?"

Passersby stared.

"Move!"

They got her into the car, into the front seat between them. Essie started the engine.

"Wait, my bike!"

"She's worried about her bike," Carla said sarcastically.

"We can fit it in the back," Essie said. "The back seat folds down."

"Forget the bike," Carla said.

"I don't get this," the woman said.

Essie waited for traffic to clear, then backed up until she reached the bike. "Don't let her go."

Carla stared at the woman coldly. "She ain't goin' nowhere, are you, sister?"

Essie folded down the seat, got the bike, shoved it into the car.

"What do you want?" the woman demanded.

Essie started driving. "Cut the game. We know you know."

"What do you mean, know? Know what?"

"She's shaking," Carla said. "You know it's over, don't you, Slick?"

"Oh, God, who are you people?"

"I thought you were older. You're kind of young for this sort of crime, aren't you?"

"Are you police?"

"You'll get police if you don't cooperate with us. Do you want to tell us where it is?" They were on Pacific again, going east.

"Where what is?"

"I'm sure it's not in the john of the Grace Cathedral."

"I don't know what you're talking about."

"She doesn't know what we're talking about, Essie, did you hear that"

"Yeah, I heard."

"Can't you see the game is over, Slick? Why don't you just tell us about it?"

"Tell you about what? I have no idea what you're talking about."

"You know, as far as I'm concerned, once we get the statue, you can disappear. We're not interested in punishing you. We just want the Winged Dancer and once we have it, you can be a free woman."

"I imagine the police would feel differently about that," Essie said. She pulled onto a side street and stopped. "Talk to us, Slick. What's Marinda going to find at the Cathedral? Another note, right? What does it say? Save us time, Slick. Where's the statue?"

"Why do you keep calling me *Slick?*"

"What would you like us to call you?"

"I'd like you to tell me what this is about."

"What's your name?"

"Deidre. Deidre Johansen."

"Do you have some identification? You got a wallet on you? Check her pockets, Carla."

"Is this a robbery?"

"Hey, girlie, do you think everyone is a thief, just because you are? Her pockets are empty," Carla said.

"My wallet's at my mother's. What do you want from me?"

"You don't know, huh?"

"I have no idea."

"Okay, I'll play. Why were you following our friend, then? And why did you try to run away when you spotted us?"

"You were following me! I tried to get away when you were driving right next to me. That's when I went up onto the sidewalk. I thought you were nuts. I was afraid you were going to run me over or something."

"What were you doing at the gas station at Broadway near Baker?"

"Broadway and Baker? I don't even know where that is. I never heard of Baker."

"You don't say."

"I'm just visiting here. I don't live in San Francisco. When was I supposed to have been at this gas station?"

Essie looked at her watch. "Exactly thirty-five minutes ago. At nine-forty-five."

"At nine-forty-five I was having breakfast with my mom."

"You don't say? Let's go, Essie. She's going to do this the hard way. Let's go to the Cathedral. Marinda should be getting close to there by now."

A half block from the Cathedral, they saw the white

Toyota parked in a red zone. Essie stopped in another no-parking area a half dozen car lengths from the Toyota. "There's Marinda," she said.

They watched her going up the stairs of the huge church.

Marinda opened the heavy doors. The church was dark inside. It took awhile for her eyes to adjust. She found the stairway going down. Took it. Found the washroom. On the wall, in felt tip pen, was a message. *For WD, check shelf.* It was the only graffiti in the room. Marinda moved along the sinks, feeling underneath the shelf that ran the length of the mirror. Near the end, she found the envelope. The note read, *Take Jones to Market, then 7th Street to Howard. There's a warehouse there on Howard. The alley between 7th and 6th leads to the side door of the warehouse. Go there and wait.*

Marinda checked the stalls. The washroom was empty. She looked into the corridor. No one. She went back into the john. "This may be it," she said. "I'm supposed to go to a warehouse between sixth and seventh on Howard. There's an alley that goes to the side door. My route is Jones to Market then down seventh. Be discreet. My guess is that that's where she's going to pick me up."

"What a runaround," Elizabeth said. "Seventh and Howard is still a long walk from here."

"That's a crummy neighborhood," Jordan said. "There's Essie. They're right behind us, a few cars down." She chuckled. "They probably stopped for a burgie."

"Jesus, it looks like there's someone in the car with them!" Elizabeth said.

"Oh, great. What the hell are they doing? Here comes Marinda."

"Okay, we'll let her walk a little ways and then signal Essie."

As soon as she saw Jordan's hand, Essie moved the

Ford forward. She double-parked next to the Toyota. "Meet Slick," she said.

"What!"

"That's right. She tried to get away but we got her."

"That's Slick?" Elizabeth stared at the young, athletic-looking woman in the navy blue jacket.

"She was following Marinda. We were keeping an eye on her but when she realized it, she tried to get away."

"She admits it?"

"No, she denies everything. But she'll talk eventually."

"Can you explain this to me?" the woman said to Elizabeth. "I have no idea what's going on and what you people are talking about."

"She was there near the phone booth back on Baker and then we spotted her again near the restaurant where Marinda stopped. She's been following Marinda the whole time."

The woman said desperately, "I was with my mother until about ten o'clock and then I went out for a bike ride. These women started harassing me. When I tried to get away from them they came after me, twisted my arm and threatened me with a knife."

Elizabeth got out of the car and beckoned Carla to join her. They went to the sidewalk to talk. "You sure you saw her back on Baker?" Elizabeth asked.

"Yes. She's the one. Didn't you notice her there at the gas station?"

"I did see a woman on a bike. She had a green jacket on though."

Carla's brow furrowed. "Green? Are you sure?"

"The one I saw had a green jacket. I'm positive. She was putting air in her tires."

Carla looked uncertain. "Maybe we should call her mother. She says she's visiting from Indianapolis, that she just got here yesterday."

Elizabeth shook her head. "I think you two made a big mistake," she said, "and I think we better get after Marinda. Slick might decide to pick her up somewhere en route. We have to go. Why don't you and Essie check out this woman's story and then, assuming she's not Slick, give her a giant apology and hope she doesn't press charges. Meet us in the area of Sixth and Seventh Streets and Howard when you're finished. If we're already gone, we'll try to leave you a note."

"You're sure it was green?" Carla said.

They returned to their cars. "Where does your mother live?" Carla asked the woman.

"On Steiner, off Union Street."

"If she turns out to be Slick, then bring her along, by all means," Jordan called out.

Meredith was in the back seat laughing.

"We'll meet you at the warehouse," Carla called. "Be careful, huh?" Carla turned to her captive. "Is that jacket reversible?"

\* \* \* \* \*

They had left Highway 116 near Guerneville and were on a county road. The countryside was rolling hills. Some of the trees had taken on their fall colors. "It's a dirt road," Doralee said, "on the right after the next curve."

Amagyne slowed even more.

"There it is." Bushes made the entrance to the narrow road almost invisible. "Keep going, though. We can park up a ways where there are some trees."

"This would be easy to miss," Amagyne said. She continued on another hundred yards and parked off the shoulder among trees that concealed the car.

"It's about a half mile walk," Doralee said. "I'm almost positive no one will be there because of the welcoming ceremony." Doralee had told Amagyne about the two new

124

members and the ceremony being held for them that day at Jamma's house in San Francisco. "But better safe than sorry."

They walked quietly through the woods. The chirping of the birds made Amagyne think of home and of her bird, Dia, who lived in the Dome Building garden. She mentioned the bird to Doralee and Doralee became tearful. "She would sit on my shoulder, that little bird," Doralee said.

When the cabins came into view, Doralee stopped abruptly. She took Amagyne's wrist. "There's a car!" she said. "Someone's there." She tugged Amagyne off the road and several yards into the woods. "We can't go farther. They'll see us." She spoke in a whisper.

"Where is the place where the statue is?" Amagyne asked, whispering also.

"The other side of the cabins."

"Then we must go around."

"We can't. There are open fields all around it. The only way to get to the statue without going over the fields is through this section of woods, but then we have to go near the cabins. There's an open area we'd have to cross. It's visible from anywhere in the cabins."

"What do you suggest, Doralee?"

"I don't know. I was sure no one would be here."

"Perhaps we can leave for a while," Amagyne suggested, "and when we return they will be gone."

"It would be very risky to try to sneak by them. Of course they could be sleeping or watching TV or something. It's possible we could do it and not be seen."

"Do you have any idea who is there, which of the women?"

"Carrie and Lilia. It's Carrie's car we saw. Lilia is her lover and they're always together." Doralee let loose a whispered chuckle. "They look alike too. I call them *Carlilies, the clones.*"

"Do you think it is just them?"

"Probably."

"And how would they react if they saw us walking by?"

"I think I am not very trusted, Amagyne. If they saw me I think they'd be angry. I think they wouldn't let us pass. They'd probably phone the others."

"Would they stop us by force?"

Doralee thought a moment. "Yes, I believe they would."

Amagyne nodded. "It's ten-forty now. Let's go away for an hour or so, then return. Perhaps they will be gone. If not, perhaps we will have thought of a plan by then."

Quietly the two women walked back through the woods towards their car.

* * * * *

Marinda was dragging by the time she arrived at her destination. The alley was deserted. She leaned against the wall near the door at the side of the warehouse, looking in every direction. The few parked cars in the alley were all apparently empty. She tried the warehouse door. It was locked. There were no windows at ground level. At one end of the alley she could see Howard Street and at the other end Folsom, each with a moderate amount of traffic. The white Toyota was parked on the other side of Folsom, clearly visible, but a discreet distance away.

Marinda took out her handkerchief and talked as she pretended to blow her nose. "There's no message. I think this is the last stop. It better be; I'm exhausted. The Winged Dancer might be here in the warehouse, but I doubt it. I expect a car to come any minute and stop and she'll tell me to get inside. Can you hear my heart pounding?"

Marinda put the handkerchief away. She looked up along the rooftops. Narrowing her eyes, she tried to see inside the windows of the stark brick buildings. Nothing. She turned her eyes to the traffic on Howard.

Fifteen minutes passed and then Essie and Carla arrived in the Ford. Deidre was with them. They parked at the mouth of the alley, on Howard. They hunched down in the car, eyes glued on Marinda.

"I wish we had some way of letting the others know that Deidre isn't Slick," Essie said.

"They know," Carla said. "We're the ones that got paranoid."

In the Toyota, Elizabeth and Jordan were pretending to be discussing the map which, again, they had spread out on the dashboard. Only Meredith seemed relaxed. She appeared to be dozing.

They waited. They waited for over an hour. Marinda blew her nose again. "I can't figure it," they heard her say. "Where the hell is she?" As she was returning her handkerchief to her pocket, a car turned into the alley from Howard Street. Marinda straightened. She watched it coming toward her, a Chevy. It came halfway down the alley and stopped. There were two men in the car. Marinda's breath came rapidly. The car began to move toward her again.

* * * * *

It was almost noon when Doralee and Amagyne returned and again walked the road through the woods. As soon as they saw Carrie's car, they turned around, retraced their steps, and returned to their car. They then drove up the road to the cabins. Carrie came out immediately. "Doralee," she said. "What a surprise."

Then Lilia emerged from the cabin. The two Kwo-amjamites looked very much alike, both medium height with long brown hair tied back, tiny noses and large chins. Amagyne and Doralee got out of the car.

"I'd like you to meet my friend, Camille," Doralee said. "Camille, Carrie and Lilia."

The women smiled and shook hands.

Doralee held candles in one hand and sponges in the other. "We've come for a cleansing ceremony."

"Oh, I see." Carrie frowned.

"Camille is learning about our truths. They are striking a good chord in her."

"Welcome, then," Carrie said to Amagyne. "We didn't expect anyone today, because of the ceremony at Jamma's. Lilia is not feeling well."

"I'm sorry."

"She's resting here today. Come in. I can help you with the preparations." Carrie turned to her double. "Why don't you go lie down, hon. I'll tend to them."

"Oh, don't bother yourself," Doralee said. "We'll use the other cabin. We don't want to disturb you."

"No, I insist. Come in with us."

The cabin was airy and bright, the furnishing simple but very comfortable. "Sit," Carrie said, "I'll heat the water for you."

Amagyne took a chair near the window. Lilia excused herself and left the room.

"I'll help with the tea," Doralee said.

"No, you sit with your friend. I'll let you know when it's ready." Carrie went to the kitchen.

Doralee sat near Amagyne. "She might be making a phone call. I can't read her. I can't tell if she's suspicious or not. If she tries to stall us, then I think we should run for the statue and try to grab a quick picture and get out of here."

Five minutes later Carrie returned to the living room. "The tea is steeping," she said. "You should meditate first. Out on the balcony. I have the tape ready. You should meditate for at least an hour and then maybe nap before you begin. Have your tea and then do the meditation."

"We planned to do the meditation outside," Doralee said, "out in the grass by the rocks."

128

"It is better that you do it here. So Jamma has said. *From within the shelters we have made, then moving slowly to the earth Kwo-am has given us.*"

"I've never heard that," Doralee said.

"It is from the Sage. You must follow the way Jamma speaks for the cleansing to be complete."

"But we don't have to meditate for an hour. That's too long."

"It takes the time that it takes. I will tell you when it is time to go outside for the cleansing. You know I am very experienced at this, Doralee." She looked at Amagyne. "Have you known Doralee long?"

"Long enough to know she is a woman very dear to me," Amagyne said.

Carrie scrutinized her. "You live in San Francisco?"

"I'm visiting," Amagyne said, "from back east. And you?"

"Oakland," Carrie said. "Why did you choose today for the cleansing, Doralee? Weren't you expected at Jamma's?"

"This felt more pressing. Though you may not see our coming as an intrusion, Carrie, I'm feeling uncomfortable. My wish is that we take our tea and then that Camille and I go right outside and begin."

"After the meditation," Carrie said. "I will tell you when it's time." She left again for the kitchen.

"She's not going to let us out there. She's called Jamma, I'm sure. I bet the others are on their way."

"Shall we push it further? I don't read her as one who would try violence to stop us."

"We'll meditate for a half hour to appease her, then we'll insist on going outside. We'll see what she does."

Carrie returned with the tea.

* * * * *

Marinda's body didn't move as the car came closer.

129

Elizabeth and Jordan were leaning toward the radio receiver, staring at the Chevy which had now stopped next to Marinda.

"Hey, baby," they heard. "Come on, get in. Come on with us."

There was a pause, then Marinda's voice. "Where to?"

"We'll have a good time."

They could hear a car door opening.

"Jesus Christ, they're trying to pick her up," Jordan said.

"I'm waiting for the police." It was Marinda's voice.

"The police! You're shittin' us. What for?"

"Someone grabbed my purse."

Pause. "Hey, let's get out of here, Kenny."

The car door closed. The men drove off.

"*Puercos,*" Marinda said under her breath. She leaned against the wall again. She watched. Up and down the alley. Essie and Carla and Deidre watched also. Up the alley and up and down Howard Street. Elizabeth and Jordan watched. Down the alley. Up and down Folsom Street. Meredith was reading a novel.

Another hour passed. And part of another.

"I'm hungry," Carla said.

"It's after one o'clock," Essie said.

Marinda was sitting on a sheet of cardboard, leaning against the warehouse wall. Elizabeth was leaning heavily on the steering wheel. Jordan's eyes were glazed over. They watched as Marinda stood and brushed herself off.

"She's not coming," they heard Marinda say.

"Surprise," Meredith said.

"Goddamn," said Jordan.

"What time is it?"

"One-thirty."

"Shit."

Marinda was walking towards them. Elizabeth started the engine and met her halfway down the alley.

"You think she saw us?" Elizabeth asked as Marinda got in the back seat with Meredith.

"I don't know," Marinda said. "What a waste."

"Oh, it may have served a purpose," Meredith said.

"What purpose?"

"I don't know," Meredith said coyly.

The Ford drove up the alley. "A no-show," Elizabeth said.

Carla introduced Deidre and explained to the others how she and Essie had gone to Deidre's mother's house on Steiner Street and confirmed Deidre's story.

"She's from Indianapolis," Essie said.

"You must be pissed as hell at these crazy women," Elizabeth said to Deidre.

"They explained everything to me," Deidre said. "I think it's fascinating. I asked to come along."

"What a bust it turned out to be," Elizabeth said. She shrugged. "Let's go get some lunch."

\* \* \* \* \*

Amagyne and Doralee sat cross-legged on mats on the balcony. The tape went on endlessly — soft flute music with ocean sounds and sounds of the wind.

"Enough," Doralee said, finally. She stretched, then got up and turned off the tape. She took her pack. "Let's go."

Amagyne grabbed the candles and sponges. She and Doralee were in the kitchen filling the plastic bucket with warm water when Carrie came.

"Already?" she said.

"Yes, we're going outside."

"You shouldn't rush the preparations."

"We're prepared enough," Doralee said. She swung the full bucket from the sink. "We'll see you in a while."

"Kwo-am is with you," Carrie said.

"And with us all," said Doralee.

131

Amagyne followed Doralee to the back door and outside. Carrie watched them from the kitchen window.

"Wait!" Carrie called.

They turned.

"Do you have incense?"

"Yes," Doralee said.

They continued toward the back. The trees and bushes were thick. There were many rocks. "Through here," Doralee said.

They stepped into the open spot surrounded by trees and bushes and boulders. There was grass, there were flowers and a fire pit. But there was no statue.

Doralee stared at the flat empty spot where she had expected the Winged Dancer to be. She looked at Amagyne. "I was so sure."

"So was I."

"Damn!" Doralee set the bucket down on the ground.

"It's beautiful here," Amagyne said. "Very peaceful."

They sat in the grass for a long time without speaking, then Doralee asked, "Would you like me to show you the cleansing ceremony? They say it dilutes zetkap."

Amagyne was staring at a flower. "Perhaps I need it," she said. "Perhaps I'm guilty of misfounded suspicions." She looked at Doralee. "On the other hand —"

"Yes," Doralee interrupted. "They could have hidden it somewhere else."

Amagyne nodded.

Doralee set three candles on a rock. She lit the incense then began to hum softly. Amagyne joined in the humming.

* * * * *

Elizabeth was exhausted when she got home. She told Jane what had happened and how frustrated she was.

"There's a weird message for you on the answering machine," Jane said. "It might relate to this."

Elizabeth dashed to the machine, rewound and listened. "Check the mailbox on Waller and Noe," the voice said. That was all. The voice was distorted and nasal sounding.

"Slick," Elizabeth said.

"I'll go with you," Jane said, grabbing her jacket.

A note was taped underneath the mailbox. *I hope your friend enjoyed her walk and all of you who were following her had a pleasant time hanging around the alley. Surely you didn't think I'd fall for your silly trick. The statue is safely tucked away where it will remain until I have what I asked for. Or until I give up on you, which may occur first. You truly are trying my patience. While you've probably surmised that I would prefer that the statue survive, I am flexible. My advice: Stop pushing me. I hope not to hear from you again until delivery day. Since you claim you are raising the money yourselves, I'll give you the benefit of the doubt and allow a time extension. You have until October 31. That's the final date. You will receive another note from me on that day with directions on how to deliver. You know the way it has to go: cash, unmarked, non-sequential serial numbers, mix of older and newer bills. I want about 50% $100's, 40% $50's, and the rest $20's. Slick.*

# Chapter 14

Randy spent much of Saturday getting her bike in shape. She'd had the motorcycle for five years but didn't use it often anymore. She changed the plugs and the oil and polished all the chrome. It's no big deal, she kept telling herself. I'm just taking an out-of-towner for a ride to see the city. Nothing to get excited about. She was more excited than she'd been in a long time.

The next morning she had brunch with Marce, who was in almost as good a mood as Randy was. She seemed eager to tell Randy about the latest chapter in the Winged Dancer story. She prefaced it by saying she probably shouldn't be telling Randy because the thief seemed to find out everything but then she told her anyhow — about Slick having sent a note saying Marinda could come and see the statue, about Marinda going on a wild goose chase all over the tallest hills in the city and then waiting in some alley for hours and Slick never showing up. Marce thought it was a riot. Randy didn't see the humor in it at all.

"So, what's going to happen now?" Randy asked.

"I guess we'll do what Slick said in her latest note," Marce said. "Quit bugging her and get the money ready by October thirtieth. That's a two-week extension. I thought that was pretty soft of her, but we had told her we needed time to raise the money. I guess she believed it." Marce slid half a bacon slice into her mouth, seeming quite self-satisfied.

"So that's that," Randy said.

"There's more," Marce said.

Randy waited while Marce ate some more of her omelette and got a refill on her coffee. She knew there was no way she could hurry Marce and besides, she wasn't enjoying what she was hearing. She kept thinking about Marinda waiting in that alley. This Slick is a real bitch, she thought.

Marce finished off her hashbrowns, then announced, "Meredith accused Marinda of being the thief."

"Oh, great," Randy said.

"She thought Marinda had taken the statue and shipped it back to Marigua, that she wanted it for her own private collection." Marce laughed as she talked. "So she goes to where Marinda is staying and asks Marinda to come with her to the bedroom, Marinda's bedroom. I can imagine what Marinda thought about that. So they go there together and Meredith goes straight for the dresser drawer and pulls out a piece of paper, a receipt. She waves it in Marinda's face and tells her to 'fess up and that she and Amagyne will try to help her. Meredith had dragged Amagyne along on this."

Randy nodded, saying nothing, feeling bad for Meredith.

"Apparently Marinda laughed in her face. I guess that was after she gave Meredith a piece of her mind for going through her things. Then she laughed at her for her suspicions and her *egregious* error, as she called it. That woman has quite a vocabulary for a foreigner."

Marce finished her omelette and asked why Randy wasn't eating.

"I'm not hungry," Randy said. Marce eyed her nearly full plate. "Help yourself," Randy told her, and Marce immediately scooped up the remaining egg and potatoes.

"The receipt was written in Spanish." Marce laughed heartily. "God, I wish I'd been there. So Marinda translates it for them. It was for a refrigerator, a commercial refrigerator she bought and had shipped to a friend of hers in Marigua."

"I see." Randy was feeling quite sad. "Poor Meredith," she said.

"Poor Meredith is right. The girl cracked up. Right there in front of Marinda and Amagyne. Just started shaking and crying. Amagyne took her off some place to console her."

"Is that why you're being so nasty about this?" Because Amagyne was kind to Meredith?"

"I'm not being nasty. Amagyne can be whatever she wants to whoever she wants. It makes no difference to me."

"Oh, really?"

"Look, Randy, the woman caught my eye. That's all. She's a good-looking woman, you have to admit that. But she and I could never be a number. I found her attractive in a rather exotic way, but to tell you the truth, I'm no longer interested."

Something must have happened that I don't know about, Randy thought, wondering if Amagyne had given

Marce the brush-off. "How did you learn about all this?" Randy asked.

"From Meredith. The host committee had another meeting last night — to ponder the latest development about the statue. Afterwards, Meredith and I went for a drink. Actually, quite a few drinks. She talked. She told me the whole story."

"I hope you didn't laugh at her."

"Of course not. I didn't even laugh when she told me she finds Amagyne's religion appealing. Looks like the Kwo-amians are getting another convert." Marce laughed.

After Marce ate the two meals, she wanted to go to her place for a while but Randy told her she had plans. She chose not to mention with whom. Even if she had nothing to do, she wouldn't want to be with Marce. She knew what would probably happen — they'd make love and then Marce would dismiss her. She didn't need that and certainly wasn't feeling loving towards Marce.

* * * * *

When Randy arrived home the phone was ringing. The caller asked for Jay. That still happened from time to time and it really annoyed her. After she told the person that Jay didn't live there anymore and hung up, she kept thinking about Jay, wondering where she was and how she was doing. Reminiscing. Feeling sad, hurt, angry. Making excuses for her, then feeling angry again. She remembered times when Jay had been very tender and loving. How could one person be so delightful and also such a total shithead?

Not my concern, she told herself. I've got better things to think about. It was two o'clock. In two hours she would be with Marinda Sartoria. She went to her closet and stared at her clothes. It ended up taking her over an hour to find just the right outfit — jeans, a black pullover sweater, ankle-high boots, the rope and bead bracelet, and the thin leather jacket Jess had given her for her birthday a few years ago.

Randy arrived at Lancy's right on time. Marinda offered her tea and they sat in the kitchen. Marinda also was dressed in jeans.

"Jordan tells me you do biological research," Marinda said, as she set the teacup in front of Randy. "You're a biologist?"

"Of sorts," Randy said. "I have a bachelor's degree in biology." She couldn't take her eyes off Marinda, and the sound of her voice was like beautiful music.

"You like the work?"

"It's not bad. Actually, it's pretty boring. My real love is graphic design."

"Is that so?" Marinda seemed genuinely interested. "And have you pursued this love?"

"I've been taking courses in it," Randy said. She pulled out her wallet and handed Marinda a business card. "I made this for Marce."

Marinda studied the card. "That is an excellent logo," she said, again sounding quite genuine. "You have talent."

They talked for almost an hour before going for their ride. The more time she spent with Marinda, the more comfortable Randy became. She loved showing Marinda her city and Marinda seemed delighted by the sights. It was dark when she brought Marinda back to Lancy's and said goodbye.

She drove home on a cloud. There's something there, she told herself, something very special. She felt happier than she had in many months.

# Chapter 15

Monday night, Randy got home from work at about five-twenty. She was planning to have a bite to eat, read for a little while, then go over to Jess's to play Hearts with her and Judy and a couple of other friends. She had just hung up her jacket when the doorbell rang.

"Randy Van Fleet?" the man said.

"Yes?"

He showed her a badge. "I'm Detective Turillo with the San Francisco Police Department."

He introduced the man with him but Randy didn't catch his name. Turillo said he wanted to ask Randy a few questions and asked if they could come in. She led them to the kitchen. Turillo was a big man, very hairy. It felt weird having two macho straight men sitting around her kitchen table.

They told her they were investigating the theft of an art object from the Indian Museum. Randy nodded, not telling them that she already knew this and a lot more, too.

"You live alone?" Turillo asked.

She nodded.

"How long have you lived here?"

"Five years."

"Have you ever had a roommate, someone who lived here with you?"

"I've had roommates," Randy said. "Why?"

"Do you know a Jay Horne?"

"Yes . . ." Why on earth was he asking about her, Randy thought.

"Does she live here?"

"No."

"Did she ever live here?"

"Yes."

"Where does she live now?"

"I don't know. Can you tell me why you're asking these questions? What are you interested in Jay for? I thought this was about a theft."

"We'd like to talk with her."

"Yeah, so would I," Randy said.

"Do you know how we could reach her?"

"No."

"When did you last have contact with her?"

"Not for a long time," Randy said. "Six months or so."

"She was your roommate and then you stopped seeing her, is that right?"

"That's right."

"Would you tell us what happened, why she left?"

"Nothing happened," Randy said. "She moved on."
Randy was wracking her brain trying to figure out what they were after.

"The uh . . . friendship ended, the relationship you had with her?"

"That's right. It ended."

"That happened when?"

"Six months ago," Randy said.

"And you haven't seen her since?"

"No."

"Or had any contact?"

"No." Randy thought about the postcard and the letter, but didn't feel like mentioning them — not yet, at least.

"Is she in San Francisco?"

"I believe she left town," Randy said.

"When was that?"

"Six months ago."

"And she didn't return as far as you know?"

"Not as far as I know. Did she return?"

"Where did she go when she left town?"

Randy was starting to get annoyed. "Would you tell me why you're asking about Jay?" she said. "If I knew maybe I'd feel better talking about her."

Turillo seemed to be thinking about that but instead of answering, he asked if he and his partner could look around the house first. "Would you mind?" he asked.

"Yes, I'd mind," Randy said. "Why would you want to do that? What are you looking for? Do you think I have the Winged Dancer hidden in my closet? Really, what's the story?" She was feeling pissed.

"So you know about the statue," he said.

"Yes, I know it was stolen."

"How do you know?"

"I heard from friends."

"What friends?"

141

Randy did not like being asked all those questions without knowing what he was after. "Friends," she said, irritably.

"We're trying to get the statue back," Turillo said. "To do so we need information. I assume you'd like us to get the statue back. Wouldn't you?"

"Sure," Randy said, "but I don't know why you want information about Jay or why you want to look around my house. What does that have to do with the statue?"

"Maybe nothing. Maybe a lot," the other cop said. "Can you account for your whereabouts on Tuesday, the twenty-ninth of September, between five and eight p.m.?"

"That's the day it was stolen," Randy said.

"That's right. Two weeks ago tomorrow."

"I was here."

"Was anyone with you?"

"No."

"Did anyone see you here during that time or call you on the phone?"

Randy remembered that she had asked Marce to go out with her that night, but that Marce had been busy with her friend across the Bay. Randy had stayed home. "I don't remember any phone calls," she said. "No one came over. I doubt that anyone saw me. Maybe a neighbor saw me come in, but I doubt it."

"What time was that? When you came home?"

"Between five-twenty and five-thirty," Randy said. "That's when I usually get home from work." This questioning was giving her the creeps.

"What neighbor might have seen you come in? Would you give us names and addresses?"

She gave them some names, the couple next door, Tom and Sandy Phillips, and the people across the street, a couple of gay guys named Steven and Don. She didn't know their last names. She thought it unlikely that any of them had seen her come home that night, or even if they had, that they'd remember it.

"We'll check it out," Turillo said.

"Do you think I had something to do with the theft?"

Turillo and Randy stared at each other. "Are you connected with Other Ways?" he asked her.

"No, but I know about it through friends."

"Through Jay Horne?"

"No. Do you think Jay's involved with the burglary?"

"We think she might be."

Randy was shocked. "You can't be serious." He looked very serious. "What makes you think so?" she asked.

"We have reason to believe she was in San Francisco on the day of the theft," the other officer said. He was partly bald and had saliva in the corners of his mouth. Randy didn't like looking at him.

"I seriously doubt that," she said.

"Why is that, Ms Van Fleet?"

Randy shrugged.

"Who are some of Jay Horne's other friends in San Francisco? Could you give us some names?"

Randy didn't answer. For some reason, she didn't want to. It felt like *squealing*.

"Does she know any of the other people involved in the Other Ways Conference?"

"She might. She knows a lot of people."

"Can you give us their names."

"Why do you suspect Jay?" Randy asked.

"If I told you, would you be more cooperative? I think you think you're protecting her by telling us so little."

Randy thought he was right. She didn't know if she would tell him more or not if she knew why they thought Jay was involved. "If I thought there was any possibility that she actually could have stolen the statue then, yes, I might be able to tell you more," she said.

143

Turillo looked at her for a long time. "We have a witness who states that on the night of the burglary, a sixteen-foot U-Haul truck was parked at the loading dock at the Indian Museum. This was at four-thirty p.m. Another witness saw a truck of the same description pass by his home a block away at approximately seven-thirty p.m. We ran a check on U-Haul truck rentals in the area on or about that day. Jay Beth Horne rented a sixteen-footer on the twenty-ninth of September at seven-thirty-five a.m."

Randy was flabbergasted. "You're sure?"

"Yes ma'am."

"It couldn't have been somebody else using her name?"

"Very unlikely. You have to show your driver's license to rent a vehicle."

"But why would she be renting a truck?"

Turillo just stared at her. Was Jay really back in San Francisco, Randy wondered. She was beginning to feel very angry. "You think she used the truck to steal the statue?"

"It's a possibility that we're checking out," Turillo said. "Perhaps if we talked to her she could clear herself."

"Yes, right, you should talk to her. I'm sure she could explain . . ." This was feeling extremely weird to Randy.

"Any idea where we might locate her?" Turillo asked.

Randy shook her head. It couldn't have been Jay, she thought.

"Any friends of hers who might know?"

"Last I heard she was in Canada," Randy said.

One of Turillo's bushy eyebrows went up. "Where did you hear that?"

"She wrote me from Canada."

"When?"

"A few months ago."

"She was living there?"

"She didn't say. She just sort of ran off and I got a postcard and a letter but they didn't say much at all. So she's back in San Francisco."

"Was," Turillo said. "She's apparently in Canada now. That was her destination. The truck was turned in in Calgary on Friday, the third of October."

Randy shook her head. She didn't know what to think.

"Will you help us try to locate her?"

"How?" Randy said. "I don't —"

"Names of any of her friends here, family, anyone who might know her whereabouts."

"It sounds like you should be checking in Calgary, Canada," Randy said.

"We haven't been able to locate her there or in Banff. Any names for us?"

Randy thought of Lenore Zemke and Marilyn Albro, two of Jay's old roommates before she moved in with her. She thought of Jordan. "No," she said. "I don't know any of her friends." Of course, if the police did talk with Jay, she probably could explain everything, Randy thought. Jay could always explain everything. Could she have been so ridiculous to have stolen that statue? Randy felt a strong need to talk with Jess or Marce. She was feeling intensely distraught. Could Jay really possibly have done it?

"If your memory improves, give me a call," Turillo said. He handed Randy a business card.

"I imagine a lot of people rent U-Haul trucks every day," Randy said, "for all kinds of reasons."

"They don't all have a friend who's friends with people who knew all about the statue," Turillo said.

"That's just coincidence," Randy said.

"Maybe so. How involved are you in it, Ms Van Fleet?"

"In what?" Randy said. She was starting to despise him.

"We'll find out," he said. "Call me if you want to talk. It would be to your benefit to cooperate."

"Am I a suspect?"

"We haven't ruled you out. Don't leave town, huh?"

That fucker, she thought. The duo left and Randy

watched them through the window. They went next door and rang the doorbell. Randy went to her phone and called Marce.

* * * * *

She had only told Marce the first few sentences when Marce insisted that Randy come to her place. All Randy had said was that the police thought Jay might be the thief because they found out she'd rented a truck the day of the theft. Marce wanted her to come over right away. Randy didn't want to leave while the cops were still in the neighborhood. She thought they'd follow her or something and it gave her a shitty feeling. She went to the window and could see them across the street talking with Dan. Dan looked up at Randy's house from time to time as he talked. He kept pushing his Siberian husky back into the doorway with his knee. Randy wondered what he was saying. After a few minutes, the cops left.

She phoned Jess and told her she'd be late for the card game, to go ahead and start without her.

"I hope it's important," Jess said teasingly.

"It is," Randy said. "I'll tell you about it soon."

She drove almost as fast as Marce always did. It was about six-thirty when she got to Marce's house. "Have you eaten?" Marce asked.

"No, I'm not hungry," Randy said. Marce was chewing on a giant submarine sandwich. She had a very big appetite.

"Okay, tell me all about it," she said after she swallowed. They were at her kitchen table.

Randy told Marce everything the cops had said and everything she had said, the best she could remember.

"She was using the truck to move," Marce said when Randy finished.

"What do you mean? How do you know? What do you know about it?"

"That shit!" Marce said.

"What is it? Tell me."

Marce leaned back, smiling to herself. It irritated Randy immensely but she knew she had no choice but to wait. She watched Marce take a big bite of her sandwich. Marce chewed for a long time. What did she mean that Jay was using the truck to move, Randy wondered. What was she talking about?

"Jay was indeed in San Francisco on September twenty-ninth," Marce said at last, "and she indeed rented a U-Haul truck."

"How do you know?"

"Sue told me."

"Sue who? You mean the one on the committee?"

"Mm-hm."

"When? What do you mean? Tell me."

Randy had to wait while Marce took another bite and then a big slug of beer.

"After the statue arrived at the museum," she finally said, "I gave Sue a ride home. She told me Jay was staying at her place, that she'd come to help someone move to Banff."

"Who?"

"A woman named Barbara. Here's the part that makes me wonder —"

"She was here in San Francisco and you knew it and didn't even tell me? You fucker!"

"Right, I'm a fucker."

"How could you not tell me?"

"I'm a fucker."

"Quit saying that."

"I considered telling you. I decided it would do more harm than good, that it would do no good, in fact."

"*You* decided! Well, who the hell are you to decide what's good for me and what isn't? Jesus, Marce, that's the most arrogant, controlling —"

"Hey!" Marce sat up and glared at her. "Cool it, kiddo!" She leaned back in her chair again. "I made the judgment that confronting Jay about the money was fruitless," she said.

"I resent your making that judgment for me," Randy responded.

"I can understand that."

"There was more than money between me and Jay. Can you understand that?"

"Barbara was moving to Canada to live with Jay," Marce said.

Randy let that sink in. She was feeling slightly sick to her stomach.

"You're much better off without her," Marce said. "The other day, when I was talking with some of the committee women about who told who about the statue and the museum security procedures . . ."

Randy was trying to listen, but her mind was on Jay — Jay and *Barbara*. As absurd as it seemed, she was feeling terribly jealous.

". . . and called her from Canada too."

"What?"

"I said she told her everything."

"Who?"

"Jay, Sue. Sue told Jay, or Barbara rather, but then I'm sure Barbara told Jay."

"Don't you hate that name — *Barbara?*"

"Randy, are you hearing me?"

"What? Sue told *Barbara* all about the Winged Dancer. So?"

"So have a beer," Marce said. "Loosen up your mind. Are you still in love with her?"

"Of course not."

Marce wouldn't talk anymore until Randy drank some beer and calmed down. Then she said, "I wouldn't put it past Jay to steal the statue, would you?" She seemed to be smirking.

Randy started to smile. "If she did it, she could be in big trouble," she said. "She wouldn't like prison."

"She might."

"I can imagine her contemplating stealing it," Randy said. "Listening to Sue and playing with the idea of sneaking in there and loading that crate onto her U-Haul, then taking off for Canada."

Marce was leaning back with her hands folded over her belly.

"But I can't picture her actually doing it." Randy stared into space. "She used to come up with all kinds of crazy schemes. Some of them quite illegal. I don't think she ever did any of them, though."

"She did you," Marce said.

"True," Randy acknowledged, "though I'm sure she has every intention of paying you off. At least, she thinks she does."

"Right. And stealing the statue for San Francisco is her contribution to the city."

Randy smiled.

"And the four hundred thousand is her fee for services rendered."

Randy shook her head. "You think she did it, don't you?"

"What do *you* think?"

Randy shook her head. "That she did it."

Marce laughed.

"What should we do?" Randy asked.

"Stop her."

"How?"

"Find her. Get her to bring the statue back."

"I wouldn't want her to go to jail."

"Softie."

"Would you?" Randy asked.

"Not especially," Marce said.

"Do you think she's planning to pay you off with part of the four hundred thousand?"

"Perhaps," Marce said.

"I bet she is. She does feel guilt, you know, when she fucks someone over."

"How noble of her."

"She probably took the statue to Canada and then came back to collect the money." Randy laughed. "Pretty slick. You have to admit she's a character."

"She's a character. What do you mean about her fucking people over. You're not the first?"

"She told me about an ex-lover in Chicago who she . . ." Randy stopped.

"She what?" Marce prodded.

"Never mind."

"Randy, you little wimp. I can't believe you're actually protecting the woman after what she did to you."

"She never really intends to hurt anyone."

"Oh, I see."

"She told me she'd changed. She talked about how guilty she felt for some of the things she'd done. Back in Chicago. But that was all in her past, she said."

"Well, her past has come to haunt you, my gullible friend." Marce shook her head.

"I guess some people just never quite get a handle on ethics," Randy said.

Marce laughed. "So true."

"I thought she loved me."

"I think she was very fond of you, Randy, but love may be something a bit beyond her."

"I wonder who this *Barbara* is."

"Some chippie."

"Marce, that's disgusting."

Marce laughed again. "Well, if we can find Jay, we may not only get the statue back, but also the van and the computer and whatever else of mine she ripped off when we split."

"She took my leather suitcase."

Marce shook her head.

"The cops may find her first, you know," Randy said.

"We have several advantages." Marce's hands were still folded over her belly. "For one thing, we know she's trying to extort money. So far the police don't know that. We also might be able to trace her through the community better than the cops could. We also know her style."

"Her *modus operandi*. You know, now that I think of it, those letters from Slick sound just like Jay. And that mannequin bit, that's her."

"A bundle of laughs."

"I guess Jess is right. That Jay's a narcissistic asshole."

"Well put," Marce said.

"I wonder if we should tell the others. Yes, of course we should. We need to comb the city, put out the word. You can be sure someone in the community knows where she is."

"I've got a better idea." Marce reached over to the counter for a sheet of yellow paper. "I started working on this after you called. *Dear Slick Jay,* she read, You know we know. So far the fuzz are in the dark. Must we shed a little light on you for them, or will you come forward? Better you deal with us than with the cops or the insurance folk. We're willing to trade. Come in from the cold. For the Personals in the *Chronicle,*" Marce said.

"If she's smart, she'll do it," Randy said. "She might just run, though."

"She'd know she'd be caught eventually. She *is* smart."

"This will blow people's minds. I wonder if any of the other women on the committee know her, besides Jordan."

151

"I don't know." Marce held up the note. "I'm going to call this in to the *Chronicle*," she said. "I'll sign it, *Marce*."

"Don't you think we should talk to the others first?"

"I don't think I could endure another one of the decision-making discussions. I think we should just proceed on our own."

"You know, she could be in Canada now and be working with someone else here. That's possible. Someone else could be playing *Slick* in San Francisco. If Jay's in Canada, the cops may find her before we do."

The more Marce and Randy talked, the more Randy realized that she believed Jay had stolen the statue. Never a dull moment with Jay, she thought. What a character. What a jerk.

# Chapter 16

Randy ended up skipping the card game that night. Instead she went home and was sitting in front of the TV brooding when Meredith phoned. "I really need to talk," she said. Randy invited her over.

Twenty minutes later, in Randy's living room, Meredith told her about accusing Marinda of being the thief, and then about Marinda convincing everybody that Meredith was sorely mistaken, that it was a refrigerator, and not the statue, that she'd had shipped to Marigua.

"She'd convinced me, too, and I felt miserable about being so wrong, but now I'm not so sure," Meredith said.

"I've been thinking a lot about this, Randy. The receipt could have been falsified. Maybe Marinda paid off the shipping agent."

"Oh, come on, Meredith."

"I just know she did it."

"Let it go," Randy said. "It was definitely not Marinda who took the statue."

"You don't know that for sure," Meredith said. "She's deceiving everyone."

"I know it for sure."

"How? The receipt doesn't prove anything."

"No, not because of the receipt. Because I know who *did* take the statue."

"Oh? You sound as certain as I am. Who do *you* think took it?"

"My ex-lover," Randy said. "Jay Horne." She proceeded to tell Meredith about her visit from the police, the U-Haul, even Jay's involvement with Barbara.

"I'll be damned," Meredith said when Randy finished.

"I suppose it could be just coincidence about the truck," Randy said.

"You don't sound like you believe that."

"Everything fits too well, including the wording of the notes and the mannequin stunt. Definitely Jay's style."

Meredith was shaking her head. "And I was so damned sure it was Marinda. I think I was obsessed with the idea. But if what you're telling me is true, then I guess . . . well, then obviously I've been wrong. I misread her."

"I think you did," Randy said.

Meredith nodded. Both women were quiet awhile, then Meredith said, "This must be really hard on you, Randy, learning about Jay."

"Yeah, not only does my lover desert me and leave me saddled with her debt, but she runs off with another woman, and, to top it all off, turns out to be a goddam felon."

"You must be pissed as hell."

"I think it hasn't completely sunk in yet."

Meredith shook her head. "I wonder what we should do now?"

"Marce is sending Jay a message," Randy said. "In the personals. Telling her we're on to her."

"She is? Without talking to anyone else? That doesn't seem right. Don't you think Elizabeth and the others should know what's going on?"

"I suppose," Randy said.

"Really, they should know."

"I've got real mixed feelings about this, Meredith. Partly I want Jay to get nailed. I hope the police catch up with the bitch and slam her goddam ass in jail. Partly I feel like I want to protect her, take care of her . . ."

"Yeah, I know. It's hard when you hate someone you love — or used to love."

"If we can get the statue back without Jay going to jail, I guess I'd prefer that. I'd like to pulverize her, but I don't wish prison on anybody."

Randy realized Meredith was no longer listening. She was staring off into space. "What are you thinking?"

Meredith didn't answer right away. Finally she murmured, "Yes, that's what happened." She looked at Randy. "They did it together, Randy. Marinda and Jay. They took the statue together."

\* \* \* \* \*

Elizabeth and Carla were fuming.

"Calm down," Marce told them. "Elizabeth, sit, let me get you something to drink." Marce rose from behind her desk. "You were on my list of things to do today."

"List of . . . I can't believe it." Elizabeth paced around the office.

Marce went into the adjoining room. "Beer, pop, juice? What would you like?"

Carla was in one of the leather chairs across from Marce's desk, her leg flung over the arm. "I could use a beer," she said.

Marce returned with an assortment of drinks. "So what did Randy tell you?"

Carla took a beer. "She didn't tell *us* anything. She told Meredith."

Elizabeth sat. Marce pushed a sheet of paper across the desk. "This is what I· put in the ad."

Elizabeth read it then handed it to Carla. "You're not much of a team player," she said to Marce.

Marce laughed. "I never was. It'll be in tomorrow morning's paper. I expect to hear from her by tomorrow night."

"What if you don't?" Carla said, putting the paper back on the desk. "Even if this Jay is the thief and she reads this, I'm not so sure she'll contact you."

"Worth a try, I figured," Marce said. "Did Randy tell you the details?"

"She told Meredith about the U-Haul."

"You know Sue's been keeping Slick updated. She's a regular news service," Marce said scornfully.

"If Jay is Slick and if she's in Canada, then how could she —"

"She's not in Canada."

"That was days ago. She came back."

"Or maybe she has someone here reading the personal ads for her, and mailing us the crate boards." Elizabeth said.

"And sending Marinda on wild goose chases around the city," Carla added.

"Possible, but I doubt it." Marce rested her arms on the desk. "I think she's in town and that I'll get a call from her tomorrow. Now that she knows we know, she'll want to save her skin. And that means we'll get the statue back."

"And what if you don't hear from her?" Carla repeated. "If I were her and I got this message . . ." She gestured toward the sheet of paper. ". . . I'd cut up the statue and disappear."

Marce stroked her chin. "Possible," she said, "but very unlikely. Putting in the ad was a risk I thought worth taking."

"You should have consulted us."

"I suppose I should have. Do you want to try to stop the ad?" Marce reached for the phone. "I could tell . . ."

"It's too late to cancel it," Elizabeth said. "I already checked."

Marce shrugged. "So now we just wait and see what happens. Do the others know?"

Elizabeth nodded. "Sue's a basket case. Feels as guilty as Lady Macbeth."

Marce smiled. "Do you think it'll teach her to talk less?"

"We all talked to people," Carla said. "There's no sense blaming Sue, she feels bad enough already."

"She tried to phone Barbara in Canada this morning," Elizabeth said. "Got a recording."

"Why'd she do that?" Marce snapped.

"I asked her to. Sue says Barbara told her she and Jay were going on a camping trip."

"They're not on any camping trip," Marce said. "At least not Jay. I bet she's within five miles of us right now. Does Marinda still think her pal from Marigua swiped the statue?" Marce opened a can of grapefruit juice and poured a glass.

"Not really," Elizabeth said. "We called Turillo as soon as Meredith told us about Jay. Marinda talked to him. He told her —"

"She didn't tell him about Slick, did she?" Marce's eyes flashed angrily.

"No," Carla said. "Some of us don't make unilateral decisions that might mess things up for everyone else."

"Touché," Marce said, "but nothing's messed up, Carla. We'll get the statue back. So what did Turillo have to say?"

"He confirmed Randy's story about Jay. About the U-Haul. Marinda didn't tell him anything. He doesn't know some of us know Jay. Jay is a friend of Jordan's, you know."

"Yes, I know." Marce grinned. "What does Jordan think of her buddy now?"

"She thinks Jay is crazy. She says she's not totally surprised though. I guess this Jay is a real flake. Marce, we need to figure out the best way to proceed. We're meeting tonight at my house. If Slick — Jay — does respond to your message, we have to be ready. I think we should guarantee her that we'll protect her if she returns the statue, that the police will never know."

Marce tilted her head. "You don't think she should be punished?"

"I'm not sure we *can* protect her," Carla interjected. "The police already suspect that she did it."

"We'll have to cover for her," Elizabeth said. She was frowning pensively. "That shouldn't be too hard. We can say the burglar contacted us, a man, and we met with him and —"

"And he gave us back the statue because he had a change of heart," Marce said. "Yeah, right." She took a drink of her juice.

"We'll figure out a way," Elizabeth said.

"We might have to say we gave him some money," Carla said. "Maybe we should tell the insurance guy, Redman, about Slick but tell him she agreed to settle for two hundred thousand. We get the money from Redman, go retrieve the statue, and then —"

"Have a big party," Marce said. "Two hundred thousand dollars is a lot of money. We couldn't return it to the insurance company, obviously."

"That's true," Carla said. "We'll think of something."

"I'm sure we will." Marce folded her hands on the desktop. "So you're saying you want to let Jay get off scot-free?"

"I don't know. We'll talk some more about it tonight." Carla swung her leg around and sat up straight. "What's she like anyway, this Jay Horne? Is she crazy?"

Marce laughed. "Just a bit sociopathic. She has a certain charm if you like her type. I do, actually. I like the woman. She's got balls — pardon me, ovaries."

"She sounds like a real gem," Elizabeth said. "According to Meredith, your friend Randy would like to cut Jay's throat."

"Nah, Randy's not a violent person."

"Figuratively speaking." Elizabeth folded her arms. "I don't know the details, but apparently Randy and Jay were lovers and Jay ripped Randy off royally."

Marce's buzzer rang. She talked to her secretary, then told Elizabeth and Carla she had to take a call. "*Muy grande* real estate deal," she said. She walked the two women to the door. "To be continued. See you both tonight. Not to worry, huh? Everything's cool."

# Chapter 17

On her way home from work on Thursday, Randy stopped at the Safeway for some groceries. She was thinking about Marinda, feeling deeply disappointed that she hadn't heard from her. She had phoned her on Tuesday and left a message; Marinda hadn't returned the call.

In the Safeway parking lot, Randy ran into Lou Bonnig, the Wisconsin woman she'd met at the party a couple of weekends ago.

"So do you think she did it?" Lou asked after they greeted each other. "Is Jay Horne the thief?"

"Word sure travels fast," Randy said.

Lou introduced her to her companion, a woman named Christina. Christina spoke with an accent Randy couldn't identify. "We were just going to get a bite to eat," Lou said. "Would you like to join us?" Randy hesitated, not sure she was in the mood to socialize. "Come on," Lou coaxed. "We're good company, aren't we, Christina?"

"The best."

They went to a restaurant just up the street.

"Jordan would like to wring Jay's neck," Lou said after they were seated, "for being such a jerk."

"I second that," Randy said.

"Amagyne thinks Jay may be involved with some spin-off group of her religion," Lou continued. "She thinks they may be working together."

"Oh, really?" Another conspiracy theory, Randy decided, thinking of Meredith.

"Yes," Lou said, "the plot thickens. Apparently one of the sect members — a woman named Doralee — told Amagyne that Jay Horne was friends with another sect member, Carolyn something. This Doralee is convinced that her group — the Kwo-amjamites — took the statue because it has some religious significance for them. So now Amagyne thinks that maybe Jay and the Kwo-amjamites stole it together, with the agreement that the Kwo-amjamites get the statue and Jay gets the extortion money."

"Curiouser and curiouser," Randy said.

"You heard about Meredith accusing Marinda?"

"Yes."

"I'm concerned about Meredith," Lou said. "I might have to have a talk with her. Apparently she identifies with Marinda for some reason, thinks Marinda has some empty part in her that she was trying to fill by possessing the Winged Dancer."

"But you think it's really Meredith who has the missing part?"

161

"Could be." Lou glanced at the menu then back at Randy. "What do you think?"

"I'm not sure what Meredith's problem is, but I know Marinda certainly isn't involved in the theft." Talking about Marinda made Randy sad. She'd thought Marinda felt the attraction too. But apparently not. "So tell me about your group in Wisconsin," she said. "Marce says it's a collective farm. Called De Nova, right? Do you live there too, Christina?"

"At Lou's place," Christina said. "But just temporarily."

"Christina is Greek," Lou said.

"We met in Athens." Christina looked fondly at Lou. "That was one of the best days of my life," she said. "She invited me to come and visit De Nova. It's a wonderful place. There's nothing like it in Greece, at least that I know of."

"Tell me more," Randy said. She listened with moderate interest as the pair talked about life at De Nova. "It sounds pleasant enough, but not real tempting to me personally," Randy said. "I think I'm too much of an individualist for collective living. I like having my own space and making my own decisions. I'd guess the same is true for you, Lou, since you don't actually live at the farm."

"You could be right," Lou said.

"I'm surprised De Nova's doing so well financially," Randy said. "I thought small farmers were having a rough time of it."

"We were in deep trouble for a while," Lou said. "Several years ago, we got bailed out by a friend of mine who suddenly came into some unexpected wealth."

Randy laughed. "That's great. I wish I knew someone with money to give away. So would you say your farm is a —"

"De Nova is not *my* farm," Lou interrupted.

"Excuse me, *the* farm, would you say it's a utopia?"

Lou tilted her head. "That depends on what you mean by utopia."

"An ideal community," Randy said, "a place where the way of life is exactly how you want it, that reflects all your values."

"Pretty close," Lou said.

"Really? Everybody gets along and agrees on everything? There's no strife?"

"That would be unrealistic," she said.

"Well, aren't utopias unrealistic?"

"Not the way you defined it."

"I think of utopia as purely imaginative," Randy said, "not based on reality, not based on what people really are, but on visionary dreams of what someone wishes people could be or thinks they should be."

"And what do you think people really are?" Lou asked.

"Trouble," Randy said. "Opportunistic, selfish, aggressive, unreliable, spiteful, disloyal, competitive."

"Mm-mm."

"Insensitive, unreasonable, uncaring," Randy added. "And small-minded."

"Hm-mm, all of us?"

"To some extent. It varies, I suppose."

"Are you that way?"

"Me? No, I don't think so. Sometimes, maybe."

"To the extent that you are any of that string of adjectives you named, do you like it that way? Would you want to change?"

"Sure, I'd rather not be spiteful or insensitive, or any of the things I said."

"Now we're talking utopia," Lou said, smiling broadly at Randy. "Process, not product."

Randy was silent for a while, then said, "I got disillusioned by the women's community."

"So much for illusions," Lou responded. "So I take it you're not too enthusiastic about the conference."

"I'm curious," Randy said. "I'll probably attend some of it. I noticed your name on the program. Several times, actually. A workshop and emceeing the show at the end."

Lou nodded. "I hope we get the Winged Dancer back before the conference begins," she said. "So many people are looking forward to seeing the real thing."

"Like Michelangelo's *Pietà*," Randy said.

Lou raised her eyebrow at that.

"Different symbols," Randy said.

"Right," Lou said.

"They're trying to raise the money for the ransom," Christina said. "De Nova will make a nice contribution. And Amagyne's people in Colorado will, I'm sure. They're the most affluent members of Other Ways."

"So will all the Other Ways utopias contribute?" Randy asked.

Lou shook her head. "Some of them are barely making it financially. We have to make contributions to them."

"Do you do that?"

"Sure."

"Does that mean any group that gets together and calls itself a utopian community can tap Other Ways for money?"

"We have our standards," Lou said.

"The Credo," said Christina.

"Credo? Sounds heavy," Randy said.

"You want to hear it?" Christina asked.

"Sure, why not?"

"Non-violence and non-coerciveness," she said. "Acceptance of diversity. Respect for interpersonal rights. And, let me see, there's one more . . ."

"I promise to love you if you promise to love me," Randy suggested.

"Very amusing," Lou said. "Conflict resolution by dialogue and negotiation. That's the fourth one."

"Only four rules to make a utopia," Randy said. "Not

bad. We have about thirty at work just for keeping the lab clean."

Lou chuckled. "I hope you come to the conference, Randy. Maybe you'll learn something."

"Well, I'd certainly like to see the Winged Dancer."

"Are you worried about Jay? That she's going to end up in jail?"

"Not at all. Jay's as innocent as a baby. She would never rip anyone off. I think it was really you De Novans who took the statue. It's probably standing in your apple orchard right now."

"Right," Christina said, "eating apples. Or maybe it was Amagyne's Colorado group that took it."

"Naw, I think it was Elizabeth," Lou said, "or maybe Marce."

"Or Sue."

"Or maybe you, Randy."

"Or the pope," Randy said.

# Chapter 18

Randy spent Saturday morning washing storefront windows with Jess. Afterwards they took a stroll on the beach near Seal Rock. Randy still had not heard from Marinda and was making every effort to exorcise her from her mind. There had also been no response from Slick to Marce's message in the *Chronicle*.

"Maybe Jay decided to melt the statue down after all," Randy commented.

"Or maybe Marce did hear from her," Jess said, "and they made a deal."

"Very funny." Randy watched a group of Asian boys roughhousing on the beach.

"I'm not kidding," Jess persisted. "From what I know of Marce, I wouldn't put it past her at all."

Randy laughed. "The whole world's getting paranoid," she said.

* * * * *

That night Randy had a date with Marce. Their plan was to go to a movie and then dinner. As soon as Randy arrived at Marce's house, she knew Marce had other things in mind. She had that look in her eye. It only took a few kisses for Randy to be as interested as Marce obviously was.

Marce had a large, wheat-colored, tweed sofa in her living room which in one quick motion could be converted into a bed. Just moments after Randy's arrival, they were on the sofa bed together, naked, absorbed in the sensations each created for the other.

Half an hour later, Marce said, "Want to order a pizza?"

They made love again while they waited for the pizza to arrive, and again after they stuffed themselves on it. Afterwards Randy felt warm and cozy, lollingly content. Her head was resting on Marce's chest, one leg flung over her. "This feels good," she said. "Much better than a movie." She gave Marce's cheek a kiss and sighed.

Marce pulled herself to a sitting position. "Reach me my shirt, will you?"

Randy grabbed it with her toes and pulled it up to Marce. "Are you cold?" she asked.

Marce didn't answer. Still sitting on the sofabed, she slipped on the tank top. Then she stood and put on her jeans. "Want to go to Bawd's?"

"Really?" Randy said. "You want to go out?"

Marce already had her jacket halfway on. "Sure, it's still early." She yawned and stretched. "I suppose you heard about the flak I'm getting from my co-committee members." She tossed Randy her sweater.

"I know they weren't happy about your putting the ad in the paper," Randy said. "So what's the latest? Since you haven't mentioned it, I assume Jay still hasn't contacted you."

"Never assume," Marce said.

"You mean you heard from her?"

Marce nodded. "I thought it would be by phone but it wasn't." She was sitting on a footstool, bent over to tie her shoes.

Randy felt that familiar anger when Marce dragged out telling something she knew Randy wanted to hear. Randy knew Marce wouldn't respond to pushing, so she just waited until Marce went on.

"Don't you read the papers?" Marce asked.

"She answered via the personals?"

"That's right."

Randy waited.

Marce tossed her the newspaper. She had circled the ad. Randy read it. *Marce — You tread dangerously on unknown ground. Better butt out. Nothing has changed. Payment is due Oct. 31. — Slick.*

Randy looked at Marce. Marce shrugged. "So what next?" Randy asked. "Apparently she won't be intimidated."

"We're putting the word out. Jay Horne, wanted dead or alive." Marce chuckled. "We'll find her. The grapevine has innumerable branches. Someone will tip us off."

"Maybe so," Randy said, "but then what? Even if you find her, how are you going to get her to admit she took the statue? How are you going to get her to give it back?"

"We have our ways," Marce said, chuckling again.

"Would you actually turn her over to the cops?"

"Perhaps," Marce said. "Get dressed, girl, let's go."
Obviously the conversation was over.

\* \* \* \* \*

At the bar, Marce got into a long conversation with someone about mutual funds and real estate investments. Randy played a video game, and then she spotted Jay's pal, Jordan. Jordan came up to her.

"So do you think she did it?" Jordan asked. "I do."

They talked about Jay for a while, Jordan's eyes wandering around the bar the whole time. Then Jordan changed the subject, started telling Randy about the different types of women she was attracted to.

"I like them butch inside, but a touch of fashion dyke on the surface," she said. "Like that one." She pointed to a very pretty and seemingly self-assured woman who was playing pool. "And I like them feisty and a little raunchy. Separatists and ReaLesbians, I can do without."

"Real lesbians?" Randy asked. "What does that mean?"

"You know, crew cuts and hairy warts, crystal and tofu and goddesses. ReaLesbian — it's one word, like *ReaLemon.*"

Randy laughed. She was beginning to understand why Jay and Jordan had been friends; they both had serious gaps in their consciousness. "Do I hear a touch of stereotyping," Randy asked, "followed by perhaps a tad of discrimination?"

"Oh, save me," Jordan said, rolling her eyes. "We all discriminate, Randy. It's human nature, just a matter of preference, really. I can't imagine you with a diesel dyke, for example. Wait, I take that back — I forgot about Marce."

Randy looked across the bar at Marce who was still deep in conversation. "You consider Marce a diesel dyke?"

Jordan laughed. "Just kidding. No, Marce is your basic

middle-of-the-road, capitalist feminist, well-laced with butch. She's one with a very eclectic taste in women, wouldn't you say? I used to think she preferred the femmier types, but I'm not so sure lately." Jordan tilted her head way back as she took a slug of beer. "There was the tweed blazer one Marce used to hang around with, a Bay Area Career Woman type. Then there's you — Ms. Androgyny. And there's that yuppie in Marin. I think she's also a bit taken with head-in-the-ozone Amagyne, the *spiritual* one. And then there was some polyester number she had over at her house a while back. I think Marce's taste is really broadening out lately."

"Who's the polyester one?" Randy asked, feeling mildly jealous.

"Someone I saw coming from Marce's house one day and driving off in Marce's car. Lipstick and heavy makeup, permanented curly suburban housewife hair. I saw the woman the day of the theft. Then after that, the statue was all anybody talked about, so I forget to ask Marce about the housewife type."

"They're still talking," Randy said.

"Mm-m, look at that one." Jordan gestured toward a tall blonde near the jukebox. "Excuse me, Randy, I think she wants to dance with me."

Randy played another game of Ms. Pacman, and then told Marce she was ready to leave.

"Go ahead," Marce said. "I'll get home on my own."

That wasn't the first time Randy and Marce had gone out together and left separately. It was fine with Randy. She was tired anyway, and tired of Marce too.

# Chapter 19

She dreamed of Marinda again. This time they were on a boat sailing off somewhere on calm waters. And then they were in the water, making love, going up and down with the great, gentle waves. Randy awoke breathless.

It was Sunday, a week since they'd gone on the motorcycle ride. Maybe Lancy hadn't given her the message, Randy thought. Perhaps today she would call Marinda again. She rehearsed what she'd say — invite her to go for another ride, tempt her by describing how beautiful the views are from the Marin Headlands, suggest they have a picnic there. She had just about made up her mind to make the call when the phone rang.

"Hello, Randy," the deep, beautiful voice said. "Is your garden really as wonderful as you said?"

"A verdant paradise," Randy answered.

"I could pick up some bagels and we could sit out there and eat them. And maybe cream cheese and lox."

"And some black olives?"

"Of course. You sound hungry."

"Starved," Randy said. Her heart was pounding.

"When would be a good time?"

"When can you get here?"

"In an hour."

"That would be an excellent time."

It turned out to be one of the best times Randy ever had. They sat in the garden eating and talking. The more she learned about Marinda, the more she liked her. There was depth and softness along with the strength, a beautiful soul beneath the beautiful skin. Marinda was becoming increasingly real to Randy and the reality was even better than the fantasy.

"When you didn't return my call, I thought maybe you found me boring," Randy said at one point.

"That's about the last thing I find you," Marinda replied, looking very warmly at Randy.

Afraid she would blush, Randy looked away. She stared at the view. The Bay Bridge was clearly visible that day.

"Tell me more about that backpacking trip," Marinda said. "I get great vicarious enjoyment hearing of adventures like that."

Randy told highlights of the European trip she and Jess had taken three years before. Marinda seemed absorbed in the stories, and spoke about her own travels. Then they talked of other things. Randy felt surprisingly comfortable confiding in Marinda. They learned they had much in common, including a series of failed romances.

Later, Randy showed Marinda through the house. Marinda admired the cozy rooms, the unpainted woodwork, the bay windows. She talked about her love of architecture and her work in Marigua as a draftsperson. Randy showed her some of the graphic design work she'd done and Marinda seemed genuinely impressed.

They did not make love that day, or kiss, or even touch, but there was unmistakable sexual energy between them. When they parted, Randy had no doubt there was more to come between her and Marinda Sartoria. Much more.

# Chapter 20

Marce arrived fifteen minutes late for the meeting Wednesday night. She grabbed a handful of cookies, poured herself a mug of coffee, then sat on the one remaining chair.

"Jordan, you were saying someone thought they saw Jay Horne," Elizabeth said.

"Well, she was very uncertain about it," Jordan said. "It was out near the zoo. This woman knows Jay only slightly. She says she thought she saw her in the passenger seat of a grayish-blue car — a Toyota, she thought. She gave a beep but there was no response."

"Anybody know anybody who owns a gray-blue Toyota," Carla asked.

No one answered.

"I think Jay's in deep seclusion," Essie said. "She's not about to go running around to the bars or strolling down Castro Street."

"The police aren't having any more luck than we are," Elizabeth said. "Neither are the Canadian police. All they've found out is that Jay has an apartment in Banff, that she operates a tour business there, and she's been out of town for the past few weeks, on a camping trip supposedly. They put the word out to campgrounds in the area, but so far no luck."

"Camping in October?" Essie said. "In Canada? Do the cops really believe that story?"

"A lot of people do fall camping," Elizabeth said, "but, no, the cops don't believe the story."

"They sure don't," Jordan said. "They gave me the third degree, even implied I might be the one who told Jay about the security procedures at the museum."

"Don't they know Sue took care of that?" Carla said.

"Sue had no way of knowing," Elizabeth said, "and we all told people about the statue, so attaching blame will get us nowhere."

"Tell us about the latest correspondence," Essie said.

Elizabeth picked up some newspaper sections from the table. "After Slick sent that message to Marce about butting out and nothing having changed, we put in the ad that said . . ." Elizabeth looked at the newspaper. "*Slick — Your contacts with us remain secret. Cops are questioning U-Haul renters. We can promise you safety from prosecution if you return the item unharmed and drop your demands.* We signed it, Other Ways. We got no response on that one so we put in another. "*Slick — Are you still listening? We need to know the status of things.* Signed, Other Ways. Slick responded . . ." Elizabeth took the next section of folded newspaper. *"Other Ways — Status unchanged although I'm growing impatient with your silly attempts to avoid the inevitable. My demands are non-negotiable. This is my last contact until delivery instructions."*

"Well, at least she's not saying she destroyed the statue," Meredith said. "I would assume she knows the cops suspect her since they've been asking around about her."

"But didn't she say she'd cut up the statue if the cops found out about her?" Sue said.

"That was a bluff," Marce said. "Obviously."

"So what next?" Meredith asked.

"That's what we're here to decide," Marinda said.

Meredith's eyes met Marinda's for the first time. She smiled weakly. Marinda nodded to her.

"I think it's time to let the insurance company know what's going on," Elizabeth said, "and be prepared to pay Jay the money if she isn't caught before D-day."

"I wonder how she thinks she can get away with it," Essie said. "She knows we know who she is and she probably knows the cops are looking for her."

"What does she have to lose by trying?" Carla said. "If she has to run from the cops anyway, I'm sure she'd rather do it with a pile of money to help her out."

"Yes, but if she turned herself in now, don't you think things would go easier for her than if she waits until she actually gets the money?" Essie took another cookie. "These are great, Sue."

"Obviously she doesn't intend to get caught," Marce said.

"If we tell the insurance company, don't they have to tell the police?" Sue asked.

"I think it's time *we* tell the police," Carla said. "I don't feel any need to protect Jay Horne."

"I'd hate to see her go to jail," Jordan said.

"Maybe it would teach her not to fuck over her sisters," Carla responded angrily. "And I don't think we'd be risking losing the statue by telling the cops. Jay obviously wants the cash rather than the gold."

"I wonder why she doesn't just cut up the statue and forget about trying to get the money from us," Sue said.

"I think Jay has some limits," Jordan responded. "I think her conscience won't let her destroy the statue. That would be going too far, even for her."

"You still feel some loyalty to her, Jordan?" Marce asked.

"I wouldn't call it loyalty, I just don't think she's all that bad. She did something stupid, but she's not really a criminal. She's not a sociopath."

"That's debatable," Carla said. "To me there's no longer any reason not to tell the cops about the notes. We have had absolutely no success on our own. Our attempts to trace her through the post office and the *Chronicle* didn't get us anywhere. And talking to people who live around those mailboxes didn't either. Maybe the police could do better."

"Maybe so," Meredith said. "It does seem we'd have nothing to lose at this point and maybe something to gain."

"Do you believe if we pay the four hundred thousand she'd return the statue?" Elizabeth asked.

"I do," Sue said. "If she wanted the statue she would never have contacted us."

"I agree," said Essie. "Maybe Jordan's right. Maybe Jay couldn't bring herself to actually destroy the statue. I don't think we have anything to gain by telling the police about Slick. Even if they catch her, what have we gained? I think the chances of our getting the statue back are better if the police don't know."

"So you think we should just pay her the money?" Elizabeth said.

"Yes. If the insurance company will go along with it. If they won't, then we should tell the cops."

"It won't work that way," Jordan said. "If we tell the insurance company about Slick, which we'll obviously have to do to get the money from them, then they'll tell the cops."

"Right," Elizabeth said. "*They'd* certainly have something to gain if the cops caught Jay."

"So what do we do?" Sue said.

"Tell the insurance company and let them do what they can to find Slick," Meredith said, "including telling the cops everything. If she's caught, fine. We get the statue back that way. If they don't catch her, we pay the money and get the statue back that way."

"That makes sense," Sue said.

"I wonder if there's a chance that, if they caught her, she wouldn't tell where the statue is," Elizabeth said.

"No way," said Carla. "Turning over the statue would be her ticket to a lighter sentence."

Elizabeth was frowning. "Maybe Jay would have a good enough alibi to avoid getting convicted."

"Right, then once she's in the clear, she melts down the statue and becomes rich," Sue said.

"That, unfortunately, is a possibility," Marinda said. "I suggest we try to get the insurance company to refrain from telling the police. Get them to pay Slick the four hundred thousand. Then afterwards, they can tell the police and try to catch her. That way the insurance company isn't risking having to pay the full nine hundred fifty thousand, and we're not risking the cops prematurely arresting her and her clamming up about the statue."

"Right, and our never seeing it," Sue said.

Several people nodded.

"I agree," Essie said.

"Yes," said Amagyne.

"That does seem to be the best route," Elizabeth said. "Everyone agree?"

"I just hope the insurance company will see it our way," Carla said.

"It seems we have no other choice but to try," Elizabeth said.

The others concurred. Elizabeth phoned Frank Redman while the rest of the women listened. She made an appointment to meet with him the following morning.

# Chapter 21

Late Saturday morning Marinda and Amagyne sat near the shore at Fort Point. The fog was lifting to reveal a clear blue sky.

"You seem happier, Marinda. Lighter."

Marinda smiled.

"Perhaps doing some letting go?"

Nodding pensively, Marinda said, "Yes, I think so. I rarely think of Galia lately, and when I do I don't get that heavy feeling."

"I'm glad."

"I think my talk with you helped. You made me face

the reality of Galia's choice. I did a lot of thinking after that talk. You were right, I hadn't accepted it." She took a deep breath. "Things are moving along," she said. "Despite my agony about the statue, I've been having an enjoyable time here." She talked about the women she was getting to know — Lou Bonnig, Elizabeth, Lancy, Randy Van Fleet. She talked the most about Randy. "I sense a happy ending to all of this," she said. "I think we're going to get the statue back and live happily ever after."

Amagyne smiled and squeezed Marinda's shoulder. "I predict much happiness for you," she said, "but I'm not so sure about the statue. I think the Kwo-amjamites might have taken it to one of their other locations — San Diego, maybe, or Seattle."

"Oh?"

"And that Jay Horne will take the money and run. I suspect the Kwo-amjamites are providing refuge for her until she collects the extortion money."

Marinda frowned. "I didn't know you still suspected the Kwo-amjamites. I thought that woman had been able to account for her time the night of the theft."

"Carolyn, yes. Doralee questioned her and her story was convincing. They didn't use the Kwo-amjamite's truck for the theft. Apparently a rented truck was used. And I don't think Carolyn was with the ones who actually took the Winged Dancer, but I think she was involved. I think she and Jay Horne developed the plan together. I have no proof though. Only what Doralee told me."

"She's the Kwo-amjamite who told you about Carolyn, isn't she?"

"Yes. Doralee also told me there's a big house in Oakland that belongs to the Kwo-amjamites. Apparently it's primarily for the Inner Circle. They've been renovating it and some of the Inner Circle group live there. Doralee thinks that may be where they are keeping the statue. She wants us to go there and find out. I've been thinking about

181

it, although I think it's more likely they moved the statue out of the San Francisco area."

"You think Jay Horne is at that house?"

"I wouldn't be surprised," Amagyne said. "You heard that she was seen in Oakland."

"Yes. Jordan saw her in a car with two other women. She tried to pursue them but lost them in traffic. That's what I heard, anyway. I wonder if it really was Jay."

"I think it was. And from Jordan's description, I believe one of the women with her was Carolyn."

"Really? Hm-mm. Have you told the others you suspect that Jay Horne and the Kwo-amjamites might be working together?"

"Some of them. They don't seem to take me seriously. They think my attitudes towards the Kwo-amjamites are biased — Elizabeth does, I know, and Carla."

"Well, the Kwo-amjamites claim that the statue belongs with them, don't they?"

"They do."

"And now with Jordan seeing Jay and a Kwo-amjamite together . . . it might be worth checking out. We don't seem to have any other leads." Marinda smiled sardonically and shook her head. "You know, initially I was sure it was Andrea Herrara who took the statue. It still crosses my mind that she might be involved." She looked pointedly at Amagyne. "Sometimes it's hard to give up certain ideas."

Amagyne held Marinda's eyes. "You think I might be stubbornly holding on to mine — about the Kwo-amjamites?"

"Not stubbornly," Marinda said. "I don't know." She leaned back on the bench. "I wouldn't be surprised if Meredith still thinks I'm the thief."

Amagyne laughed. "There might be a corner of her mind that can't quite let go of the possibility."

"The corners of our minds," Marinda repeated, slowly.

"I hope my corner is dead wrong. If Andrea Herrara took the statue, we very likely will never see it again."

Neither woman spoke for a while, both very pensive. Marinda's eyes wandered to the flock of sailboats passing beneath the bridge. "Shall we make an expedition to Oakland?" she said at last.

"I imagine the house is well-guarded." Amagyne ran her fingers through her coal-black hair and sighed deeply. "My last expedition in search of the statue was not very productive."

Marinda smiled. "So I heard. But that doesn't mean we don't keep trying. What do we have to lose by checking out that house? Maybe we'll find Andrea there too."

Amagyne looked surprised. "Do you really think so?"

"No." Marinda chuckled. "But it is hard to give up blaming our favorite enemies for things that go wrong. I can't think of anyone I despise as much as Andrea's brother."

Amagyne nodded. "For good reason. But I don't think I consider the Kwo-amjamites my enemies."

"Rivals? Competitors? Turncoats?"

"No, I don't think so."

"Why does Meredith see me as *her* enemy?"

Amagyne stretched her legs, half burying her moccasins in the tall grass. "It isn't you," she said. "It was part of herself that Meredith thought she saw in you . . . that's what she was responding to."

"Mm-mm. Maybe that's what we're all doing. Projecting."

"I think it is not so simple."

"Maybe not."

They were quiet for a while, looking at the water. "You know," Marinda said, "I thought that if I ended up getting involved with anyone, it would be you."

"But now you feel differently."

"I don't think it was meant to be, not for either of us."

"Meant to be?" Amagyne smiled. "Hm-mm. Do you see yourself as a religious woman?"

"No," Marinda said firmly, "and I don't intend to become one."

Amagyne laughed. "I suspect you fear a sermon coming your way?"

"Should I?"

"No."

"You didn't read the book I gave you, did you?"

"The *Words of Kwo-am?* I glanced through it. It's not for me, Amagyne."

Amagyne nodded. "That's all right. We don't have to know Kwo-amity to be moved by Kwo-am's energy." They were silent again. "Does Randy know how you feel about her?" Amagyne said at last.

Marinda frowned. "How I feel? About Randy?" She shrugged and said no more. Amagyne poured them each another cup of cider.

"Did you check the paper this morning?" Marinda asked.

"The personals? Yes. There was nothing from Slick. It looks like you and Marce were right — that she won't respond to our counter-offer of two hundred thousand. I hope Redman was correct in his assumption that trying wouldn't do any harm."

"I think he was wise to agree not to tell the police about the extortion until after the payoff," Marinda said.

"Yes, Slick is slick, isn't she? It looks like the insurance company will end up paying. And then, to quote Elizabeth, 'We cross our fingers hoping we get the statue back.' If my suspicions are accurate, though, that won't happen." Amagyne paused. "Unless . . ."

"I'd be willing to go to Oakland," Marinda said. "It'll certainly feel better than just doing nothing. Why don't you call Elizabeth and see if you can gather a dyke SWAT squad to storm the Kwo-amjamite house? We can give Slick and her cohorts a stern lecture, liberate the Winged Dancer, and then have a big celebration party."

Amagyne laughed. "Maybe so," she said. "Dawn tomorrow morning is what I had in mind. Do you think we can get ten or fifteen adventurers to rouse themselves that early?"

"Maybe two or three," Marinda said. "The rest will still be up from the night before."

"How about you? Will you come?"

"Of course." Marinda frowned. "We'll need a plan, you know."

"I know. Could you come tonight? I'll ask everyone to come for a planning meeting at Robyn's house. At seven o'clock."

"I'll be there," Marinda said.

# Chapter 22

They'd had several long wonderful phone conversations during the week. Randy felt a thrill each time she heard Marinda's voice. Several times Randy had suggested they get together, but each time Marinda had said she wasn't able to make it. It confused and troubled Randy. She's torn, Randy decided. Clearly drawn to me, yet fighting it. She's afraid of getting hurt.

Randy was beginning to think they'd never be together again, but then on Saturday afternoon, not long after Randy got home from another miserable morning of window washing, Marinda called and suggested they meet at the Artemis Cafe.

Randy arrived at the cafe first and took a window table. Several minutes later she watched as Marinda parked Lancy's car and walked toward the door. She looked magnificent.

Their conversation was light and impersonal at first. Randy told Marinda about how crazy the Castro area gets on Halloween night and asked how they celebrated Halloween in Marigua. Marinda said they didn't. Then they talked about the Winged Dancer. Marinda said Amagyne thought she knew where Jay was and maybe the statue. Randy told her Jordan had seen Jay in Oakland, which Marinda already knew. Randy talked some more about her relationship with Jay. Marinda couldn't understand how someone could behave the way Jay had toward Randy.

As the conversation proceeded, Randy felt an energy between them so strong it was like a series of wires stretched almost to the breaking point. She was about to suggest they go to her house and do what both of them obviously wanted very strongly to do when Marinda said, "Let's go for a motorcycle ride."

"Sure," Randy responded.

They drove in their separate cars to Randy's house.

"Do you want to come inside for a while first?" Randy asked.

Marinda didn't answer right away as if weighing the possibilities. Finally she said, "No, let's ride."

Randy took the bike down Divisadero to the Bay and then west to the Golden Gate Bridge and across to the Marin Headlands. They marveled at the views; they sat on a hill and talked; they hiked a very steep trail. After the hike, Randy was exhausted. She lay in the grass. "My legs are killing me," she said. "I think you're in better shape than I am."

Marinda leaned over and began massaging the muscles of Randy's calves and upper legs. Randy closed her eyes to concentrate fully on the feel of Marinda's fingers on her flesh. She was so turned on she could barely breathe. "Let's go to my place," she blurted.

Marinda took several deep breaths. She said nothing. Then suddenly she looked at her watch. "Yes, it's getting late. We should go. I have a meeting tonight at seven."

Randy felt a sinking disappointment.

* * * * *

When they got back to Randy's house, Marinda went directly to her car. "There's going to be some action tomorrow morning," she said, "at dawn." She told Randy about the plan to make a surprise visit to the Kwo-amjamites. "If you feel adventuresome, why don't you come along?"

"It would be some adventure if we found Jay," Randy said. "Yes, I'd like to go."

"I'll call you tonight after the meeting . . . about where to meet and what the plan is. Will you be home?"

Randy had tentative plans to go dancing at Wild Blue Yonder that night with Marce. She didn't feel particularly enthusiastic about it. "Yes, I'll want to get some sleep if we're really going out at dawn."

After Marinda left, Randy took a hot, hot bath. Her legs were still sore. Then she called Marce to cancel their plans.

"Why?" Marce demanded. "Surely you don't think you've found somebody better, do you?"

Randy told her she was worn out from hiking in the Marin Headlands. Marce asked who she'd gone with. Randy told her.

"I heard the Marin Headlands were named after

Marinda," Marce said, "because she gives good head. Is that true?"

"And I have to get up early tomorrow," Randy added. "That's another reason I'm not up for going out tonight."

"The raid brigade," Marce said. "Are you part of that?"

"Yes," Randy answered. "Are you?"

"Hell no. You know I never get up before noon on Sundays." Randy knew that wasn't true but she didn't say anything.

Marce's parting shot was about Marinda. "She'll break your heart, kiddo," she said.

Randy didn't respond to that either. She was becoming increasingly less tolerant of Marce.

# Chapter 23

Eleven women went to Oakland. Randy rode with Marinda, Elizabeth, and Carla. They told her the plan on the way over. Randy would be one of the women stationed outside the house to guard the windows and make sure no one tried to escape. She was given a stun gun and told how it worked. It looked like a flashlight, with an on-off switch, but had two prongs instead of the light bulb. Carla explained that it would send a current of electricity through a person's body when you touched them with the prongs.

"It doesn't do any permanent damage," she said, "but

it sure as hell slows you down. You want to see what it feels like?" Randy said she'd take a pass.

The mansion-sized Kwo-amjamite house was in the middle of the block on Everett Street. It was six-thirty a.m. and still very dark when they got there. They parked the three cars in different places nearby, and went in pairs and trios to the house.

Meredith was already there when Randy's group arrived. She had brought some pieces of rope for all the outside people. She and Randy were stationed near each other along the east side of the house, Randy at the front and Meredith back by the garage. When everyone was in place, Marinda and Elizabeth rang the doorbell. Randy crouched behind some bushes staring at the three windows she was supposed to guard. If anyone tried to climb out, she was to show herself and tell them to stay inside. If they came out anyway, she was to stun them with her gun, then use the rope to tie them up.

"Call for help if anything happens in your area," Marinda had told her. Randy truly hoped she wouldn't have to. It wasn't that she was opposed to the plan in general, but the idea of violence made her very uneasy. She kept staring at the windows and wondering if Jay would try to climb out of one of them. After Marinda and Elizabeth and the others who were on inside detail had been gone for several minutes and nothing seemed to be happening, Randy sat down on the ground. Crouching had become uncomfortable. The ground was a little damp, but she didn't mind.

More time passed and still nothing happened. Randy fingered the stun gun wondering how big a jolt it gave. She wondered if Jay actually was inside and how she'd react if she was. Suddenly she heard activity on the front porch. She got into her crouch position. About a half minute later Carla came towards her.

"Marinda wants you," Carla said.

"What's happening?"

"Not much. They're very pissed at us. We rounded them up from all the bedrooms. They deny knowing anything about the Winged Dancer, but we got them to tell us where Jay Horne is — a motel in San Pablo. One of the Kwo-amjamites said she gave her a ride there the other day. That's all they'd say. Elizabeth and I are going after Jay."

Randy sucked in her breath. So I'll see her soon, she thought. She went into the house. What a weird scene. About ten women were sitting in the living room chanting some sort of mantra with their hands folded in their laps. Some of them had their eyes closed. They were chanting the word, *Kwo-am,* over and over. Amagyne was there also, standing near Marinda. She wasn't chanting. Randy went up to Marinda. She looked as if she was in complete control of the situation. She also looked gorgeous.

"Go check the garage, will you?" she said to Randy.

"All right."

"Be careful, huh?" Marinda warned.

Randy went out the front door and around the side. The sky was growing lighter. She told Meredith what was going on in the house, then told Jennifer, who was stationed at the back door. The garage was huge, two stories high, with what appeared to be an apartment on the second floor. The side door was locked. Randy tried the big door but it was locked also. She looked at the upper windows. They had heavy curtains over them, as did the downstairs windows. She tried to look through one of the locked lower windows but all she saw was heavy black cloth. She went back into the house to see if she could get the key. Marinda asked the chanters where the key was but they ignored her.

"Go look around the house," she suggested. "Maybe you can find it."

That chanting sounded very eerie. Randy could hear it from the kitchen as she searched through drawers. Essie came and helped her but they didn't find any keys.

"Let's go break a window," Essie said.

"You think someone's hiding in there?" Randy asked.

"Could be. We should have thought to look sooner. If someone was there, she could have gotten away by now."

"Jay, maybe," Randy said.

"Who knows? She might be at that motel where the Kwo-jammies told us she is, but I doubt it. Come on."

They went out the back door, scaring Jennifer. Her stun gun was in her hand and she was very jumpy.

They went to the garage. The ground floor windows were small so there was no way they'd be able to climb through one of them. There was no window on the side door at all.

"Maybe we could find a ladder and climb up to the second floor," Randy suggested. "Maybe one of those windows is open." She pictured Jay crouching in a corner up there somewhere, scared shitless. She really doubted she was there, though.

"There's probably a ladder in the garage," Essie said. "Let's bust the window and take a peek."

Randy grabbed a rock from the side of the driveway. "What will the neighbors think?" she said. There was a house about twenty yards from the garage. "Seriously, we don't want to wake them. We need some masking tape to muffle the sound."

"I saw some masking tape in the basement when I was searching the house," Essie said. "It's in a cabinet next to the work bench."

"I'll get it," Randy said.

The basement was huge, and divided into several different rooms, the main one full of building supplies and cans of paint and a variety of tools. In the tallest cabinet she finally found the tape hanging on a hook. On her way out she grabbed a rubber mallet. Instead of going back up through the kitchen she went out the basement door. Jennifer wasn't there and Randy wondered where she'd gone. She made her way around the back of the garage where she'd left Essie. Essie wasn't there either. Randy started taping the window, figuring Essie would soon show up. She had it all taped and Essie still hadn't returned. Randy went ahead and broke the window using the mallet. It made a dull thudding sound.

Once she got rid of the pieces of glass, she tried to push the drape aside, but it was big and heavy and all she succeeded in doing was pushing it inward. Finally she just gathered handfuls of it and pulled it out of the way. It was dark inside the garage and she squinted trying to see.

Slowly her eyes adjusted. What she saw made her heart pound so loudly she could hear it. "Jesus," she whispered. She kept blinking and staring. There it was — standing right there bigger than life. She was gasping. The golden statue! The Winged Dancer! No doubt about it; it looked just like the pictures she'd seen.

The statue was partially draped in black cloth, the head and center part of the body covered, but Randy could see outstretched arms and part of a feather cape. It was entirely gold.

She whistled through her teeth. It's actually here and I found it, she thought, knowing how delighted Marinda would be. She ran inside to tell the others.

As soon as Randy got into the kitchen she knew something was wrong. Before she had the chance to have another thought, someone grabbed her arms. Two women held her and pushed her toward the front of the house. One of them took the stun gun from her pocket.

"We found another one," the woman said as she escorted Randy down the hall.

The situation in the living room had changed considerably since Randy's earlier visits. No one was chanting. The room was jammed. Amagyne, Meredith, and Sue were sitting on the sofa. Essie was in an easy chair near the windows, Jennifer next to her on another chair. Marinda sat on the arm of the sofa, her arms folded. Standing all around them were about twenty women, Kwo-amjamites, Randy assumed. The one who had grabbed Randy pushed her toward the center of the room and told her to sit. She sat on a straight-backed chair near the coffee table.

"Where did she come from?" one of the Kwo-amjamites asked.

"From out back. We must have missed her."

Randy felt frightened. She looked at Marinda who gave her a big smile. Marinda seemed very calm, bored almost.

"Continue, Dee," someone said to a black woman in a big white T-shirt.

"All right," the T-shirt woman said, "let me reiterate." She looked from one to the other of the non-Kwo-amjamites, her eyes angry and fierce. "We do not want you or any of your friends ever to come around here again!" She emphasized each word. "Or to harass us in any way. I repeat — we will not be pushed around! We will not be annoyed or intimidated by a bunch of Zetka-inspired outsiders. And believe me, if you ever try anything like this again, we won't let you off so easy. We want you out of here and out of this area and out of our lives."

After the speech, the Kwo-amjamites herded the intruders out to the front porch and to the sidewalk, and stood there in a group as the non-Kwo-amjamites walked toward their cars. Randy walked next to Marinda who seemed very amused by the whole situation. As soon as they were out of earshot of the Kwo-amjamites, Randy whispered to her. "The Winged Dancer is in the garage."

"What!" The amused expression left Marinda's face.

"I saw it through the window."

Marinda's mouth was part way open. Then she was

smiling broadly, showing her beautiful white teeth. She looked back toward the house. The army of Kwo-amjamites were still standing there watching the retreat. Almost to the car, Marinda motioned to Amagyne. "Follow us," she said.

Marinda, Randy, and Jennifer got into the car that Randy had come in. Marinda asked Randy exactly what she had seen. Randy told her about breaking the window and about the statue, how it was draped with a black cloth but only about half-covered.

Marinda drove to the corner, turned right, went another block, turned left, then stopped the car. The other car pulled up behind her. Everyone gathered in a huddle and Randy told them what she'd seen. They stared at her with wide eyes. Someone patted her back.

"Great job, Randy," Amagyne said.

Then everyone started talking at once, excitedly, about what to do next, about the other women who had gone to find Jay, about whether to call the police. Essie was afraid the Kwo-amjamites would see the broken window and know that they knew the statue was there.

"They might try to move it out of there," Marinda said. "Was there a truck in the garage?" she asked Randy.

"No," Randy said, "no cars either. Where did all those other Kwo-amjamites come from?"

"One of the women who was upstairs must have phoned them before we got to her," Meredith said. "That's how I figure it."

"Did anyone get zapped?" Randy asked.

"No," Sue said. "They took us by surprise. They all know karate. You should have seen —"

"I'm going to call Detective Turillo," Marinda said.

"He'll need a search warrant," Essie said.

"Maybe not," Meredith said. "With the evidence we have it may not be necessary — *probable cause*."

"I'm not so sure," Essie said. "And, you know, since

this is Oakland, not San Francisco, Turillo would probably have to involve the Oakland police."

"It may take awhile, then," Marinda said. "Watch the street in front of the house until the police arrive. If you see a truck come to the house —"

"Yeah, what do we do then?" Jennifer said. "How would we stop them? I don't think we could do it by force."

"No, of course not," Amagyne said.

"We could lie down across the driveway," Sue said. "Refuse to move."

No one acknowledged her comment.

"There are no alleys," Meredith said. "The only way they could get that statue out of there is by way of the street. If they come and take the statue before the police get here, we'll follow them."

"Maybe they won't see the broken window," Sue said.

"We also need to intercept Elizabeth and the others," Amagyne said, "so they don't walk into the clutches of our angry Kwo-amjamite friends."

"Are they coming back here?" Sue asked.

"Yes," Marinda said. "You're right, Amagyne, we must intercept them."

"I wonder if Jay will be with them," Randy said.

"Does everyone agree I should call Turillo?" Marinda asked.

Amagyne raised the possibility of going back and telling the Kwo-amjamites that we'd seen the statue and giving them the opportunity to turn it over to us voluntarily. "That way they could avoid prosecution," she said.

There was a brief discussion of this, but the group ended up deciding the risk wasn't worth it.

"We'd be crazy to have another confrontation with them," Essie said.

"Yeah, they were some mean broads," Sue said.

Randy agreed that they should bring in the police. "I

197

know what we can do in case the Kwo-amjamites try to bring in a truck to move the statue," Sue said. "We can park one of our cars in the driveway and block their way. And we can lock ourselves inside of it with the brakes on and keep beeping the horn until the police come."

Marinda gave Sue a big smile. "That's not a bad idea," she said. "Maybe without the horn-beeping though. We want to give Turillo time to get here."

Sue was beaming. "See, sometimes I have good ideas."

Amagyne gave her a warm smile. "Of course you do, Sue."

The group talked a few more minutes, reviewing the plan, and then everyone left. Marinda and Randy went to find a phone to call the police; the others got into the other car to go back to Everett Street.

Randy spotted a phone booth at a gas station on Broadway. Marinda and Randy made the call. Turillo wasn't available but they talked to his partner, who questioned Randy closely. He told her there should be no problem getting the search warrant and that they would meet her at the gas station. He took the phone booth number just in case something went wrong and he needed to contact her.

Marinda leaned against the car. "Well, it's almost over," she said.

"Yeah, what a relief, huh? I wonder what will happen to the Kwo-amjamites. I suppose the museum will press charges."

"Very likely."

"And they admitted knowing Jay. It looks like they did it together."

"Looks that way," Marinda said.

"I feel sorry for Jay."

Marinda raised her thick black eyebrows. "You do? After what she did to you?"

Randy shrugged. "I don't want her to go to jail."

Marinda smiled. "Well, you can be a character witness

for her then. Maybe that will help her get a light sentence. Tell the judge what a fine, upstanding woman she is."

"She does have a lot of good qualities."

Marinda looked pointedly at Randy. "Are you still in love with her?"

Randy felt like folding herself into Marinda's arms and telling her, *No, I'm in love with you, you idiot.* "No," she said. "Not at all. I just feel sorry for her."

"So you said."

"I'm sure she would have paid Marce what she owes her if she had gotten the money."

"You're very magnanimous, Randy."

Randy watched the traffic passing on Broadway. It was still early and there weren't many cars. She was still thinking about Jay.

"I really was afraid we'd never get it back," Marinda said. "That would have been a tragedy." She told Randy about her friends in Marigua who had figured out where the missing statue had once been hidden. It was quite a story and Randy listened with fascination. Some time later, the police arrived in two squad cars.

Turillo again went over with Randy what she'd seen, how she knew it was the statue, whether she had seen it clearly. Then he and the rest of the cops followed Randy and Marinda to Everett Street.

Carla and Elizabeth and the other women had returned from the trip to the Realia Motel on San Pablo Boulevard. Jay wasn't there, they said, but two women had stayed at the motel a couple of nights ago, the manager had told them. One of them might have been Jay, but they couldn't be sure. Meredith said that no truck had come while Randy and Marinda were gone.

Turillo and his partner and a couple of uniformed officers would go to the house. The women were to wait where they were, at the corner of the block. Everyone was very excited. Meredith had her camera and was filming people as they talked. Marinda was so delighted about the statue that her whole face glowed. Randy thought she looked more beautiful than ever.

After about ten minutes, one of the uniformed cops came down the street towards the women and beckoned to them. Everyone was too excited to talk except Sue, who kept chattering about finally getting to see the statue.

Turillo's partner was on the porch. He told Marinda, Elizabeth, and Randy to come inside and ordered the others to wait. A group of Kwo-amjamites was sitting in the living room with Turillo in the midst of them. Turillo glared at Randy when she walked into the room. What was his problem, she wondered. He stood up. "Come on," he said, still looking at Randy.

Randy followed him through the house and out the back door. Marinda and Elizabeth and a couple of the Kwo-amjamites came also. The side door of the garage was open. Randy glanced at Marinda. Marinda caught her eye and smiled happily and gave her arm a squeeze. This was a great moment in both their lives.

Turillo went into the garage first. The lights were on, dim, amber-colored. The room was huge and beautifully decorated. Randy gasped the moment she walked inside. She could not believe what she saw.

Where the statue had been, there was only a ladder with a black cloth draped over it.

"Where is it?" She choked out the words, looking at Turillo, then at Marinda, then back at Turillo. "What happened? How did they get it out of here?" Her heart was pounding rapidly.

Turillo looked at her coolly.

"It was here!" Randy said. "They moved it. They hid it somewhere." She looked frantically around the room.

Everyone was staring at her. Marinda was shaking her head. The light was gone from her eyes. She looked a little sick.

"Son of a bitch," Elizabeth muttered. "It was just a goddam ladder."

"No!" Randy shouted. "I swear it was the statue. I saw it clearly. I know I saw it!"

Turillo gestured for them to leave the garage. Randy's whole body was shaking. This couldn't be happening, she thought. It was like a nightmare out of Kafka.

No one said a word as they made their way back to the house. In the living room the black Kwo-amjamites in the T-shirts talked to Turillo about harassment and pressing charges. Something was said about a restraining order. Randy couldn't really listen, she was feeling so miserable. She had a terrible ringing in her ears and wondered if she was going to faint. No one said anything to her. Marinda didn't look at her the whole time they were in the Kwo-amjamite living room and then the whole time they walked back to the car.

Randy climbed into the back seat with Carla. Marinda and Elizabeth were in the front. It was deadly silent.

"Well, what now?" Elizabeth said after they'd driven a couple of blocks.

"They got it out of there somehow," Randy said.

"Oh, come on, Randy," Carla said impatiently. "Accept it. It was dark, you saw the ladder and thought it was the statue. You made a mistake. Accept it, for Christ's sake."

Randy sighed and looked out the window. No one said anything. "Is that what you think, Marinda?" Randy said at last.

"There's no other explanation," Marinda said. Randy had expected her voice to have a hard edge but it didn't.

She pictured the statue, the way it had looked through the window. Sure, it was dark but there was enough light to see what I saw, she thought. It was no ladder. I saw the feathered cape, the upraised arms. I saw the gold. Suddenly she felt like crying. I did see it, didn't I? Oh, shit. Tears were slipping down her cheeks. She wiped them away.

Carla patted Randy's leg. "Hey, we all make mistakes," she said. "You saw what you wanted to see, that's all."

"It's all right, Randy," Marinda said.

"Something must be wrong with my mind," Randy said.

Marinda laughed. "You on anything?" she asked.

Carla laughed too and nudged Randy. "Yeah, Randy, did you drop a little acid this morning?"

"It's not funny," Randy said.

"It better be," Carla said. "We have to keep our sense of humor about this."

"Are we in trouble with the cops?" Randy asked. They were crossing the Bay Bridge. She wished she were at home. She wished she were just stirring in her bed and thinking about maybe getting up and having a nice breakfast.

"We will be if any of us contact the Kwo-amjamites again," Elizabeth said.

There wasn't much conversation the rest of the drive. Marinda dropped Randy off first. Randy crashed on her sofa, feeling absolutely wretched.

# Chapter 24

Randy felt despondent all day Monday and Tuesday. She had no contact with any of the Other Ways women except Marce, who called and teased her about her "hallucination."

On Tuesday evening Marinda called and asked Randy to meet her at the Heartland Cafe on Steiner Street. Randy's mood lifted immediately. She put on her red blouse that Jess always said made her look very sexy. She moussed her hair.

Marinda was already at the cafe when Randy arrived.

She looked at Randy admiringly. "You look . . . delicious," she said, her eyes sparkling.

Randy sat across from her. "You're not angry any more?"

"I have some news," Marinda said, smiling.

"Oh?"

"You weren't mistaken. The Winged Dancer *was* in the garage."

"All right!" Randy exclaimed. "I knew it." She felt wonderfully vindicated. "So, tell me. How did they manage to get it —"

"*A* winged dancer, I should say," Marinda amended. "The Kwo-amjamites have a copy of it. One of their members is an artist. She'd reproduced the statue using chicken wire and papier mache. Apparently it's a very good replica."

"I'll be damned."

"The garage is their ceremony room. Their effigy of the Winged Dancer is part of their altar. It was just recently completed and they're planning an unveiling ceremony soon. Amagyne learned all this from Doralee."

"A replica," Randy said. "That never crossed my mind."

"No one else's either. The Kwo-amjamites found the hammer you'd left outside the garage, and they saw the broken window. According to Doralee, they moved the replica out of there to make fools of us. They knew we'd be back. They moved it into a neighbor's garage. I guess they just picked it up and carried it. Doralee told Amagyne the Kwo-amjamites got a good laugh out of the whole thing."

"The fuckers," Randy said. "You know, I was beginning to doubt my own mind."

"Are you angry at me?" Marinda asked. "For not believing you?"

Randy looked into her beautiful black eyes. "I was."

"Forgive me?" She smiled at Randy. It was a very warm smile.

"It must have been terrible for you," Randy said, "to believe you had the statue back and then . . . what a let down. I know you were angry at me."

"Briefly. Mostly I felt disappointed and frustrated . . . about the Dancer."

"I know." Randy had a powerful urge to reach over and caress Marinda's beautiful face. And to kiss her wonderful, sensuous lips. Does she have any idea how I feel about her, she wondered.

"Amagyne still thinks the Kwo-amjamites took the real statue."

"Oh yeah?" And to feel Marinda's naked body softly moving against her own. "Do you?"

Marinda shook her head. "At this point, I have no idea. Redman, the insurance investigator, said he'll have the cash ready by Saturday — twenties, fifties, et cetera."

The waiter came and the women ordered capuccino.

"Won't the insurance guy tell the police about Slick?" Randy said. "I'd think he would."

"Not until after the payoff. He's fairly certain Jay Horne is the thief but he says the evidence against her is slim. He did the same thing we did, checked at the post office, went to the *Chronicle*. Nothing. He also talked with the neighbors around Sue's place. A couple of them noticed there was a U-Haul truck parked there a month ago, but none of them knew when it came and went. He's afraid that if the police get involved and succeed in finding Jay, they won't have enough evidence to prosecute and she may never reveal where the statue is. He wants to go through with the payoff because he thinks that's the most likely way of getting the statue back. Then he'll tell Turillo everything."

Randy was smiling. "What do I do if I get six thousand dollars in the mail? After Jay gets the payoff."

Marinda shrugged.

"That woman is such a piece of work," Randy said, chuckling.

"You sound like you're still attached to her," Marinda said. "Maybe still in love with her."

"I told you I'm not," Randy retorted. "I mean it. Jay is part of my past." She looked deeply into Marinda's eyes. "I'm moving on."

"Good," Marinda said. Then she looked at Randy in an unmistakably seductive way.

Randy returned the look. Neither woman spoke for some time, just continued looking at the other. Finally Randy broke the spell. "You know I have a terrible crush on you," she said. "I did from the first moment I saw you."

"I hope it's more than just a crush," Marinda said.

"I suspect it could be a lot more," Randy responded.

Marinda grinned. "If I were home now, this is the point when I'd suggest we go to my place."

"And what would I say?" Randy asked coyly.

"You'd say, *Let's go.*"

"Let's go," Randy said. "Will my place do?"

*  *  *  *  *

The moment Randy closed the front door, they held each other and then found each other's lips. The power of that first kiss shocked Randy. She felt a joyful, filling, erotic, confirming bliss that grew with the next kiss and the next. Soon they moved to the bedroom.

They made love slowly. First, removing each other's clothes, one garment at a time, exploring each part of the other's body as it became exposed. Lips on nipples. Skin against skin. Slow, sliding movement. Fluttering fingertips on smooth backs and legs and buttocks. Fingers inside. Juices. Tongues everywhere.

Although they got little sleep that night, Marinda had to leave early in the morning for a breakfast date with Amagyne. After she was gone, Randy lay in bed, contentedly, feeling Marinda's aura. She stretched her naked body languorously, remembering the feel of Marinda's skin, the tenderness of her touch, the intense passion they had shared. Not since Katherine had she felt anything like it; not even with Katherine had it felt so good and so right.

She had to force herself to get out of bed and go to work. At ten-thirty Marinda phoned her at the lab. "Lunch?" she asked.

They met in Golden Gate Park. They ate the sandwiches Marinda had brought, and they talked and watched the ducks. Randy was twenty minutes late returning to work.

At five o'clock Marinda was waiting outside the hospital. They spent the night together. And the next night and the next.

# Chapter 25

The instructions from Slick arrived as promised. The mail carrier was still on the porch when Elizabeth had the envelope out of the mailbox. She wore thin leather gloves and held the envelope by its edges. She removed the letter and then handed the envelope to Redman who also wore gloves. Holding the typewritten paper by its edges, Elizabeth began to read aloud.

"*Sue Silverman is to be the courier. Dress her up entirely in red, keeping her sweet face visible and recognizable. She's to carry an American flag, at least two feet long. Gift wrap the money securely, in 'plain brown paper,' four packages, and put it in a Safeway bag. With the sack of money in hand, and the flag, Sue is to go alone to The Bushes on Castro Street at exactly nine o'clock, tonight, Halloween night. She's to go into the bar and ask for Sammie. After that she's to go to the phone at 19th and Noe and wait for it to ring."*

Elizabeth moved to the sofa and sat. Elizabeth's lover, Jane, Carla, and Redman were gathered around her. Elizabeth continued reading. *"If this is done, and I get the money, and it's all there, and if there are no police following Sue, and no Redman, then you will have the Winged Dancer tomorrow. Soon after that I expect to see it dancing near the Bay. Happy Halloween. Slick."*

Redman had slid the envelope into a plastic bag. When Elizabeth finished reading, he took the letter from her and slid it into another plastic bag.

"Sue's going to love it," Carla said.

"What do you think?" Elizabeth asked Redman. "Does it sound as foolproof to you as it does to me? Slick will have Sue take the money somewhere where there are thousands of people, then she'll grab it and disappear into the crowd. Damn slick."

"I think she blew it," Redman said.

"What do you mean? Do you know what the scene is on Castro Street on Halloween?"

"I've never been there but I've seen it on the news," Redman said. "A regular Mardi Gras."

"This year will be no exception," Elizabeth said.

"Unless you want to go as a fairy godmother," Carla said, tittering.

"I'm going to go to Castro Street right now, as an insurance investigator," Redman declared. "To The Bushes and have a nice chat with Sammie."

Elizabeth was shaking her head. "Bad idea. If he's a friend of Slick and you show up and question him, it could blow the whole thing."

"I know what I'm doing," Redman snapped. "I guarantee Sammie will be very happy to talk with me rather than the district attorney."

"Unless Slick promised him a big chunk of the money," Jane said, folding a piece of gum into her mouth.

"My guess is that he doesn't even know Slick," Redman replied. "I think Sammie's role is to be a mailbox."

Carla was nodding. "Could be," she said, "like the runaround Slick put Marinda through. She might do the same thing to Sue."

"That's right," Redman said. He put the bags with Slick's letter and envelope into his briefcase. "Only this time she'll show up."

"Are you going to try to trace the typewriter?" Carla asked.

"Yes," Redman said. "After tonight, I'll turn these over to the police. Once Slick is caught, they'll see if they can find the typewriter she used to write the letter." He stood. "Sit tight, ladies, I'm going to go find out what Sammie's supposed to do when the woman in red shows up."

"I think *I* should go," Elizabeth said, standing also. "You'd stick out like an onion in a petunia patch at The Bushes."

Redman laughed. "I probably will but that's no problem. I don't want Sammie to be comfortable with me."

"I think we should leave well enough alone," Carla said. "We agreed not to try to catch Jay until after we have the statue. You said yourself she won't be able to hide for long. Why take the chance? Why not wait and get her afterwards?"

"I agree," Elizabeth said. "If Sammie tells you what he's supposed to do when Sue gets there, so what? What have we gained? If we catch Jay red-handed, picking up the money, then we've done what we said would be too risky — apprehending her before we have the statue."

"Not true," Redman retorted. He was still standing, but

leaning against the doorway. "That was if the police picked her up. I'm not the police. If I get her, I'll negotiate, cut a deal that I like better than the one she's proposing."

"Like what?" Elizabeth demanded.

"Like she gets half the money now and half when the statue is safely returned."

"She won't go for it."

"Or I turn her over to the cops."

"I don't go for that."

"Just a threat," Redman said, "to get her to negotiate. They always do that when you have them trapped."

"How are you going to keep her from just running away?" Jane asked.

Redman reached into his pants pocket and pulled out a pair of handcuffs. "I have the authority to apprehend her," he said. "Don't worry about her leaving until I'm done talking with her. You know, I'm being very patient with you. I don't owe you all these explanations. You've interfered in this case enough. Trust me, huh, ladies?"

"Let me see those handcuffs," Carla said.

Redman grinned. "No time for games, kids. Get ahold of Sue Silverman. Have her meet us here at seven-thirty. Go shopping. Buy a bunch of red clothing."

Redman left. Elizabeth called Marinda and then Amagyne and told them about the note from Slick and about Redman's plan. Then she called Sue. Sue went on for about fifteen minutes, excitedly assuring Elizabeth that she knew she could do the job, that she was feeling very confident, but how surprised she was that she was to be the courier.

* * * * *

There was no one named Sammie who worked at The Bushes, the bartender told Redman, and no customer that he knew of by that name. "But if you're serious about big

211

money being involved, I'd consider changing *my* name," he added, "although I'm very partial to my own. It's Robert."

"Who's working tonight?" Redman asked.

Robert frowned and looked petulantly at Redman. "I don't think I want to give out that information," he said. "What's this all about, anyway? Are you a cop or something?"

"Yeah, I'm something," Redman said.

"You're not bad but you're not my type," Robert responded. "Maybe Sammie works at Deja Vu's. They're always hiring new girls over there."

Redman drew a fifty-dollar bill from his pocket. "I really do want to find Sammie," he said.

Robert eyed the money. "I guess you do," he drawled. "If I see him, who should I say is calling?"

Redman took the fifty and wrapped it around a business card. "Tell him to call this number. He'll get a machine. Tell him to leave a number where I can reach him."

"Yes, Mr. . . ." Robert looked at the card. "Oh my, Mr. Special Investigator Gregory Moersch. I love it, Greggie."

"Just give him the message," Redman said.

"Roger Wilbur, over and out, Mr. Special. Do come back, you hear?"

Redman left the bar. Three hours later, at four-ten, he got the message. *This is Sammie,* it said. *Ask for Peter when you call.* A phone number followed. Redman dialed the number.

"Bushes," a male voice answered.

"May I speak to Peter, please."

"Speaking."

"This is Moersch," Redman said. "We need to talk. Right away. Can we meet someplace?"

"Talk about what?"

"The woman in red, *Sammie.* You've gotten yourself

involved in a crime that could mean serious trouble for you."

Peter agreed to meet with Redman in a half hour at a deli down the street from The Bushes. He was a slim, short-haired man with a trim mustache, in his early thirties.

"So tell me what you know," Redman began after they were seated.

"What do you know?" Peter retorted.

"That you have a rendezvous with a woman in red tonight at nine o'clock."

Peter nodded. "What's it all about?" he asked. "What kind of crime are we talking?"

"Kidnapping," Redman said. "Ransom."

Peter whistled. "The big time, huh?"

"What do you know?"

"I know I should keep my nose out of other people's business," Peter answered. "Especially if forty bucks is all I get out of it."

"Go on."

"A woman calls a couple nights ago. A practical joke, she says. She asks me if I'll be working Halloween night at the bar. Yes, I say, so? She says she's playing a joke on a friend and wants me to give this friend an envelope on Halloween night when the friend comes into the bar. She say's she'll give me forty dollars for my trouble, twenty before and twenty after. What's the joke, I ask. That part's private, she says. If the joke works out, she says, then she'll tell me what it was about. In any case, if I give the woman the envelope then I'll get another twenty."

"Could you recognize her voice if you heard it again?" Redman asked.

"It was a weird voice, high and squeaky."

"Disguised, no doubt," Redman said. "What else did she say?"

"That's about it. That this woman would come in at nine o'clock, that she'd be dressed all in red and she'll ask for Sammie. Then I give her an envelope. That's it." Peter shook his head. "Kidnapping, huh? Can you tell me who was kidnapped?"

Redman shook his head. "Confidential," he said. "Do you have the envelope?"

"Yeah, it came in the mail this morning. Along with twenty bucks."

"Let me see it."

Peter started to reach into his pocket. "You got any identification or anything. Are you FBI or what?"

"Special Investigator," Redman said. "Hired by the family." He opened his wallet and flashed a badge.

Peter handed him the envelope. It was unopened and had *Red* written on the outside. He drank the last of his iced tea and then started to stand.

"Stay," Redman said, not looking up. He opened the envelope. There were two sheets of paper. He read silently while Peter sat restlessly, watching him. Then Redman opened his briefcase, put the two pages from Slick inside, took out a sheet of blank paper, and began writing. When he finished, he folded the paper, put it into a fresh envelope and sealed it.

"Okay, here's what I want you to do," Redman said. He wrote *Red* on the back of the envelope. "I want you to go through with it just like planned. Watch for the lady in red. When she asks for Sammie, give her this." Redman held out the envelope to Peter.

Peter didn't take it. "I'd really rather not be involved," he said.

"She'll take the envelope, read the note, then she'll leave. That will be the end of it."

"Isn't there some other way you can do it?" Peter asked.

Redman looked at him scornfully. "All right, I'll get

someone else. Is Robert working tonight? He can be Sammie."

"Oh, no, not Robert. He'd fuck it up."

Redman stared at him.

"All right, I'll do it," Peter said. "You're sure she'll leave after she reads it? There isn't going to be any trouble in the bar, is there?"

"Like I said, she'll leave and that will be the end of it."

Peter smiled. "I won't get the other twenty, will I?"

Redman reached for his wallet.

"No, no, I'm just kidding." Peter took the envelope and stood. "You can do this for me though. When it's all over, give me a call and tell me who was kidnapped and how it worked out, all right?"

"Will do," Redman said. He reached out his hand. "Thanks, Pete."

"Peter," Peter said. He shook Redman's hand. "Thanks for the tea, Gregory," he said.

# Chapter 26

Marinda left Saturday morning after breakfast to meet Farrell Pembroke who had recently returned from Kuwait. Randy sat on her back porch swing and relived the highlights of the last few evenings. *I love you,* Marinda had said last night as they lay in each other's arms, and she'd said it again that morning before she left. The words reverberated in Randy's mind. It's all happening very fast, she thought.

When she thought about the fact that soon Marinda would be returning to Marigua, she felt a sinking in her stomach. She forced the thoughts away, remembering instead Marinda's loving words, the feel of her fingers and her lips, her flesh pressed against Randy's own, her soft, strong, loving, lovable body. And she remembered the feel of her tongue and what it did to her.

Later in the day, Randy was in the middle of mopping the kitchen floor when Marinda called. "You're sounding very beautiful."

"I'm loving you," Randy said.

"I know. And I love you more today than I did yesterday."

Randy laughed. "I think you're a romantic."

"I am."

"Me too. I spent half the morning smelling you on my fingers."

"Mm-mm."

"And tasting you on my lips. You spent the morning with Farrell Pembroke. How did it go?"

"I talked about you most of the time. It went okay. Randy, I've got some Winged Dancer news — we heard from Slick. Sue Silverman is supposed to take the money to a bar on Castro Street. At nine o'clock tonight. Redman's going to try following her."

"Oh boy, I hope he doesn't blow it."

"He wants all of us to hang around on Castro and see if we can get a glimpse of Slick. Look, but not touch. Will you come?"

"Of course," Randy said. "I've got those dinner plans with Marce and Jordan, though, at seven. I couldn't get out of it. I'm sure they're planning to go afterwards to Castro. Any possibility of you joining us for dinner?"

"No, thanks," Marinda said.

"I thought not," Randy said, knowing Marinda found Marce hard to take.

"I will come by for you, though, if you'd like, afterwards."

Randy told her where they'd be and Marinda said she'd

217

be there at eight-thirty. "Do you know the song, *Woman You've Been On My Mind?* I can't get it out of my head."

"I'll sing it for you," Randy said. "Tonight, after we play spy on Castro."

"When we're finally alone again."

"I can't wait. I'm excited just thinking about it."

"Me too," Marinda said. "I'd come right now if I hadn't promised to get together with Lou. I might come anyway," she added, chuckling.

"Not without me," Randy said.

"I'm also excited about the Winged Dancer. If all goes well, we'll have it back tomorrow."

"I think we will," Randy said.

"I like your thinking."

"I like your lips."

"I like your breasts."

"I like your cuntie."

"You're delicious and sexy and also happen to be the woman of my dreams."

"I like your dreams," Randy said.

They talked for another half hour, mostly silly love talk, which to Randy felt like the most serious thing on earth to be doing. The only future they talked about was that night and the next morning. Marinda said she would not wear a costume although she would go buy a mask. "For security reasons," she said.

"A tiger," Randy suggested. "It would suit you."

# Chapter 27

Sue wore a red baseball cap, a faded red jacket, a red skirt, red tights, and red sneakers. She arrived at Elizabeth's at seven-fifteen. Redman was already there and so were Carla, Amagyne, and Meredith. Essie arrived twenty minutes later.

Redman told Elizabeth his trip to The Bushes had been a waste of time, that he had learned nothing. He also said that he wanted Sue to wear a radio transmitter so they'd be able to follow her and maybe get a chance to confront Slick.

Elizabeth objected. "We're not trying to catch her

tonight, remember? I think a transmitter is an unnecessary risk."

"The purpose of the transmitter is not to apprehend Slick," Redman stated. "It's just to give me a chance to talk with her and get a look at her. That's what will guarantee our getting the statue back."

"I'm not so sure," Elizabeth had said.

"If she knows I can identify her," Redman insisted, "she won't risk compounding the charges against her by keeping the statue."

"I'm not so sure Slick will see the logic of that," Elizabeth said. "It's possible it would have the opposite effect. That if Slick knows you can identify her anyway, then she'll figure she has nothing to lose by melting down the statue and having the money to help her evade you and the police."

"I'll explain it to her so she understands," Redman said. "Obviously the legal consequences of keeping the statue will be more severe than if she returns it, and more severe yet if she destroys it. I'll make sure she understands this."

Carla thought he might have a point. Meredith agreed. In the end it was decided that they would help Redman try to get a chance to talk with Slick, and they'd have other women available to help if necessary. They all agreed to meet afterwards at Church Street Station, a bar and restaurant near Castro.

When Sue was told, she was a little hesitant about wearing a wire. "I heard those things can short out and burn your skin," she said.

"Not true," Redman said. "It's perfectly safe, Sue."

She tugged on the brim of her cap. "Well, Marinda did it and nothing happened to her. Okay, I'll do it," she said, with an air of bravado. She looked at the four large packages sitting on Elizabeth's dining room table. "That's the money, huh? Wow, I hope I don't get mugged. Heh-heh.

Maybe I'll just take off with it and catch a plane to Tahiti or somewhere." She caught Redman's eye. "Hey, I'm just kidding."

"Don't kid like that, Sue," Redman said. He smiled at her then. "Your outfit is charming. I have to tape the wire to you now. Would you remove your upper garments."

Elizabeth stepped in. "We'll do it," she said. She and Carla took Sue to the other room.

Forty minutes later, the five women and Redman left in Redman's car for Castro Street. Redman told Sue to talk into the transmitter only when she had something important to let them know.

Essie laughed. "Impossible," she said, and Sue punched her on the arm.

The women were all in costume. Elizabeth was dressed as an aviator — leather jacket, white silk scarf, aviator cap, goggles. Carla wore a bright green running suit and a green-faced monster mask. Meredith wore black studded leather with a Darth Vader mask. Essie was dressed all in tight-fitting beige and a full head mask of Venus de Milo. Amagyne wore a red-trimmed black robe; her mask was the head of a brilliantly plumed bird.

They dropped Sue two-and-a-half blocks from The Bushes, which was as close as they could get. A section of Castro Street was closed to traffic, and rowdy crowds jammed the street as well as the sidewalks. With the Safeway sack full of money in one hand and the American flag in the other, Sue wove her way through the masses of people. Music poured from all the bars.

Sue reached The Bushes at eight-fifty. She stood for a while in front of the bar, looking from person to person, trying to spot Jay. Many of the people were in costume. Several, Sue thought, could be Jay, but it was impossible to tell for sure. At eight-fifty-five, turning her head toward the wall, she said, "I'm going in." She tried not to move her lips as she spoke. She was fairly certain no one was

221

watching her, although it was possible, she realized, that someone with binoculars could be looking at her from one of the buildings across the street.

Inside The Bushes it was wall-to-wall people, probably all men, Sue thought, although many of them were in full drag. She pushed her way toward the bar. It took her awhile to get a bartender's attention. "I'm looking for Sammie," she said. She had to yell it because of the tremendous noise in the bar.

The man looked her up and down, nodded, then held up his index finger, indicating that she should wait. Several minutes later, someone with rouge, lipstick, and false eyelashes, but a real mustache, came to her.

"You looking for somebody?" he asked, scrutinizing her.

"Sammie," she said.

He looked grimly serious as he took an envelope from his pocket and handed it to her. Sue thanked him and elbowed her way back to the street which was almost as crowded as the bar. She found a place in a doorway and opened the envelope.

*Hello Sue,* she read silently, *Be at the phone booth on Castro and 20th by 9:30. Wait for the phone to ring. When you answer it, say, "Hello, this is Little Red Riding Hood." I'll talk to you then, Sue. Yours truly, Slick.*

Facing the door, her back to the crowd, Sue spoke: "It says I'm to go to the phone booth on Castro and Twentieth, to be there by nine-thirty, and she's going to call."

Redman had parked his Buick on Collingwood near Twentieth Street. Elizabeth and Carla had remained with him while Amagyne, Meredith, and Essie had gone on foot to Castro Street.

"We'll stay parked here," Redman said. "We'll be able to hear her all right when she reaches the phone."

* * * * *

Randy and Marinda were standing in the midst of chaos on the corner of Eighteenth and Castro, eyeing everyone near them. Elizabeth had called Marinda earlier that evening and asked her to be at that corner to watch for Sue and see what she could see. Randy was dressed as an astronaut. Marinda wore all black and a tiger mask. They had left Marce and Jordan at the restaurant half an hour earlier. Marce and Jordan were supposed to mill around on Eighteenth Street near Collingwood. Jordan had dyed her full head of hair green and wore brown pants and a brown jacket. She had a homemade mask painted to look like a big maple leaf. She said she was a tree. Marce's only costume was a wolf mask. She had on black pants and a Gay and Lesbian Pride 1992 sweatshirt.

"There she is," Marinda said. Sue had passed within five feet without noticing the women. She was pushing herself through the crushing crowd, the flag rising a foot above the mass of bobbing heads.

Marinda and Randy followed her down Castro until they were out of the thick of the crowd. They went no farther, remaining on the fringes of the mob, and from there, watched Sue walk toward Twentieth. A minute later a figure in a black robe and bird mask came by.

"That's Amagyne," Marinda said, pushing back her tiger mask and taking hold of Amagyne's arm.

"Who's your friend?" Marinda asked Amagyne, gesturing to meredith in her Darth Vader mask.

"Zetka," Amagyne said.

Meredith pushed up her mask. "We've been following Sue," she said. "Did you see her pass?"

"Yes." Marinda pulled her mask back down. "I don't think we should risk going any further. We can keep an eye on her from here."

\* \* \* \* \*

By the time Sue reached the phone, she was panting from the uphill climb. The corner at Twentieth Street was nearly deserted, just a few passersby now and then heading north toward the action on Castro.

Sue stood near the phone, scanning the area in all directions. It was nine-twenty-two. "I'm at the phone," she said, partially covering her mouth.

Jordan came up to Marinda and the others. "I lost Marce in this madness," she said.

"We lost Essie," Meredith said. "This scene is too crazy."

"Well, if we don't run into them, we'll see them at Church Street Station," Randy said.

"I think it's time for you to go to the car," Amagyne said to Meredith.

"Okay. You all wait here," Meredith said, "and when I find out what the message was, I'll come right back."

"We'll be here," Amagyne assured her. "Don't get lost."

Ten minutes after Sue arrived at the phone, it rang. "Hello, this is Little Red Riding Hood."

"Hi, Sue. Go to the phone booth one block up. Twenty-first and Castro. Wait for the ring." Click. The voice was very low and muffled.

As soon as Sue hung up, she relayed the message, then she trudged her way up the hill toward Twenty-first.

"She *is* slick," Redman said. "Switching phones in case there was a bug."

When she arrived at the second phone, it was already ringing. "Little Red Riding Hood," Sue said.

"Hi again, Sue," the hoarse, muffled voice responded. "I want you to do some more walking now. Go back down to Castro and Seventeenth, then turn left on Seventeenth and go to Collingwood. Keep walking and keep turning left at each corner. You'll be going around and around the block until I tell you the game is over. Listen again. Castro to

224

Seventeenth, to Collingwood, to Eighteenth, to Castro, to Seventeenth, and so on. You got it, Sue?"

"I got it, around and around the block."

"Walk on the sidewalk. Keep on the left side of the streets. Okay?"

"Okay. Left side."

"Wave that flag, Sue. And just keep walking until I tell you the game is over. 'Bye now."

As Sue headed back downhill on Castro, she spoke, repeating exactly what Slick had said.

"She's going to grab the money and disappear into the crowd," Elizabeth said. "Just like I thought."

Redman started the car. "I want to get closer."

He drove a couple of blocks and ended up parking in a driveway on Diamond between Seventeenth and Eighteenth. Elizabeth and Meredith left the car. Jane, Karen, and some other women were waiting at Eighteenth and Collingwood. Elizabeth headed toward them. Meredith returned to Amagyne, Marinda, and Randy, where she had left them on Castro near Nineteenth.

The plan was for the women to place themselves in pairs at various spots along Sue's route. One pair would follow Sue until they came to the next pair, who would pick up the trail until they came to the next pair, and so on. Redman had given Elizabeth and Meredith a supply of masks, U.S. presidents, for the women to wear so they could recognize each other. If anyone witnessed the money exchange, one member of the pair was immediately to give Redman and Carla a description of Slick, via Sue's transmitter, and tell them the direction Slick was going. The other member of the pair was to follow Slick, but not try to stop her.

The crowd was boisterous as Sue began her second trip around the block. Abraham Lincoln and Teddy Roosevelt followed ten feet behind her.

Periodically, Redman and Carla heard Sue report her location. It was difficult to hear her. "I wish she'd shut up," Redman said. "Slick could be three feet from her right now."

Amagyne and Meredith followed Sue from the middle of the block at Seventeenth to the corner of Collingwood where they came upon Washington and Jefferson who picked up the pursuit. Jane and Elizabeth stayed with Sue until they neared Eighteenth and saw FDR and JFK.

Sue continued circling the block, holding the flag aloft, the Safeway bag held close to her body. She scrutinized the people she passed, wondering when Slick would appear. Occasionally she reported her location. She was on her fourth trip around the block, on Castro between Eighteenth and Seventeenth. Thirty yards earlier, Randy and Marinda, as Woodrow Wilson and Eisenhower, had taken over the job of tailing Sue. Sue was passing through the throng of people in front of the White Elephant Cafe when a black-caped figure began walking in step with her.

"Hi Sue, the game is over. I'll take the bag now." The voice was very low and muffled through the fanged, blood-dripping mouth of a Dracula mask.

Sue felt shaky. She handed over the bag and Dracula immediately moved into the thick crowd that was milling in the street. Randy ran up to Sue, pushed back her Woodrow Wilson mask, and spoke into Sue's chest. "Slick got the money. She's wearing a black cape and a Dracula mask. She went onto Castro Street. I've lost sight of her. I can't tell which direction she went. Marinda is following her."

"Was it Jay, do you think?" Sue asked, when Randy finished conveying the message.

"Yes," Randy said. "I think it was. What do you think?"

"The height was about right, but I couldn't tell from the voice."

Marinda saw the caped figure disappear into the bar on

the northeast corner of Castro and Seventeenth. Still wearing her Eisenhower mask, she followed Dracula inside then frantically scanned the raucous mob. There were nuns and ballerinas and clowns but no sign of any Dracula. Marinda pushed her way through the crowd, searching for the rear exit. She glanced back periodically toward the front door. She was heading down a hallway which she figured might have a door to the outside when the devil in front of her bent and picked up a piece of black fabric, a cape. On the floor near the devil's feet, Marinda saw the discarded mask, white, fanged, the mouth dripping with blood. "Shit," she mumbled.

She elbowed her way to the hallway, to the door in the rear of the bar. It was locked. She backtracked to the front entrance where she and Dracula had come in. Outside, she looked up and down the street, then made her way across it, back to Randy and Sue.

"She got away," Marinda told them. "She dumped the cape and mask. Who knows what she's dressed in now. Did you see anything?"

"Nope," Sue said. She shook her head. "She was too slick for us."

They walked up Castro until they came to Monroe and Adams. "She got away," Marinda told the two presidents. Jane and Karen removed their masks. The group continued around the block gathering up the other pairs of presidents. Then they headed to Church Street Station.

Marce and Essie were already there, sitting on stools in the bar. Sue excitedly told them everything that had happened. ". . . and then she slipped away into the crowd. She could have been Cleopatra at that point or Tarzan or who knows? I want to take this thing off my chest now."

Elizabeth went with Sue to the john to help her remove the radio transmitter.

"What happened to you?" Marce asked Jordan. "You suddenly disappeared."

"I thought you were right behind me," Jordan said defensively. "As it turned out you didn't miss much. Elizabeth was right. Slick just disappeared." Jordan shook her head and the green hair flicked around like jungle vines.

"So will we hear from her again?" Meredith asked. "Want to place your bets?"

"If Dracula was a Kwo-amjamite, we will not hear from her," Amagyne said. "I'd bet on that."

"Do you still think it was Marinda?" Marce asked Meredith.

Meredith's eyes flashed angrily. She didn't answer.

"It was Jay Horne," Elizabeth said, "and she's probably safely back at her hideout by now."

At that point, Carla and Redman came into the bar. Redman did not look happy. "Where's Sue?" he asked.

Sue appeared and handed him the little box with wire wrapped around it. "Mission Impossible," she said. "But we gave it our best shot. Could you hear me all right?"

"You did fine, Sue," Redman said, taking the equipment. "I'll be leaving you folks now. Keep in touch," he said to Elizabeth. "Let me know the minute you hear anything."

"*If* she hears anything," Jordan said.

Redman left the bar. Sue asked Amagyne to dance.

# Chapter 28

The feel of Marinda's body against her own when Randy awoke Sunday morning was like fitting in the last piece of a thousand-piece jigsaw puzzle. Randy's head was cradled in the nook of Marinda's shoulder. She looked at Marinda's sleeping profile and felt tingly with the sense of completeness and contentment. She dozed off again and the next time she awoke, Marinda was looking at her. Marinda kissed her good morning. Randy kissed in return and the kisses grew longer and deeper. The passionate excitement Randy felt when they made love sprung, she knew, from the deep liking she felt for Marinda, the genuine appreciation she had of the person Marinda was. Randy would fly and yet she felt grounded, solid, like jumping into a cool pond in the middle of a flowering meadow that was home. She was in love.

They breakfasted on coffee and sliced fruit in the garden. They were talking about Slick and the Winged Dancer and wondering if and when they would hear, when the phone rang. They both dashed inside. It was Elizabeth asking for Marinda.

"Stay on the line," Marinda said to Randy, "I'll pick up the other phone."

"You're not going to believe it," Elizabeth said. "Slick called Sue. Here's what she said, and I quote, 'Surprise, the statue was never stolen. Ha-ha-ha. Tell them to check the storage area ve-r-ry carefully.' End quote."

"What's that supposed to mean?" Marinda sounded irritated. "Is that all she said?"

"Yes . . . oh no," Elizabeth amended, "she also told Sue she looks adorable in red."

"What is she trying to pull?"

"Got me. She couldn't have brought the statue back, that's for sure. I don't know, Marinda. It doesn't make any sense, but we're going to the museum to have a look around. I've already talked to the curator — Hefferman. Carla and I are meeting him there in an hour."

"Is it actually possible she could have hidden it somewhere in that storage area? I can't imagine where," Marinda said.

"Hefferman can't either," Elizabeth said. "Nor I, but we're going to check it out anyway. Want to come along?"

"It doesn't make any sense at all," Marinda said. "Okay, yes, I'll go with you."

Randy thought it must be some sort of stupid sick joke, and was feeling utter contempt for Jay. Elizabeth said she'd stop by for Marinda. She invited Randy to come along.

* * * * *

The four of them arrived at the museum at 10:45 a.m. and went directly to the curator's office. He and the security guard, Felix, accompanied them downstairs to the storage and shipping area, Hefferman saying it would surely turn out to be a waste of time.

"My biggest fear," Carla said, "is that Slick cut the statue into pieces, and that's what we're going to find."

"We won't find anything," Hefferman said.

The first thing they did was thoroughly check the room where art works were stored, looking into boxes, going through the contents of each shelf, examining particularly the area in the corner where the larger works of art were kept. Nothing.

While Hefferman, Carla, and Elizabeth went to check out the shipping area, the others went into the junk room where two-by-fours and tools and paint cans were kept. They looked around halfheartedly, behind sheets of plywood, underneath pieces of tarp. It was ridiculous. They were looking for a seven-foot-high statue, not a little vase or a diamond brooch.

The junk room was L-shaped. Felix stood at one corner staring fixedly at the back wall of the L. Randy was watching him and so was Marinda.

"What is it?" Marinda asked.

Felix didn't answer but walked over to the back wall and tapped on it with his knuckles. Then he stood back a few feet still staring at the wall. "I might just be imagining this," he said, "my mind playing tricks because I want to find that statue, but I have the sense that this room used to be longer." He started moving things out of the way until there was a clear view of the wall. "It looks freshly painted," he said.

Randy noticed that the edges of the wall didn't fit

exactly. She looked upward, following Felix's eyes. Like the storage room they had just left, the ceiling of the junk room was very high, the same height as the shipping area ceiling, about twelve feet or so.

"Does the wall look different from usual?" Randy asked.

Hefferman had entered the room. "Find something?"

"This wall, sir," Felix said. "Look at the paint. It looks fresher than the side walls. And look here, at the edges. I might just be fooling myself but it seems to me this section of the room is smaller than it used to be."

Hefferman moved past Marinda and Randy and stood next to Felix. "A false wall?" he asked.

"Could be."

"Knock a hole in it," Hefferman said. "Let's take a look."

Elizabeth and Carla had joined the others in the junk room. Marinda handed Felix a hammer and a chisel. He put the chisel against the wall about two feet from the right corner and began tapping it with the hammer. The plaster board cracked. Pieces fell onto the floor. When the jagged hole was about six inches in diameter, Felix asked for the saw hanging on a hook near Carla.

He cut out a square section of wall about two feet to a side, then shone his flashlight inside. "There's a room back here," he said, "and there's a big crate."

The excitement in the group was electric. Randy was sweating. Felix began moving more things out of the way and the others helped, moving cans of paint and pieces of board, power tools, boxes filled with nails and fittings. When the area was clear, Felix started hammering vigorously and pulling out sections of plasterboard, assisted by Marinda and Randy. Soon they had a big enough area ripped out of the wall to walk through. Felix went first. "It's the crate from Marigua all right," he said. "son of a bitch."

Part of the plasterboard that had been the false wall was nailed to the crate. Marinda was standing next to the crate, staring at it, her face glistening and her eyes full of tears. Several of the boards from the crate had been removed. Marinda took the crowbar Randy was holding and began pulling off more pieces until she could see inside.

"It's here," she said, her voice cracking.

The statue was wrapped in cloth and tied to the crate with ropes, but Marinda had revealed a section of it and Randy could see it clearly — gold, beautiful glittering gold. Randy thought of the replica in the Kwo-amjamite garage. "This is the real thing," she whispered.

"It certainly is," said Marinda.

"Son of a bitch," Felix said.

Hefferman was brushing plaster dust from his suit pants. "We've never had a theft at the museum," he said. "Never once."

* * * * *

Hefferman tried to get Elizabeth to allow the museum to display the statue for at least several days, but Elizabeth was firm. "Today is the day it was originally scheduled to be transferred to the conference hall," she said, "and that's how it will be."

And that's how it was. They called for a crew to come and transport the Winged Dancer to the Embarcadero Convention Building. The opening address of the conference was scheduled to take place at three that afternoon. The statue would be there in time.

Marinda was so happy she seemed to be floating above the ground. From the museum, Elizabeth drove everyone to Randy's place where they had some celebration food and drink. Elizabeth made several phone calls, spreading the news. Jordan had some news for her. Jay Horne had been arrested. The police had found her at an apartment in the

Sunset District. The news made Randy's stomach sink and her palms sweaty. Elizabeth called Detective Turillo to get the details. The others listened anxiously.

"She denies everything," Elizabeth said when she hung up.

"Surprise," Carla said.

"Turillo says the charges will be breaking and entering with intent to extort, destruction of museum property, extortion, and probably a few others," Elizabeth said.

"So what is Jay saying?" Randy asked.

"She claims she left San Francisco September thirtieth," Elizabeth said, "and was in Canada until two weeks ago. She and Barbara were supposedly on a camping trip. Jay called her answering machine to check her messages and learned Barbara's sister was in a car accident, so they flew back here. Jay denies any knowledge of or involvement in the theft — the *relocation,* I should say, or the extortion."

"So she's not denying she was here the day of the theft," Carla said. "Does she have an alibi?"

Elizabeth shook her head. "What she's saying is that she was alone at Barbara's apartment in San Francisco the entire evening and night of the disappearance of the statue. Watching TV. No witnesses."

"Her goose is cooked," Carla said.

"You'd think she'd have a better story than that," Marinda said.

"The police found Jay at Barbara's aunt's in the Avenues. That's where they were staying. Jay admitted she knew the police were after her. The fact that she stayed in hiding really clinches her guilt for Turillo. He says according to the D.A. there's a fairly good chance for a conviction. They're busy checking her fingerprints now. She also admits she was on Castro Street on Halloween night, dressed as a clown, she says."

"At least she's got the money for a good lawyer," Carla said.

Marinda said, "She won't be able to use that money."

"I hope she's smart enough to tell them where the money is," Randy said. "If she refuses I bet they'll give her a longer sentence. I hope she doesn't actually have to spend time in jail."

"If she's convicted, I imagine she will be sent to prison," Elizabeth said, "whether she returns the four hundred thousand or not. We'll see how it goes." Elizabeth looked at her watch. "Time for me to go," she said. "Conference registration begins in an hour and I have the forms." She and Carla stood. "See you two at the conference."

* * * * *

When they arrived at the Embarcadero Conference Center, Marinda and Randy went straight to the main lobby. A huge crowd surrounded the Winged Dancer and everyone seemed spellbound. The lobby was very quiet, people staring in awe at the statue, and occasionally murmuring something to those next to them. Even though the statue had no spiritual significance to Randy, she could understand what they were feeling. It was strange, she thought, the effect that the beautiful object had. She realized she was holding her breath as she stared at it.

The graceful figure of the dancer actually appeared to be in motion. The arms were spread wide, and from the shoulders flowed a magnificent robe made up of thousands of golden feathers. The dancer's head was thrown back in an expression of strength and joy and aliveness. The expression on the face seemed both serene and excited, and that's how it made Randy feel as she looked at it.

She glanced at Marinda and could see she was feeling the same emotion. They stayed there in the lobby until three o'clock when the opening talk began. The speaker was an Asian woman from a settlement in New Mexico, one of the original founders of Other Ways. Marinda and Randy took seats near the center of the conference hall.

The speaker was introduced and, as the emcee said, the *Other Ways 1992 Annual Conference* was officially underway. The main theme of the talk was the potential of human beings to live humanely together and how the Other Ways communities were living examples of this truth. The speaker began by talking about the Winged Dancer and how its timely return was a meaningful omen. Later she talked about the credo of Other Ways, the precepts Lou had told Randy about — no violence or coerciveness, respecting everyone's interpersonal rights, accepting and valuing diversity, and resolving conflict by dialoguing.

Somehow in this context it sounded possible to Randy. After the opening talk, people split up to go to different workshops. Randy went to one entitled *Diversity and Its Limits: Where To Draw the Line.* Marinda chose one called *Fostering New Communities.*

Randy found the workshop fascinating. There were about fifty people there, and a panel of three who gave short talks then opened the meeting up to discussion. They talked about dealing with credo violations among members, such as stealing from other members; they talked about how to respond to the needs of members with emotional problems that caused pain for themselves and others. People gave examples of how they handled such concerns at their own communities. Randy felt as if she were on another planet because everyone seemed so nonjudgmental and sincerely caring toward even the worst troublemakers. She wondered what they'd recommend doing with the likes of Jay Horne.

After the workshop, Marinda and Randy found each other in the lobby. "I missed you," Randy said. Marinda looked at her so lovingly that it took all Randy's willpower not to grab her and make wonderful love with her right then and there. She suspected Marinda was feeling the same.

"There's a big dinner here tonight, you know," Marinda said, "and then more meetings afterwards, and then a cocktail party."

Randy looked into Marinda's sparkling eyes which had a mischievous glint. "I hope they enjoy it," she said.

Marinda took her hand and they headed for the exit. They took a cab to Randy's place, ordered a pizza, and didn't leave the house until the next morning.

# Chapter 29

At work on Monday, Randy kept thinking of Jay sitting in a cell with a collection of prostitutes and junkies. Serves her right, she thought. She wondered if anyone would bail her out.

Marinda, Jess, and Randy met for dinner on Monday night at a place near the Embarcadero. Then they went to the conference to hear Amagyne give a talk about her community in Colorado. She was a dynamic speaker and handled the questions afterwards beautifully, Randy thought, even the snide ones from people who called her group a cult.

Afterwards Randy ran into Marce in the lobby. "I assume you heard about Jay," Marce said.

"You look delighted," Randy responded. "It would probably make you happy if she got ten years."

"Not at all," Marce assured her. "What makes me happy is what should make you happy. I'm going to get my money back from her."

Randy looked at her skeptically. "She certainly can't pay you in unmarked cash."

Marce chuckled. "No, no, not that money. She has another source. When I get it, you'll be getting a reimbursement from me. I hope you appreciate what I'm doing for you."

Randy was having trouble believing it. "How did you pull this off?" she asked.

Marce looked supremely smug. "Easy. I went to her preliminary hearing this morning. She was pretty shaken up. After her girlfriend bailed her out, I told her I could get her a good lawyer. I also mentioned that it would look better for her if the prosecutor didn't find out about her defaulting on her loan. She's being very cooperative with me. Oh, and get this — she said she was planning to begin sending me payments anyway. Isn't that rich?"

"Where'd she get the six thousand?" Randy asked. "That in itself ought to be enough to convict her."

"From Barbara Keegan," Marce said. "Barbara has almost twenty-thousand in a passbook account. The Bank of America, right here in San Francisco. She says she built up the savings over the last ten years, that her account will show that. Tomorrow, six thousand of it will be mine."

"I see."

"So you're off the hook, my dear." Randy was about to respond when Marce said, "Oh-oh, there's your new girlfriend looking for you. I better disappear — you know how jealous those Latinas are." Marce started to walk away, then called back over her shoulder. "Give me a call some lonely night when Marinda's back in South America. See you around, kiddo," she said.

\* \* \* \* \*

That night Randy and Marinda took a shower together, then went to the bedroom. They were eager for each other, and their lovemaking was especially passionate that night. Randy was falling deeper in love by the minute.

At midnight, sitting up in bed, pillows propped behind them, Randy said how relieved she was about the money. "Marce certainly did move in swiftly on Jay, didn't she?"

"Of course," Marinda said. "Taking care of her investment."

It was then that Randy broached the topic that had been constantly on her mind. "I'm feeling very invested in *you*," she said.

Marinda chuckled. "I sensed that, my love." She kissed Randy on her bare shoulder. "And I'm finding myself rather taken with you, in case you hadn't noticed."

"Invested in me?" Randy asked.

Marinda pulled her head back and looked at her. "Of course," she said. "What are you getting at?"

Randy didn't answer.

"Are you thinking about the future?"

Randy felt very nervous. Had she crossed the line? Would Marinda back off now and say, *It was nice while it lasted, Randy, but be realistic; you live here and I live there. Call me if you're ever in Marigua.*

"Yes," Randy said. "Do you think that's stupid? I know we hardly know each other."

"We know a lot about each other," Marinda said. "I too have been wondering about what the future holds." She was looking into Randy's eyes.

"You have?"

240

Marinda looked askance at her. "I'm not playing with you, Randy. Don't you know that?"

Randy did but was afraid to believe it. She nodded. "Any suggestions?" she asked.

Marinda shrugged. "Marigua's a beautiful country. Do you like warm weather?"

"Mmm-hmm," Randy said, "especially the warm Octobers in San Francisco."

"I was afraid of that."

"And you?"

"The weather actually was rather pleasant here last month." She smiled at Randy. "You think you'll still love me tomorrow?"

Randy's eyes teared. "Every tomorrow."

Marinda took her hand. "I haven't been very lucky in love," she said. Randy started to protest that this would be different, but Marinda interrupted. "But this seems different." She looked tenderly at Randy, then looked away and spoke. "There's a woman in Marigua whom I was in love with. *Obsessed* might be a better word. I think I was still in love with her until . . . oh, I guess, until our first motorcycle ride."

"And now you're over her?"

"Yes," Marinda said. "I've moved on." She was still holding Randy's hand and looking intently at her. "I truly do love you," she said. She took off her silver bracelet and slipped it onto Randy's wrist.

Randy's eyes brimmed with tears. She smiled through them as she removed her own rope and bead bracelet and slid it onto Marinda's soft, smooth wrist.

That night Randy dreamed she was swimming in a clear pool pond in the middle of a field of wildflowers, and then floating into a warm mist with Marinda, laughing, both of them laughing gaily and looking into each other's eyes.

241

* * * * *

Randy called in sick at work the next day, and she and
Marinda didn't get out of bed until after ten. There was a
panel discussion at the conference at one o'clock that
Marinda was planning to attend, another one on forming
new communities.

"You seem very interested in that topic," Randy
commented.

"Mm-hmm. Do you want to know why?"

"Because you want to start one," Randy teased.

"That's right," she said.

"You're kidding. Where?"

"San Francisco, California," Marinda said. "Like the
location?"

"Are you serious?"

"There's a whole group of us trying to get it off the
ground. Including Elizabeth and Carla."

"How long have you been planning this?" Randy asked.
"Does this have anything to do with me by any chance . . .
with us?"

"Egotist. We started talking about it the day I arrived
in the States, before I ever met you or knew I'd fall so
totally in love with you. Elizabeth wants to model it on the
settlement in Marigua."

"Interesting," Randy said. "Tell me more."

"Come to the meeting today. I'm on the panel. I'll tell
you then."

Randy feigned anger at her. "What other secrets do you
have?"

"Many," Marinda said, kissing Randy deeply. "Many,
many secrets," she murmured, "and one by one they will
all be yours."

* * * * *

They arrived twenty minutes late for the meeting, because of Marinda's dawdling. Randy was afraid she'd soon pick up Marinda's attitudes about time, but that didn't especially bother her. Marinda was the third speaker. There were sixty or seventy people in the audience. As Marinda spoke, she seemed as comfortable as she did in Randy's living room. Marinda was in the middle of her talk when someone tapped Randy on the shoulder. Jordan. She asked Randy to come outside with her.

Randy followed her outside the meeting room and Jordan told her she'd just talked to Elizabeth. "The charges against Jay have been dropped," she said.

Randy was shocked. "Why? What happened?" She pictured Jay talking her way out of it, coming up with some story in such a convincing way that even that hard-ass Turillo fell for it.

"Sue provided her with a hermetically sealed alibi," Jordan said. "Inadvertently. Sue was having a talk with her ex-roommate — you know who . . ."

"Barbara Keegan," Randy said.

"Sue was complaining to Barbara about some bills Barbara had left unpaid, including a phone bill. She had the phone bill in front of her — AT&T long distance. She had circled the charges for the month of September that weren't hers. One of them was a call to Grand Rapids, Michigan."

"Where Jay's parents live," Randy said.

"That's right. The date of the call was September twenty-ninth, the night of the theft. From five-thirty-two until six-forty-something, Jay was on the phone with her mother."

Randy shook her head incredulously.

"The police called Jay's mother and her mother remembered the call clearly, and the date. She said she had been relieved to finally hear from Jay because they'd been out of touch for several months. She even remembered questioning Jay about the loan and about your call to her about the money."

Randy nodded numbly.

"Jay had forgotten all about that phone call. All she remembered doing that evening was watching TV and cutting her toenails. Elizabeth said the moment Jay was told the charges were dropped, she raced over to Sue's apartment and covered Sue's face with a bunch of slobbering kisses." Jordan was laughing as she told the story. "Sue kept protesting that she hadn't done it on purpose. Then later she said of course she would have, though, if she'd made the connection."

Jordan shook her head. "Part of me never believed Jay had done it — that she was the extortionist."

Randy was still trying to let it sink in. "But if it wasn't Jay, then who —"

"Right," Jordan said. "Who the hell did it? Who's got the four hundred thou? That's what everyone's asking. Everyone was sure dead wrong about Jay."

"Where is she, do you know?"

"She's scared to see you. She and Barbara are staying at Sue's. Jay said she couldn't stand another minute at Barbara's aunt's in the Sunset District. There were doilies on the chairs there, she said, and six cats."

"Jay's allergic to cats."

"I know. Do you want to see her?"

Randy didn't answer. She wasn't sure.

"Did you hear what Amagyne did?" Jordan lit a cigarette. "She went over to the Kwo-amjamites house in Oakland — you know the one — and apologized to the women. They were slow in accepting her apology but I guess they finally did. Amagyne must have been feeling very guilty for having accused them."

"Like the rest of us should feel about Jay."

"Well you have to admit, it sure looked like she had done it, but like I said, I never fully believed it. Did you?"

"Yes," Randy admitted.

"Well, maybe she'll forgive you if you forgive her for what she did to you. She told me if she had known Marce was actually going to insist that you make the loan payments, she'd have come back immediately and stopped it."

"Yeah, yeah," Randy said. "What a bullshitter."

"Yeah."

"I don't think I want to see her."

Jordan nodded. "She is a bit of a shithead, even though she's not Slick. You know she's selling the van, don't you, and giving the money to Barbara? That blows her business in Banff. She's talking about starting a new one, a pizza place with a laundromat attached."

Randy rolled her eyes.

"That's Jay," Jordan said.

# Chapter 30

"The police have a new suspect," Marinda said the next night at dinner. "Elizabeth learned about it from Turillo."

"Oh, really? Not Andrea Herrara?" Randy said.

"No. Her name is Cassandra Lee."

Since the statue was safe and since Jay hadn't been involved, the whole topic of the extortion seemed rather anticlimactic to Randy. "So who is she?" Randy asked, only mildly curious.

"She lives in Pacific Heights," Marinda said. "Forty-eight years old, divorced, wealthy background."

Marinda filled Randy in on the other details. After Jay

was cleared the police had gone back to checking U-Haul renters. They broadened their search beyond San Francisco and turned up somebody who had rented a truck in Concord on September twenty-ninth at two-twenty in the afternoon. A woman named Jacqueline Dietrich.

That name rang a bell for Randy but she couldn't place it.

"It turned out that Jacqueline Dietrich had been in the hospital at the time the truck was rented," Marinda said. "She said she hadn't loaned her driver's license to anyone nor had it been stolen. While she was in the hospital, she said, the license was in her home in Pacific Heights, in a wallet, along with her credit cards and such. So the police started checking everyone who could have had access to the license. That's where Cassandra Lee comes in. She's a friend of Dietrich's. And she had a key to the Dietrich house."

"So the police think Cassandra Lee took her friend's license and used it to rent the truck."

"That's right," Marinda said.

"Why?" Randy asked, wondering if this would turn out to be yet another mistake. "Why wouldn't she just use her own license? So the suspicion would fall on Dietrich?"

"I doubt that," Marinda said. "I don't know. So the rental couldn't be traced to her, I suppose. Not very bright, as it turned out."

"Has she confessed?"

"She denies everything. According to Turillo, though, they have a strong case against her. She admits knowing about the statue — she's an avid art fancier, goes to all the openings, keeps up on museum exhibits. She knew the Winged Dancer was coming to San Francisco and she knew when."

"That doesn't mean anything," Randy said. "Thousands of people knew that."

"True, my love, but be patient, there's more."

"Did she know about the storage room? About the security procedures at the museum?"

"I don't know," Marinda said. "It would certainly have helped to have that information but it wouldn't have been necessary."

"I suppose not," Randy said. "I suppose someone could have hung around the museum and learned quite a bit that way. Like where the shipping area is."

"Yes, I imagine so. Do you want to hear the rest?"

"Go on."

"As I said, Lee had the key to the Dietrich house so she could easily have gotten the license and could easily have returned it after she was done with it. And she has no alibis. She claims she can't remember what she did the evening of the twenty-ninth. On Halloween night she says she was home alone working on her photo album."

"You'd think she'd have come up with something better than that if she were guilty," Randy said.

"My hunch is that she was sure they'd never trace the U-Haul since she rented it thirty miles away from the city. Anyway, the most incriminating part for her has to do with motive — she was in desperate need of money — big money. She's a gambler, a regular at the casinos in Reno."

Marinda poured wine into Randy's glass and then her own. "Nobody," she continued, "including Cassandra Lee, can come up with an explanation for how or why a U-Haul truck was rented in the name of Jacqueline Dietrich, other than that it was rented in order to steal the Winged Dancer. They arrested Lee yesterday."

The name *Jacqueline Dietrich* continued to bother Randy. She was sure she'd heard it before. "Didn't the U-Haul people notice that this Lee woman didn't look like the picture of Jacqueline Dietrich on the license?" Randy asked.

"Apparently not," Marinda said. "She could have

disguised herself to look like Dietrich. Or maybe it was a poor photo."

"Hmm-m, I suppose. So, has she recently paid off her debts?"

"I doubt that," Marinda said. "She'd probably be careful not to spend a lot of money right away."

"And the police are sure she did it, huh? They think they can prove it?"

"According to Elizabeth, yes."

"So, The End, then. Case closed." Randy shrugged. "Maybe," she added. "What do you think? Do you think this Cassandra Lee did it?"

"Probably," Marinda said.

Randy nodded. "Yeah, I guess so." She shook parmesan onto her pasta. "Didn't anyone else have a key to Jacqueline Dietrich's house?"

"Just her husband and the cleaning woman," Marinda said. "No one else."

"And the cleaning woman's clean?"

Marinda laughed. "She was with her lover and some other people the twenty-ninth. Plenty of witnesses. Yeah, she's clean."

"And the husband?"

"Clean too. And no sign of the house being broken into."

Randy nodded, feeling oddly disappointed. "I really thought it would turn out to be someone that one of us knew," she said, "someone more interesting than some Pacific Heights type." She scooped more creamy dressing onto her salad.

"I've got some other interesting news," Marinda said, giving Randy a big grin. "We established a new committee today, the San Francisco Alternative Community Project Committee. I'm a member."

"Ah, so you're really going to do it." Randy smiled lovingly at her. "Bring nirvana to the west coast."

"There are twenty-five people so far who want to be part of the community. Elizabeth is acting as coordinator. I've agreed to help with the architectural design. First we need to acquire some property, but before that we have to raise some money. Other Ways has agreed to contribute five thousand dollars."

"That's a start," Randy said. "Are you trying to tell me you've made your decision?"

"About moving to San Francisco?" Marinda looked teasingly at Randy. "I'm giving it serious consideration."

"If you do move here, then I definitely won't move to Marigua."

Marinda laughed. "You're a delightful human being," she said.

Randy liked hearing that.

* * * * *

Saturday morning, Marinda left to go to the conference, and Randy stayed home to do her laundry. Mostly she wanted time alone to think. There was something nagging at her about the Cassandra Lee business.

She was folding her second load when she finally remembered how she knew the name Jacqueline Dietrich. She's heard it from Marce. Marce had told a story about a rich matron in Pacific Heights, named Jacqueline Dietrich, who smoked pot and had some other interesting habits that would probably have surprised most of her friends. Marce's friend, Sandy something, told Marce about finding some roaches in the old gal's ashtray when Sandy was cleaning her house. Gossett, that was her name — Sandy Gossett, Marce's cleaning woman. And Jacqueline Dietrich's cleaning woman. Sandy Gossett had been cleaning Marce's house for the last couple of years, Randy recalled, and they had apparently become good friends. They were neighbors too, she remembered; Sandy lived in a rented place four or five houses down from Marce.

This train of thought was getting Randy very excited. She tried to remember everything she could about Sandy Gossett. She was a real gossip, according to Marce, who loved to tell her friends stories about the rich people whose houses she cleaned. Randy had wondered what she told people about Marce. Apparently this Jacqueline Dietrich provided some good stories, Randy remembered, not only about the pot, but about the kinds of books and magazines Sandy dusted — hard core stuff, in Jacqueline's room, not the husband's. They had separate bedrooms, apparently, which also provided Sandy with some gossip material.

Once Randy started thinking about this, more memories came. She remembered Marce telling her that Sandy had said Jacqueline Dietrich was going into the hospital for surgery, and Sandy suspected it was for injuries done to herself with her latex toys while she pored over her porn magazines. Marce had found that very amusing.

More was coming back. Marce had talked about Sandy's pegboard full of keys that hung in her bedroom. A bunch of keys, all labeled, keys to her customers' houses and apartments.

"You trust her with your key?" Randy had asked Marce.

"Absolutely," Marce had said. "The woman has great integrity. I have a key to her place too, to take in her mail when she's out of town. That must mean I have great integrity."

Randy remembered thinking at the time that Marce's logic was a little off there.

The connections she was making sickened her, but she couldn't stop. Sandy Gossett had a key to Jacqueline Dietrich's. Marce had a key to Sandy Gossett's. Marce knew Dietrich had been in the hospital. Marce knew about the statue and the museum security procedures. Not only that, Marce knew Jay had rented a U-Haul truck.

Stop, Randy told herself. I'm as bad as Meredith was about Marinda. Besides, she thought, Marce was working the day it happened. Wasn't she? The twenty-ninth. And then she went to Xavier's that night. Randy remembered that clearly because she had asked Marce to go out with her that night, but Marce had said she had a date with Xavier.

The stuff about the cleaning woman and the keys is just coincidence, Randy thought.

* * * * *

An hour later, Randy met Lou and Christina for lunch. Lou recommended that Randy go to the session that afternoon on *Structure and Rules Versus Anarchy in Experimental Communities*.

Randy took her up on it and found the discussion fascinating. In fact, she was finding most of what she was learning at the conference fascinating. It made her wonder whether it would be possible for her to be part of the new San Francisco Community and still live at her house.

After the meeting, Randy found Marinda. The Winged Dancer had originally been scheduled to be shipped back to Marigua on Monday, but Marinda had gotten the date changed to two weeks later, she told Randy. Randy was very glad of that since Marinda would be accompanying the statue back home.

"So the Indian Museum will have those two weeks to show the statue," Marinda said. "That made the curator happy."

"I'll bet," Randy said.

"I want you to come to Marigua with me," Marinda said, "meet my friends, see what a wonderful place you are luring me away from. We can stay a few months or so."

252

Marinda didn't seem concerned when Randy explained that she only had two weeks of vacation time coming, and that research assistants didn't get sabbaticals. "Maybe it's time to quit that job," she had said.

"But I like to eat," Randy retorted, and Marinda just laughed.

* * * * *

That night was the conference finale, a concert emceed by Lou Bonnig. There were singers from the various Other Ways communities, including a trio from France, and a dance troupe, several poets, a comic, and a band from New York. After the concert, there was a wild party at Elizabeth's. Jay showed up with Barbara. Randy and Jay stared at each other across the room but neither of them moved.

"Do you want to talk?" Jay called. She was about ten feet away from Randy with a crowd of people between them.

"Maybe some day," Randy answered.

Jay looked a bit sad. She nodded and then she moved off with Barbara and they started to dance.

Meredith had been watching. "Do you think you'll ever forgive her?" she asked Randy.

"Mostly I already have," Randy said, "but I just don't think I want to associate with her. She's part of my past."

Jordan came up to Randy and asked her if she knew who Marce's new friend was. Randy followed Jordan's eyes and saw Marce with a long-haired Latina, very, very pretty.

"No," Randy said. "Her latest conquest, maybe." Marce looked so arrogant and cocksure.

"I hear her name is Vivian," Jordan said. "She and Marce are taking a trip together in a couple of weeks, to Bermuda."

Spending some of the extortion money, Randy thought.

She realized that part of her really believed that. "Did you ever find out who that curly-headed woman was?" Randy asked Jordan. "The one you saw coming out of Marce's house the day the Winged Dancer disappeared?"

"Oh, Ms. Polyester Suburbia, you mean?" Jordan chortled. "No, I never did. I guess that fling didn't last very long."

"What time was it?" Randy asked, "when you saw the woman? Do you remember?"

"What time?" Jordan scrutinized Randy. "Yeah, it was right after lunch, probably about one-thirty. Why?"

"You're sure?"

"Yes. I'd had lunch with a friend of mine who I wanted to do some filming with. Marce had said I could borrow her video camera so after lunch I decided to stop by her house and get the camera. It must have been about one-thirty. Why do you ask?"

"Just wondering," Randy said. "Was Marce home?"

"Yes, but she didn't answer the door. She's like that sometimes."

"How do you know she was home?"

"I heard the stereo," Jordan said.

She could have left the stereo on, Randy thought. She wondered if Jacqueline Dietrich had curly hair.

"Forget Marce," Jordan said. "Come on, let's dance."

Randy danced with Jordan and then with Essie and then Marinda. Marinda held Randy at arm's length and her eyes drank Randy in from her head slowly down to her feet and up again.

Randy felt the gaze as if it had fingers. "What are you doing, my sweet?"

"Touching your perfect body with my mind."

Soon after that they were on the street and hailing a cab. "You know what I've been thinking, Marinda?" Randy said in the taxi. "Don't laugh."

Marinda kissed each of Randy's eyelids. "What have you been thinking, my love? Of course I won't laugh."

"I think that Marce is Slick," Randy said. "Seriously. Don't laugh."

Marinda didn't laugh. "Is it hard seeing her with other women?" she asked.

"It's not that," Randy protested. "Really. Listen to this — the woman who cleans Marce's house is also the Dietrich woman's cleaning woman. Her name is Sandy Gossett. She's a good friend of Marce's and Marce has a key to her apartment. Sandy keeps the keys to her customer's houses in her apartment, including the key to Jacqueline Dietrich's house."

"Interesting," Marinda said.

"You ready for more?"

"I'm listening."

"On the day the statue disappeared, Jordan went over to Marce's to borrow a camera. She saw someone with curly hair and makeup coming out of Marce's house and getting into Marce's car. Jordan assumed it was a new lover of Marce's, but I don't think it was."

Marinda waited.

"I think it was Marce," Randy said.

"Marce? With curly hair and makeup?"

"In disguise."

"Oh, I see."

"I want to find out what Jacqueline Dietrich looks like."

"So you're thinking —"

"Yes, that Marce took the driver's license, that she rented the truck. It's possible, Marinda. I want to check it out."

Marinda didn't say anything.

"You think I should just forget about it."

She smiled. "It seems you're not feeling very fondly towards Marce Flasch these days, my love."

"It seems I'm not," Randy said, "but that doesn't change the business about the key."

"She did manage to get the money from Jay so you don't have to worry about becoming a pauper."

"I suppose I should appreciate that."

"Don't you?"

Randy shrugged. "So instead of ripping *me* off, she rips off Barbara Keegan." Randy sighed. "I guess it's really Jay I'm mad at. No," she said, "I'm mad at both of them. They're slimy."

Marinda nodded. "You knew what Marce was from the beginning, didn't you?"

"Yes. She's like Jay in a sense, somewhat morally deficient, but with a few socially redeeming qualities."

"Such as?"

Randy chuckled. "You're the one who really can't stand Marce," she said.

"She's not my favorite person, but I don't think she's the extortionist, Randy. As I recall she was easily able to account for her time on the twenty-ninth."

"You're right, I should just forget about it." Randy smiled at her. "You have very sexy lips," she said, smacking hers.

Marinda smiled lovingly at her. Then she smacked her lips also and the two of them just stared at each other.

"Perfect," Randy said. "Everything in my life is perfect right now. I'm in love with a perfect woman who's in love with me. I don't owe anybody any money. I feel happy and wonderful." She was frowning.

"But . . ."

"But there's a loose end," she said. "I can't help it, Marinda. I have this strong feeling that Marce did it, that she's the extortionist. It's not like Meredith suspecting you. This is different. I'm not projecting. Marce Flasch has four hundred thousand dollars that she has no right to, and an innocent woman is being accused."

256

Marinda said nothing. A minute later, the cab pulled up in front of Randy's house.

* * * * *

They were in bed ten minutes after they got inside with Marinda on top of Randy, burying her face in Randy's neck, giving her little nips and kisses. Marinda had taken Randy's T-shirt off and Randy was squirming beneath Marinda's warm body, raising her hips, pushing herself against Marinda. Marinda's mouth moved from Randy's neck to her breast, her hand caressing Randy through her underpants.

The gentle sucking on Randy's nipple grew from light teasing to more and more intense licking and deep sucking. Randy felt heat rising along her legs and her middle and up her neck. She was writhing with excitement, feeling herself getting wet. She'd been caressing Marinda's back and buttocks, but when Marinda kept sucking her nipples, first one then the other, pulling them into her mouth, Randy let her hands fall back on the bed, arms bent, palms up. "Your gesture of surrender," Marinda had once called it. It was then that Marinda became more aggressive. She already had Randy's pants half way down, and then she pulled them all the way off, still sucking deeply on Randy's nipple. She inserted a finger into Randy's vagina. Randy started gasping. Marinda moved her hand rhythmically and Randy matched the rhythm with her hips. Only when Randy was on the brink of orgasm did Marinda let go of her nipple and lay her head on Randy's chest with her fingers moving, more and more rapidly, until the heat became ignition and Randy felt the burst everywhere, in her cunt, her stomach, up her spine, exploding out her throat in a long low moan.

As Randy lay catching her breath Marinda mumbled how beautiful Randy's body was, her soft skin, and wonderful breasts. How sexy Randy was. Marinda was very excited, her voice rumbly and hoarse. Randy shifted positions, kissing Marinda in a jagged line from her lips to her neck, her chest, her full breasts, to her stomach and her round belly. Randy had moved down until her torso covered the lower part of Marinda's body, her breasts resting on Marinda's legs. She could feel the soft tickle of Marinda's hairs on her chin, and the trembling of Marinda's muscles as she got more and more aroused. Marinda knew what Randy was going to do next and Randy wouldn't disappoint her, but she would prolong it. She lingered around Marinda's soft thighs, kissing, licking, and along the rim of her triangle of hair, caressing with her lips, blowing, going down teasingly toward her clitoris, then back up.

At last Randy gave Marinda what she had been waiting for, pulling Marinda's stiff little clit into her mouth, flicking with her tongue, sucking, licking. She inserted one finger deep inside of Marinda, continuing to stimulate Marinda's clit with her mouth and tongue. She'd barely begun to gently vibrate her finger when every one of Marinda's muscles tightened. Randy knew she was very close. She kept at it, back and forth with her tongue, up and down with her finger, feeling Marinda pressed tightly against her, sensing her hands groping for something to squeeze. When Marinda peaked, her whole body shook and shook. The first time it had happened, the intensity of it had scared Randy. Marinda was shaking now and Randy almost came with her. Marinda gave a little laugh right after the climax ended and her muscles simultaneously let go into a sag of contented relaxation.

She pulled Randy up to her, kissed her juicy face, held her tight, stroking her back and buttocks. They fell asleep wrapped in each other's arms.

# Chapter 31

At brunch the next day, Marinda told Randy the San Francisco project needed some graphic artwork for fundraising and advertising. She had talked to some of the other members, she said, and they wanted to look at samples of Randy's work. "Perhaps you will end up making a living as a graphic artist."

"I'd love it," Randy said.

"I could support you for a while," Marinda said, "if needed, until you get established."

"Really? I thought I'd be the one supporting *you* for a while."

Marinda shook her head. "I will have no trouble getting jobs here. I've already made some contacts."

"You're a fast worker."

Her eyes glinted. *"Si, muy rapido."*

Randy touched a slice of cantaloupe to Marinda's lips. Marinda opened them slowly and caressed the fruit with her tongue.

"How does this sound, Randy?" Marinda leaned forward resting her elbows on the table. "Request a leave of absence at your job, and if they say no, then tell them you quit."

"All right," Randy said, without any hesitation. She had already decided there was no way she was going to pass up the chance of going to Marigua with Marinda. "I'll talk with Dr. Cartwright tomorrow."

"You may fall so in love with my country that you won't want to return here," Marinda said.

Randy smiled. "My Spanish is very rusty."

"We will polish it up together," Marinda said, "while we polish up other things." She wiggled her tongue obscenely at Randy and that, of course, meant that mealtime was over and it was time for other pleasures.

An hour later Marinda dozed off on the bed and Randy went to the living room to phone Marce's secretary, Elise Stein. They small-talked briefly then Randy got to the point. "It's a surprise gift for Marce," she said. "I'm charting her bio-rhythms and then I'm going to relate them to her diet."

Elise laughed.

"No, this is serious. It could be very important for her health. I've already begun to identify some patterns but I need more information. Would you mind if I ask you a few questions about her?"

"About her rhythms? I don't think I can help you much with that. Or her diet."

"I bet you could. You know her schedule, her work and

rest patterns. Isn't it true that at the beginning of each month, Marce tends to work much longer hours than she does at the end of the month?"

"Hmm-m, I've never noticed," Elsie said.

"Well, think about it. You keep a log, don't you? Do you know how much time she was in the office near the end of the month versus near the beginning?"

"Hold on, let me check."

Elise gave Randy Marce's appointment schedule and in and out times for the last few days of October and the first couple of days of November. October twenty-ninth she'd been in the office all day and into the evening with several trips away to show properties. The next day she worked at home in the morning then was in the office the rest of the day until seven. Saturday she had one appointment in the late morning then nothing again until Monday.

"She wasn't around very much Monday or Tuesday, November second and third," Elsie told me. "That seems to support your theory, doesn't it?"

"So far," Randy said. "How about the end of September?"

"Let's see." Randy could hear pages flipping. "On the twenty-eighth she had appointments all day," Elsie said, "up until six-thirty. On the twenty-ninth, Tuesday, she was here briefly early in the morning, then she worked at home most of the afternoon and evening. Then on the thirtieth —"

"Just a second," Randy said. "On the twenty-ninth, you say she worked at home most of the day."

"Yes. She had an appointment scheduled for one but she called at about eleven and asked Nina to handle it."

"This was the twenty-ninth," Randy said.

"Yes, September twenty-ninth."

"Does she ever tell you she'll be working at home but then change her mind and do something else?"

"Oh, sure. But she always calls and lets me know."

"And on the twenty-ninth of September she was definitely working at home?"

"Yes. She was working on the accounts that day. I remember because she called to ask me about some accounts receivable questions. I looked up the information and called her back."

"Do you have the times of the calls?"

Elise laughed. "Are you sure you're charting her bio-rhythms or whatever, Randy? Or are you trying to catch her playing hooky?"

"It's her business," Randy said.

"In both senses of the word," Elsie said. "I don't want to get personal, Randy, but are you worried about her . . . about other women, maybe?"

"Elsie, I'm not like that. If she wants to run around with other women, that's up to her. No one can put reins on Marce."

"You got that right," Elsie said, laughing.

"So tell me more about the calls on September twenty-ninth. Do you write down the times in your log?"

Elsie was silent for a moment. "That's the day that statue was stolen from the museum, isn't it?"

"Yes," Randy said.

"I remember that day well because the police asked me about it, about Marce's whereabouts that day."

"What did you tell them?"

"What I told you. That she was here briefly in the morning then left to go to the museum for the arrival of the statue. Then she went home and worked there. She called several times, and I called her. The last contact I had with her that day was at six-fifteen when I called to give her the accounts receivable information she'd asked for."

"You called her at home?"

"That's right. You sound like the police, Randy. What's going on?"

"I need to get the actual work times," Randy said, "to see the patterns. So you called her at home at six-fifteen."

"Yes. She was still working on the accounts. The next time I spoke to her was the following morning when she called to cancel an appointment scheduled for eleven-fifteen. She told me the statue had been stolen and she had an emergency meeting with the Other Ways group that morning. She didn't come in until four when she had an appointment with a client. Is this helpful?"

"Yes," Randy said. "I'm also going to have her keep a record of what she eats when. What I'm doing may change her life." Randy laughed to herself as she said that.

"Do you want to know more about her work schedule? Early October?"

"This is enough for now," Randy said. "Thanks, Elsie. Remember, it's a surprise. Don't tell her, all right?"

"Do I get to see the chart when you're done?"

Randy told her as soon as it was finished she'd show it to her, which wasn't a lie. After they hung up Randy realized she was disappointed. From what Elsie had told her, Marce couldn't possibly have been the one who took the statue. Randy told herself to just let it go. But she couldn't.

"Call-forwarding," she said to Marinda. Marinda had awakened and come into the living room where Randy was still sitting with the phone in her lap. "Elsie could have talked to Marce via call-forwarding."

"What are you talking about, sweet one?" Marinda rubbed her fingers through her hair and stretched her arms, yawning.

"I just talked to Marce's secretary, Elsie. On September twenty-ninth, Marce talked by phone with Elise during the afternoon and evening, but Elsie's call to her at six-fifteen could have gone through call-forwarding. Marce could have had her calls forwarded to the museum shipping room that evening."

Marinda just looked at Randy.

"And Xavier could have been confused about the time. Marce supposedly got to Xavier's house that night at seven-thirty. That wouldn't have given her much time to move the statue and build the wall and everything. But it could have been later that she arrived at Xavier's. Marce told me Xavier pays very little attention to time when she's sculpting. She was probably working on her sculpture that night before Marce got there and had no idea what time Marce arrived."

"Maybe we should see if Elizabeth has any more news about Cassandra Lee," Marinda said, "before you go any farther with this. Maybe Lee has confessed by now."

"Find out if Jacqueline Dietrich has curly hair and wears heavy makeup," Randy said. "That's what I want to know."

Marinda looked a little annoyed. Randy knew Marinda thought she was trying to implicate Marce because of her anger towards her. "Would you still love me if I had curly hair and wore makeup?" Randy asked, trying to lighten things up.

"You do have curly hair," Marinda said.

"I mean on my head."

"I'd love you if you had curly hair on your elbows," she said.

"You're so silly." The thoughts about Marce wouldn't go away. "Marinda," Randy said, "would you like to take a drive with me to Pacific Heights?" She went to the dining room cabinet where she kept the phone book. Marinda followed her. "There are a lot of Dietrichs," Randy said. "Ah, but only one Jacqueline. And a James at the same address." She wrote the address down.

"I'm not interested," Marinda said. "This is your vendetta."

* * * * *

An hour later Randy pulled up in front of a stately house on Jefferson Street in Pacific Heights. Part of her was telling herself to stop this, leave Marce alone, forget this obsessive idea that she was Slick. She rang the doorbell.

"Yes?" The woman was an inch or two taller than Randy. She wore a turquoise blue smock top, pale lipstick, a ton of makeup and her brown hair was done in curls all over her head.

"Jacqueline Dietrich?"

"Yes."

"I'm doing a survey," Randy said. She held a clipboard against her arm and a pen poised to write. "For *San Francisco Hygiene*. May I ask you a couple of health-related questions? The first one is whether you shampoo your hair first or last when you take a shower."

"I'm not interested," Jacqueline said, and she started closing the door.

"Sorry to have bothered you," Randy said.

She stopped at home to get her tape recorder and look up a number in the phone book. Then she drove to Marce's house. She knew her evidence was about as solid as the morning fog, but she felt compelled.

Marce was dressed in cutoff shorts and a wrinkled old T-shirt. She obviously wasn't expecting company. "Imagine my surprise," she said. She ushered Randy in. "I was just having a bite to eat. You're welcome to join me."

Randy followed her into her kitchen. Marce had a plate of mostociolli on the table and thick slices of Italian bread.

"No thanks," Randy said. "You go ahead."

"I intend to," Marce said, sitting and stabbing at the pasta with her fork.

Randy watched her chew. Neither of them spoke for a while.

"So what's on your mind? Don't tell me you just happened to be in the neighborhood."

"No," Randy said, looking intently at Marce. "I wanted to hear your story first, before I tell anyone else what I've learned."

Marce frowned. "What are you talking about?" She seemed mildly curious. "What did you learn?"

"That you are Slick."

Marce looked at Randy wide-eyed for a second then burst out laughing. "Oh, that's rich. Randy, sometimes you really are a stupid twit."

Randy didn't flinch. "You took Jacqueline Dietrich's driver's license. You made yourself up to look like her and went to Concord where you rented a U-Haul. You hid in the janitor's closet at the museum, cut the lock, moved the statue, built the false wall. I know all about it, Marce."

Marce shook her head sadly. "I feel sorry for you," she said. "You're worse than Meredith."

"You were seen leaving your house on September twenty-ninth at one-thirty in the afternoon wearing a wig and makeup."

"Is that so?" She shook her head disgustedly and kept eating.

Partly Randy thought she was in the middle of making a complete fool of herself. But another part of her was absolutely sure her suspicions were right. She persisted. "You had your calls forwarded to the museum storage room. I checked with the phone company.

Randy thought she saw something in Marce's face then, just a little momentary flash of fear. Then Marce smiled. "They don't give out that information," she said.

"Yes they do. You received a call at six-fifteen from

Elsie Stein that night. It was forwarded from your home phone to . . ." Randy reached into her pocket and pulled out a slip of paper, ". . . 625-0966 — the museum shipping room."

Marce wiped her mouth with a napkin. "That's ridiculous." She looked at Randy as if she were a fly speck. "What is this, some silly practical joke, Randy? If it is, it's dumb, not funny." She was still looking contemptuously at Randy, but there were tiny beads of perspiration on her upper lip.

"And on Halloween night you conveniently got lost in the crowd."

Marce took a drink of wine, half frowning and half smiling, keeping eye contact with Randy. She didn't say a word.

"The police will want you to explain the mysterious curly-headed woman who drove off in your car that day."

Silence.

"Can you explain her?"

"Randy, do you really believe this?"

Randy truly did not know if she did or not. "Yes," she said.

"No one borrowed my car."

"Jordan says differently," Randy snapped. "She saw someone come out of your house and drive off in your car that day. She thought it was a new lover of yours, but I know it was you."

"Disguised as Jacqueline Dietrich," Marce said. She laughed but it was not her usual laugh. There was a hollow ring.

"Yes."

"But, Randy, my dear, how would I have gotten Dietrich's driver's license? Broken into her house? They didn't find any broken windows as far as I've heard."

"You got the key from Sandy Gossett's house."

Marce's face fell perceptibly. She tried to cover it up,

267

grinning at Randy, but her eyes looked frightened. "If you really believed this silly nonsense," she said, "what would you do next? Try to blackmail the extortionist?" She pushed her plate away. The food was only half-eaten.

"I'm not sure what I'm going to do," Randy said.

Marce drummed her fingers on the table, staring at Randy. Then she folded her arms across her chest. "You're getting on my nerves," she said at last.

"I expect I am."

"Who else have you been talking to about this?"

"No one. Like I said, I wanted to talk with you first. I want to understand why you did it. Was it just the money? What about Jay? Would you have let her go to jail if she hadn't come up with an alibi? And what about Cassandra Lee?"

"If Cassandra Lee is innocent, she'll get off," Marce said. "The only evidence they have against her is that she had a key to the Dietrich house."

"Do the police know you had access to a key?"

Marce stared coldly at Randy. "The police know I was working that night."

"They haven't checked with Pacific Bell yet."

Randy had never seen Marce look so uncomfortable. Neither of them spoke for a good minute. Then Marce said, "That would be quite a bundle of cash to have."

Randy didn't respond.

"More than I'd need for myself."

Randy was beginning to feel as uncomfortable as she thought Marce was. *Is she admitting it? Or is she playing with me?* Marce was looking at Randy very intently. Randy still said nothing. She thought of the tape recorder running in her pack.

"What do you have in mind?" she asked at last.

Randy wasn't sure how to play it. She wasn't sure *what* she had in mind. *Do I intend to turn her in,* she asked herself. Would I let her get away with it if she gave the money back? Would I let her pay me off? She knew the last option was out of the question, but maybe she shouldn't let Marce know that. Maybe I should get her to completely incriminate herself, she thought.

"We could have a new contract," Randy said, "a partnership of sorts. Fifty-fifty, and a conspiracy of silence."

"Fifty-fifth, huh? Greedy girl."

"I think that's fair."

"You could get in trouble for this, Randy."

"I don't think so. Who'd talk?"

Marce smiled. "You're sure you haven't? No one else knows your silly story about me and the curly wig?"

"Not yet."

Marce stood and walked out of the kitchen. Randy followed her. She went to her office, to her desk, took a notepad and began to write. "If I really were the extortionist," she said, "I'd give you ten percent."

Randy waited while she finished writing. Marce pushed the paper over to her and Randy read it aloud. "*November 8, 1992. I, Randy Van Fleet, of 2306 Sanchez Street, San Francisco, California, in exchange for the sum of $40,000 paid to me this day, do hereby agree to refrain from communicating with anyone other than Marce Flasch about my suspicions regarding the activities and whereabouts of Marce Flasch on September 29, 1992.*"

"Paragraph two," Randy said. "*I, Marce Flasch of 832 20th Street, San Francisco, California, agree to pay $40,000 to Randy Van Fleet in consideration of her silence regarding her suspicions about my activities and whereabouts on September 29, 1992.*"

Randy looked at her.

"Shall I type it up for us to sign?" Marce asked.

Randy still wasn't sure if Marce was playing with her or not. "A hundred seventy five thousand for me," she said.

269

Marce glared at her. "You little bitch." She kept her eyes locked on Randy. Randy couldn't quite read the expression. "I underestimated you, kiddo."

Randy shrugged.

"I'll give you a third," Marce said. "Rounded off that's a hundred thirty-three thousand dollars. You realize that if I really am the extortionist, by signing this you will be guilty of a number of crimes — blackmail in particular."

"I don't imagine you'd turn me in," Randy said.

"That's right." Marce rolled a sheet of paper into her typewriter and began to type.

Randy's mind was racing. She still didn't know what to believe. Would Marce burst out laughing any minute and tell her the curly-headed woman in her car was her cousin from Pasadena? She finished typing, then laid the sheet in front of Randy. It looked very formal. Randy read it slowly, then signed it at the bottom over her typed name, and gave it back to Marce.

Marce signed it. "Go wait in the living room," she said.

Randy went and sat on the sofa, the one that opened into a bed, the one where she and Marce had made love many times. In about ten minutes, Marce returned, carrying a Safeway grocery bag. She plopped it in Randy's lap. It was full of piles of cash, held together in packets with rubber bands.

Randy was flabbergasted. On some level she had thought it just couldn't be true. Marce couldn't be Slick. Her heart was pounding. She was truly astounded despite her suspicions and detective work. "Why, Marce?" she said, staring dumbly at the money. "Why did you do it?"

"Count it," Marce said, "then sign the receipt."

Randy read the paper Marce put in front of her. It was a handwritten acknowledgement that on the eighth of November, 1992, Randy received from Marce Flasch, the sum of one-hundred thirty-three thousand dollars. Randy read the note aloud. She signed the note. "Why did you do it?" she repeated.

"You're looking at it," Marce said, gesturing to the sack of money. "I needed the money."

"The stock market?" Randy asked.

"No, a real estate deal. I bought a property a year ago — a very expensive property — that was supposed to triple in value when they built a new road adjacent to it. The road was never built and it's not going to be. I won't bore you with the details but I was left in a very uncomfortable financial position."

"I see," Randy said. She wasn't sure if she was feeling contempt or sympathy.

"You were clever, Randy, and greedy. What about *your* motives? Just the money, or was it primarily revenge? You did a lot of investigating. You certainly were determined." As she spoke Marce folded the receipt and put it in her pocket.

She thinks she's safe, Randy thought, and wondered what Marce would do if she knew about the tape recorder. Does she trust this transaction to keep me silent, she wondered. She decided Marce was playing the odds, figuring that if Randy told what she knew, an investigation would reveal enough evidence to convict Marce. Marce was gambling that Randy would prefer the money to getting Marce locked up. Randy didn't know if she was going to tell the police or not. "How long did you plan it?" she asked.

Marce was sitting on the sofa next to Randy. Randy had put the bag of money on the floor. Marce leaned back and looked at the ceiling. "You want to hear the story?" She didn't wait for an answer. "It was very spontaneous actually. The thought would never have crossed my mind, I'm sure, if I hadn't learned Jay Horne was in town and was about to depart for Canada in a big U-Haul truck."

271

"Sue told you that."

"That's right. After she did, I went home and thought for a solid half hour. That's how long I planned it."

"Did you figure Jay would be accused?"

"I hoped so. I made sure the U-Haul I rented was seen." Marce smiled. "But it was pure luck that Jay came back to San Francisco after I hid the statue."

"Oh, so you weren't responsible for Barbara's sister's car accident."

"Very funny," Marce said sarcastically. "She's recovering well, by the way, Barbara's sister. Having Jay in town just made it more fun for me."

"How far would you have let it go?" Randy asked. "Would you have let her go to jail if she had gone to trial and been convicted?"

Marce grinned. "I don't know. I doubted she'd get convicted though, but I enjoyed her squirming. Didn't you? And I got my money back from her. That worked out rather well for both of us."

"So you just decided to do it on the spur of the moment."

"I needed three hundred thousand dollars to bail myself out. It was a gamble I couldn't resist, getting the insurance money, getting Jay. I certainly didn't think you'd be the one to cause me any trouble."

"You do underestimate me," Randy said, thinking again of the tape recorder. She was calculating the time. She excused herself and went to the john, taking her pack along. She flipped the tape, then returned.

Marce seemed more than willing to tell Randy all about her escapade.

"The hardest part was the janitor's closet," she said. "When the security guard opened that door and checked the room, I had an idea of what an anxiety attack feels like. If the guard had lifted those overalls, it would have been goodbye Marce." She smiled. "After that it was gravy. The most fun was Marinda's wild goose chase up and down the hills. I also enjoyed everybody's speculations about who the thief was."

"Jess thought it was you," Randy said. "I should listen to her more. So you rented a U-Haul with Jacqueline Dietrich's license . . ."

"I knew she was in the hospital and I figured her husband would be at work. The first step was to get the key to Dietrich's house. Sandy wasn't home. I got the Dietrich key from her collection, went and had a duplicate made, then returned the original to Sandy's. That went smooth as pudding. My first gamble was that Jacqueline Dietrich hadn't taken her driver's license with her to the hospital. If she had, or if I hadn't been able to find it, I would have aborted the mission. But it was right there in her bedroom, in the dresser drawer. Once I had the license I went to a thrift shop on Mission Street and got the wig and the clothes, and a big maroon bag. Very tacky. I got the makeup at Walgreen's." Marce sneered disgustedly. "I hated being in drag," she said. "Next to the janitor's closet, that was the worst part."

Randy smiled. "I bet you looked lovely."

"I didn't look like me," Marce answered. "Obviously Jordan didn't recognize me. I told that woman to call first, damn her. She knows I don't like her just dropping in on me."

"I can see why," Randy said.

"So I got all dressed up and took my tools —"

"To cut the lock."

"Right, and to staple the plasterboard to the carton, and paint the wall. I made a couple of calls from the storage area and had Elise call me. Establishing my alibi just in case. So the phone company gives out that call-forwarding information, huh?"

Randy didn't say anything.

"I ought to sue."

273

"What did you do with the wig and stuff?"

"Dumped them somewhere between the museum and Marin. In a dumpster."

"And Jacqueline Dietrich's license? When did you return that?"

"Right after I got the U-Haul. Then I went to the museum."

"You didn't drive the U-Haul to Marin, I assume, after you moved the statue. Did you take it back to Concord that night?"

"No, the next day. I didn't want to be too late arriving at Xavier's. After I left the museum — that was about seven-thirty — I drove the truck to my car which I'd parked near the Powell Street BART Station. I left the truck there overnight. I drove my car to Xavier's, cleaning the slop off my face on the way. I stopped at a gas station to change my clothes."

Randy nodded. "And the business about the statue having to remain in San Francisco, what was that about?"

"To alleviate people's fears that Slick would melt it down, to increase the chances of getting the money. It worked," Marce said with a self-satisfied smile.

"The whole thing was clever, Marce, well-done, really, I'll give you that."

"I did a lot more work for my money than you did for yours," she said.

Then she told Randy about Halloween night. She'd written two notes for *Sammie* to give to Sue, she said, but apparently Redman had replaced them with a note of his own.

"I didn't know that," Randy said. "What did the original notes say?"

"I'll show them to you." She got up and left the room. It was obvious that Marce was enjoying bragging to Randy about her exploits. She returned a minute later with two sheets of paper. "I make copies of everything," she said. "Bad habit. I should destroy these."

Randy read the notes aloud. One was addressed to Sue, the other to *Turillo, Redman, Amagyne, or anyone else other than Sue.* The one to Sue said, *Sue: If it's now 9:00 Halloween night and you're alone and unwired, a happy ending is very near — the statue will be returned tomorrow, all of this will be history, and you will have played a major role. What's important, as you know, is getting the statue back — not the money, not catching me. So if anyone is with you, waiting outside, planning to follow you, hoping to see me or grab me, I suggest you persuade them to leave. If you are wired with a radio transmitter, Sue, I suggest you do not say a word to whoever is listening on the other end. If you do as I say, you'll soon see the golden statue — it really is quite beautiful — and enjoy the well-earned admiration of your friends. I hope to see you soon, Little Red Riding Hood. Be at the phone booth on Castro and 20th by 9:30. Wait for the phone to ring. When you answer it, say, "Hello, this is Little Red Riding Hood. Slick.*

"You were worried about being caught, huh?" Randy said, "and hoped this note would persuade Sue to tell people not to follow her."

Marce nodded. "As it turned out it didn't matter that Redman took the note."

Randy read the other note. "*If any of you is reading this,*" it said, "*and if I do not yet have the money, then be very careful. If I sense any chance of being caught, the game ends — I'm out of here for good, and so is the Winged Dancer. Be wise. Slick.*"

Randy put the note on the table on top of the other one. "I guess it didn't scare Redman," she said.

"Like I said, it didn't matter," Marce replied. "That huge crowd and everyone being in costume made getting the money a piece of cake."

275

"But now I've taken the frosting," Randy said.

"You took more than that, you bandit."

Randy glanced at the Safeway bag. She was ready to get out of there. She had a lot of thinking to do.

Before Marce let her go she made Randy reveal step by step how she had figured it out. Randy told her it was hearing that Jacqueline Dietrich's license was used to rent a U-Haul, and remembering that Marce had talked about Dietrich, and about Sandra Gossett. "That, combined with what Jordan had told me, got me suspicious," Randy said. "What clinched it was my visit to Jacqueline Dietrich's and seeing how she looked, and the information from the phone company." Randy didn't mention Elsie Stein.

Marce said they both would have been better off if they had never met each other, but then she changed her mind. "That's not true," she said. "It turned out very well for you, didn't it?"

It wasn't exactly on warm, friendly terms that Randy and Marce parted, but they were both coolly cordial when Randy took the grocery bag and they said goodbye.

# Chapter 32

It was 4:30 p.m. when Randy got home. Marinda had gone to say goodbye to Amagyne. She'd said she'd be back around six. The first thing Randy did was listen to the tape. It was all clearly audible.

She took the money out of the Safeway bag, piled it on her coffee table and sat there staring at it for a long time. She was having all kinds of thoughts, including figuring out how long it would take her to earn that much money as a research assistant. One hundred thirty-three thousand dollars. When she started thinking about whether it would be better to deposit it in various bank accounts or just keep the cash, she suddenly sprang into action.

She made two copies of the tape on her Sanyo tape deck, wrapped one of them in thick layers of brown paper and addressed it to her sister in Atlanta. She included a note. The other one she hid in the back of the top shelf in the pantry. Then she went and stared at the telephone.

Finally she picked it up.

Marce answered on the eighth ring. "I'm going to return the money to the insurance company," Randy said.

"Randy? What are you talking about? What money?"

"The money you gave me today."

"The money *I* gave you? What do you mean?"

"And I want you to return the rest of it. I won't say anything to anyone, but you have to give back the money, and we have to make sure they drop the charges against Cassandra Lee."

"You are talking in riddles, girl. Have you been drinking?"

"All right, all right," Randy said. "So you won't talk about it on the phone."

"Randy, what is this all about? Really, I don't get it. Are you okay? Do you want me to come over? I think I should."

"Yes, I think we should meet," Randy said, "but Marinda will be here any minute."

"I see. Well, then we'll have to make it another time, won't we?"

"There's something you should know, Marce. I tape-recorded our conversation today."

There was a long silence. "You shit."

"I've made several copies of the tape. I've mailed two of them."

"I see. You've turned into a real creep, Van Fleet."

"I hope you haven't spent any of the money," Randy said. "And you better work on a way to get Cassandra Lee off the hook. I'll talk to you later, Marce. Call me tomorrow at the lab."

Marce hung up.

Randy decided not to tell Marinda what had happened. She might think Marce should pay for her crime and that returning the money wasn't enough. Randy was sure a lot of people would think that, but despite what Marce had done, Randy did not want to be instrumental in getting her imprisoned.

When Marinda arrived, Randy evaded her questions about how her investigation had gone. Instead she got Marinda to tell abut her visit with Amagyne, who was leaving the next day for Colorado. Doralee, one of the Kwo-amjamites, was going with her. Later Marinda and Randy cuddled up and watched a movie on TV.

The next day, Randy talked to her boss. Dr. Cartwright told her a two-month leave of absence was impossible, because of university policy, and also because she couldn't manage without Randy for that long.

Randy said she understood but that, as of today, she was giving her two weeks notice. Dr. Cartwright said she hated to see Randy go and Randy had no doubt that she meant it. She was wondering about the possibility of beginning a new career as a graphic artist when Marce called.

They arranged to meet that night at a restaurant. Marce had wanted Randy to come to her place, but Randy vetoed that. She knew Marce was angry and frightened and maybe even a bit desperate. She didn't want to risk being alone with her.

* * * * *

Marce was cheerful and talkative when she first arrived at the Pacific Cafe, a restaurant on the Wharf where she and Randy had eaten together several times before. She ordered a big meal, then launched into an anecdote about one of her clients, the *low ball king*, she called him. The story was funny and Randy realized she was enjoying being with Marce.

"So," Marce said, after the food arrived, "what's this business about money that you wanted to talk with me about? Do you need a loan?" She chuckled.

"I'm not taping this conversation, Marce," Randy said, "although I did bring my tape recorder along." She pulled it out of her pack. "I want you to listen to this, just in case you think I was kidding."

She set the recorder on the table, pushed the *play* button, and handed Marce the earphone. Marce listened for a minute or so then took the cassette out of the recorder and put it in her pocket.

"I told you I made copies," Randy said.

"Leave the tape recorder on the table where I can see it," Marce said. "Come to think of it, let me see your pack. For all I know you may have another recorder hidden away."

"I don't."

She gestured for Randy to give her her pack. Randy handed it across the table and Marce looked through it then gave it back.

She cut into her slice of beef. "Okay," she said. "Go ahead, I'm listening."

"Like I told you on the phone," Randy began, "I want you to return the money. You can send it anonymously with a note saying it's the ransom money from the Winged Dancer kidnapping, and also saying something that would clear Cassandra Lee."

Marce took a forkful of potatoes au gratin. "And your cut?" she asked. "What happens to that?"

"That will be included," Randy said.

"You feeling sorry for Prudential?" Marce asked.

Randy took a bite of her crab salad. "You can't keep the money, Marce. What you did sucks."

Marce smiled at her. "You're so law-abiding, Randy. A pillar of the community."

Randy took a deep breath. "If that were true I would have sent a copy of the tape to Detective Turillo."

Marce looked at her. "Who did you sent copies to?"

Randy shook her head.

"Secret, huh?" Marce drank from her water glass. "Let's think this through, Randy. You seem not to hate me enough to want me locked up . . ."

"I don't hate you," Randy said.

"I'm glad to hear that. But you think I'm a bad girl, that what I did was naughty, and I have to atone for my sins."

"Those aren't the words I'd choose," Randy said, "but something like that. You have no right to the money."

"You're concerned about the insurance company."

"What you did was wrong. It has nothing to do with the insurance company, per se."

"Ah, it's the ethics, then, the principle."

"That's right. In addition to conning Prudential out of that money, you put a lot of people through a great deal of anguish. Don't you see that? Don't you feel any guilt about this?"

"The way I see it, a lot of people had a great time," Marce said. "I sparked up their lives. Gave them an adventure. Have you talked to Sue lately? She hasn't had so much fun in years."

"That's not the point," Randy said.

"And the statue was there for the conference, all shiny and in perfect condition. And now, I hear, even the Indian Museum is going to be able to display it. All's well that ends well, Randy. The only unhappy people are the insurance executives who will write off a relatively minor loss, and Cassandra Lee, but we'll take care of that."

"I won't try to get you to see it my way," Randy said. "That doesn't matter." She watched Marce put a big piece of pink meat into her mouth. "I want you to package up the money and we'll send it to Frank Redman at his office downtown. I have the address. Have you thought of something to say that will prove Cassandra Lee wasn't the extortionist?"

Marce didn't respond. She looked a little haggard, Randy realized. She was sure this wasn't easy for her. "You're to send a copy of the letter to the president of the insurance company," Randy said, "and a copy to Turillo. I'll help you do all this, Marce. And we'll go to the post office together. And I'll want to be present for the packaging of the bills."

"To count them."

Randy didn't answer.

"I can't imagine why you don't trust me, Randy," Marce said. "All right, listen to this." She laid her fork on her plate. "Your plan is interesting but I have a better suggestion. Why don't you and I gather some information on the Prudential Insurance Company. We can look over their profit and loss statements for the past few years. Maybe we can even find out what the top executives are pulling in annually. Then we talk to some people who made claims and see how many of them were gypped on some technicality. After that we can decide if we really want to return this money to Prudential or if we can think of something better to do with it. What do you say?"

"I told you I'm not concerned about the insurance company."

"I'm sure that the hundred thirty-three thousand dollars would help you and Marinda get a nice start on your new life together. That seems like a much wiser use of it than giving it to a rip-off organization that it will make very little difference to anyway."

282

Randy shook her head. "No," she said, "the money's not mine to use. And it's not yours."

"We could keep it for a few years," Marce tried. "Invest it and then send Prudential the principle after we've made a little profit."

"No."

"Give yourself a few months to think about it, Randy. Let's talk again when you get back from South America."

Randy shook her head.

Neither of them said anything for about half a minute, then Marce said, "I'm afraid I can't agree to send the money to the insurance company." She picked up her fork again. "It's out of the question, Randy."

What gall, Randy thought. "Marce, you're not really in a position to make that decision."

Marce took a bite of food. "You blackmailed me for a hundred thirty-three thousand dollars yesterday," she said, "and today you tried to get another fifty thousand out of me. I think I could make that sound convincing. If they get me, Randy, they get you."

Randy stared at her, taken aback by this sudden twist. Could I actually be made to look as guilty as she, Randy wondered. She thought of that stupid paper she'd signed, trading her silence for the money. But that was just to get her to admit she was the extortionist. They'd understand that, wouldn't they? They'd believe me. She was feeling a little sick to her stomach. She'd also signed the receipt for the money, she remembered. Shit. And the tape she had would just reinforce Marce's story. Of course she would insist that she had tried to get Marce to give the money back; but Marce would insist she'd tried to blackmail her for more. Who would be believed?

"I don't think you want me to go to jail, Randy, but even more, I don't think you want to be locked up yourself. Am I right? You see, you did blackmail me."

"That wasn't blackmail. It was your idea to give me money. I just went along to get you to confess, to get your confession on tape."

"Calm down, Randy. We'll work this out."

Damn, she makes me mad, Randy thought.

"I think the most sensible way is to just leave it as it is," Marce said. "You have a lot of money and I have a lot of money. No one's really hurt and no one's the wiser. You keep your mouth shut and I keep mine shut. And we live happily ever after. The end."

"If I went to Turillo right now with the tape and the hundred thirty-three thousand, he'd believe me," Randy said.

"Maybe."

"What motive would I have for blackmailing you successfully and then turning the money in?"

"I don't know," Marce said. She seemed very calm now, like she had the upper hand.

"I sent the tapes to people," Randy said. "That proves I wasn't blackmailing you."

"Does it? Maybe it just proves that you were afraid of me."

"I told Marinda I suspected you," Randy said.

"Your lover."

"They'd believe her."

"Maybe."

"You cunt."

Marce smiled.

"You're so damn sure of yourself."

"It's you I'm sure of, Randy. I'm sure you don't want me to go to jail. Being here now and trying to get me to return the money to the insurance company proves that, but I also know your views on prisons and punishments. In addition I'm sure you don't want to risk being seen as a blackmailer. And I know you're a sensible person, Randy. It's you I'm sure of, my friend."

"Cocksure," Randy said.

Marce snickered. "The rooster kind or the prick kind?"

"We can't keep the money," Randy said. "It's impossible."

"Stretch your borders, Randy. Make room for the new and amazingly possible. You have your cut, I have mine. Shall we talk of other things? How long will you be staying in Marigua?"

Randy's mind was racing. What an unexpected turn this had taken. She had thought it would be easy. She'd tell Marce what she had to do and Marce would do it. Shit. Marce was turning everything upside down, she thought. Marce was right about Randy's feelings about imprisonment. It would take a lot to get her to turn anyone over to the criminal justice system, especially a sister, and a friend, of sorts. Conning money away from a rich capitalist corporation wasn't enough and Marce knew it. Murder or rape would be another story.

"It's just money," Marce said.

She's reading my mind, damn her, Randy thought. "I'll tell everyone else that you did it," she said. "Everyone but the cops. Everyone will reject you."

Marce laughed.

"You'll be ostracized."

She stuck her lower lip out in a pout.

"Marce, I'm not going to let you keep that money."

Marce gave Randy a plaintive look, obviously fake. "What about my money troubles?" she said. "I told you I'm in a bind."

"That's not my problem," Randy said.

"I think at this point our problems are intermingled," Marce said. She had finished her prime rib and was looking at the remains of Randy's crab.

"You can't have it," Randy said.

Marce laughed. "What can't I have, the money, or your crab salad?"

"Neither."

"Let's make a deal," she said. "I won't keep the money if you give me that salad. You're not eating it anyway."

"What are you talking about?"

"You haven't touched it in the last five minutes. You have that lost-my-appetite look."

"I mean about the money," Randy said angrily. God, she's a pain, she thought.

"I mean it. If you give me your crab, then I'll relinquish the two hundred and sixty-seven thousand."

Randy handed over the plate. Marce dug right in. "Okay, here's the deal," she said. "I know your conscience won't allow you to send me to jail. But I also know your conscience won't allow you to let me keep the money. So, we've got a conflict here. Mmm-m, this is delicious."

"Go on," Randy said.

"If I simply keep the money, then your need not to let that happen might someday grow strong enough to overcome your need not to be instrumental in my incarceration. I don't want to live with that hanging over me."

"Good," Randy said, "Then —"

"Yes, I know, your first choice would be for me to give the money to the insurance company. But I reject that, Randy. You can't have your first choice. Giving the money back would be no fun at all in my view. So what's your second choice?"

"I don't know," Randy said. "What do you mean?"

"Come on, Randy. Let's deal. You're holding plenty of cards. Get with it. I'm not going to return the money to the insurance company, but I'm not going to keep it either, and you're not going to keep your share. Your conscience wouldn't allow it. So . . .?"

"So we'll give it to the Red Cross or something?"

"Fine. Is that your choice?"

"No," Randy said.

"You want to think about it some more?"

"You're confusing me. Are you being serious, Marce? You're definitely willing to give up the money, is that what you're saying?"

"Randy, I spelled it out for you. What's wrong up there?" She tapped Randy's temple. "I can't keep the money. Don't you see? I don't trust your conscience."

Randy was getting a headache. "This isn't as much fun as I thought it would be."

Marce laughed heartily. She signaled the waiter to bring the check. "Think about it," she said. "Then give me a call." She took some bills from her wallet and laid them on the table. "I've got to leave you now, Randy. I have a date. Ta ta."

Sometimes I really don't like that woman, Randy thought.

# Chapter 33

The case against Cassandra Lee had grown weaker. Elizabeth was keeping Marinda and Randy posted. For one thing, Elizabeth told them, the police had learned that Lee was singularly unhandy with tools. The chances that she could have driven the forklift, moved the statue and built the false wall seemed very slim indeed.

Then Jacqueline Dietrich's husband helped shift Turillo to another track. During his wife's stay at the hospital, he told Turillo, she had kept her house key in the drawer of her bedside table. She was a friendly woman and had talked with a number of different nurses and aides while she was recuperating, about many things, he said, including the fact that the Winged Dancer was coming to San Francisco. She had even shown several of them a newspaper article about the statue. "It's priceless," she had said.

One of the hospital employees could have taken the key, Jacqueline's husband suggested. He or she could have made a copy of it then returned it to the drawer with no one the wiser. The police obviously agreed this was possible, Elizabeth said, since they began questioning all the nurses and aides and orderlies who might have had access to the keys.

As it turned out, though, Cassandra Lee ultimately cleared herself. One week after being charged with the crime, she remembered that she had visited with a couple of neighbors on September twenty-ninth, the day of the theft. They had been together between five and six o'clock. The neighbors verified the story. Cassandra Lee was in the clear.

"Turillo's extremely frustrated," Elizabeth said, "but he's not giving up. He's going after the hospital cleaning crew now, hooking them all up to his lie detectors. I wonder if we'll ever find out who did it."

"Probably not," Randy said. "The perfect crime."

Marce was in the process of *laundering* the money. She seemed to know exactly how to do it. It would take five or six days, she said, and when they turned the four-hundred thousand back into cash again the bills would not be the original ones.

"There's no way anyone will be able to trace the money to the extortion," she assured Randy. "The insurance company will have no claim on it."

Randy had agreed to let Marce handle the money laundering but only if she would agree to sign a paper acknowledging that she was the extortionist. Marce insisted that Randy sign a statement that she had blackmailed

Marce and that later both she and Marce felt guilty and so decided to give the money away. Obviously neither had much trust in the other. Randy was learning a lot about business through Marce. They worked on the documents together until they were both satisfied.

After they signed, Marce told Randy she'd found another solution to her financial woes. "Big real estate deal," she said. "A five-story office building. You don't have to worry about me anymore, I'm solvent again. I know that delights you."

"I'm overjoyed," Randy said.

"The other money's piling up too. By tomorrow noon I'll have it all. Come for lunch and we'll pack it up together then take a trip to the post office. The day after that, I'm off to Bermuda."

\* \* \* \* \*

The night before their ship was to sail to Marigua, Jess had a small going-away party for Randy and Marinda. Marinda and Jess were becoming friends, which pleased Randy greatly.

Much of the conversation at the party was about the four hundred thousand dollars that had been sent anonymously to the *Other Ways San Francisco Project* in care of Elizabeth. There was much speculation about who the donor was, but nobody came even close. Everyone was delighted, of course, that the San Francisco Project would now be able to buy some property and get started. Marce offered to be the broker, which made Randy laugh. That was almost as funny as Jay asking Marce to lend her some money for her pizza delivery business. Needless to say, Marinda would be centrally involved with the architectural design of the living space for the San Francisco Project.

She was also helping with the charter for the new community. Randy would do the graphics.

The day after the party, Jess drove Randy and Marinda to the dock. She gave Randy a big bouquet of flowers and told her to promise she'd be back. Randy promised.

The ship set sail. Marinda and Randy were sitting near the bow, holding hands. Randy was wearing the silver bracelet Marinda had given her and Marinda was wearing the rope and bead one from Randy.

Like everyone else, Marinda continued to wonder who Slick was, and it was on her mind as they sat there feeling the movement of the sea beneath them. "She surely is a friend of Other Ways," Marinda said. "No doubt about that. An altruist who took a very big risk for us."

Randy looked into her beautiful eyes. "You and I have a lot to talk about, my love."

"Oh?"

"But you probably won't believe me."

Marinda smiled. "You think you know who Slick is?"

"Can you keep a secret?"

"Of course."

"No one else can know," Randy said.

Marinda looked at her as if she wasn't sure whether to laugh or to prepare herself for a very interesting story.

"Promise?" Randy said. "No one else can know."

Still looking very skeptical, Marinda promised that the secret would just be between the two of them. Randy took her tape recorder from her pack and handed Marinda the earphone. She pushed the *play* button. As Marinda listened Randy watched her beautiful face and thought of all the days ahead for them.

Randy looked out at the sparkling Bay water. They had left the Golden Gate behind, the Winged Dancer tucked safely in the hold below, and were heading for the open sea. They were on their way, but they would return. The stairs of Randy's back porch needed paint, and she had a new career to pursue, and Marinda had a nirvana to build.

Marinda was shaking her beautiful head as she listened to the tape, her mouth slightly open. Soon Randy would kiss that mouth.

A few of the publications of
THE NAIAD PRESS, INC.
P.O. Box 10543 ● Tallahassee, Florida 32302
Phone (904) 539-5965
*Mail orders welcome. Please include 15% postage.*

STAYING POWER: LONG TERM LESBIAN COUPLES
by Susan E. Johnson. 352 pp. Joys of coupledom.
ISBN 0-941-483-75-4    $12.95

SLICK by Camarin Grae. 304 pp. Exotic, erotic adventure.
ISBN 0-941483-74-6    9.95

NINTH LIFE by Lauren Wright Douglas. 256 pp. A Caitlin
Reece mystery. 2nd in a series.    ISBN 0-941483-50-9    8.95

PLAYERS by Robbi Sommers. 192 pp. Sizzling, erotic novel.
ISBN 0-941483-73-8    8.95

MURDER AT RED ROOK RANCH by Dorothy Tell. 224 pp.
First Poppy Dillworth adventure.    ISBN 0-941483-80-0    8.95

LESBIAN SURVIVAL MANUAL by Rhonda Dicksion.
112 pp. Cartoons!    ISBN 0-941483-71-1    8.95

A ROOM FULL OF WOMEN by Elisabeth Nonas. 256 pp.
Contemporary Lesbian lives.    ISBN 0-941483-69-X    8.95

MURDER IS RELATIVE by Karen Saum. 256 pp. The first
Brigid Donovan mystery.    ISBN 0-941483-70-3    8.95

PRIORITIES by Lynda Lyons 288 pp. Science fiction with a
twist.    ISBN 0-941483-66-5    8.95

THEME FOR DIVERSE INSTRUMENTS by Jane Rule.
208 pp. Powerful romantic lesbian stories.    ISBN 0-941483-63-0    8.95

LESBIAN QUERIES by Hertz & Ertman. 112 pp. The questions
you were too embarrassed to ask.    ISBN 0-941483-67-3    8.95

CLUB 12 by Amanda Kyle Williams. 288 pp. Espionage thriller
featuring a lesbian agent!    ISBN 0-941483-64-9    8.95

DEATH DOWN UNDER by Claire McNab. 240 pp. 3rd Det.
Insp. Carol Ashton mystery.    ISBN 0-941483-39-8    8.95

MONTANA FEATHERS by Penny Hayes. 256 pp. Vivian and
Elizabeth find love in frontier Montana.    ISBN 0-941483-61-4    8.95

CHESAPEAKE PROJECT by Phyllis Horn. 304 pp. Jessie &
Meredith in perilous adventure.    ISBN 0-941483-58-4    8.95

LIFESTYLES by Jackie Calhoun. 224 pp. Contemporary Lesbian
lives and loves.    ISBN 0-941483-57-6    8.95

VIRAGO by Karen Marie Christa Minns. 208 pp. Darsen has
chosen Ginny.    ISBN 0-941483-56-8    8.95

WILDERNESS TREK by Dorothy Tell. 192 pp. Six women on
vacation learning "new" skills.　　ISBN 0-941483-60-6　　8.95

MURDER BY THE BOOK by Pat Welch. 256 pp. A Helen
Black Mystery. First in a series.　　ISBN 0-941483-59-2　　8.95

BERRIGAN by Vicki P. McConnell. 176 pp. Youthful Lesbian–
romantic, idealistic Berrigan.　　ISBN 0-941483-55-X　　8.95

LESBIANS IN GERMANY by Lillian Faderman & B. Eriksson.
128 pp. Fiction, poetry, essays.　　ISBN 0-941483-62-2　　8.95

THE BEVERLY MALIBU by Katherine V. Forrest. 288 pp. A
Kate Delafield Mystery. 3rd in a series.　　ISBN 0-941483-47-9　　16.95

THERE'S SOMETHING I'VE BEEN MEANING TO TELL
YOU Ed. by Loralee MacPike. 288 pp. Gay men and lesbians
coming out to their children.　　ISBN 0-941483-44-4　　9.95
　　　　　　　　　　　　　　ISBN 0-941483-54-1　　16.95

LIFTING BELLY by Gertrude Stein. Ed. by Rebecca Mark. 104
pp. Erotic poetry.　　ISBN 0-941483-51-7　　8.95
　　　　　　　　　　ISBN 0-941483-53-3　　14.95

ROSE PENSKI by Roz Perry. 192 pp. Adult lovers in a long-term
relationship.　　ISBN 0-941483-37-1　　8.95

AFTER THE FIRE by Jane Rule. 256 pp. Warm, human novel
by this incomparable author.　　ISBN 0-941483-45-2　　8.95

SUE SLATE, PRIVATE EYE by Lee Lynch. 176 pp. The gay
folk of Peacock Alley are all cats.　　ISBN 0-941483-52-5　　8.95

CHRIS by Randy Salem. 224 pp. Golden oldie. Handsome Chris
and her adventures.　　ISBN 0-941483-42-8　　8.95

THREE WOMEN by March Hastings. 232 pp. Golden oldie. A
triangle among wealthy sophisticates.　　ISBN 0-941483-43-6　　8.95

RICE AND BEANS by Valeria Taylor. 232 pp. Love and
romance on poverty row.　　ISBN 0-941483-41-X　　8.95

PLEASURES by Robbi Sommers. 204 pp. Unprecedented
eroticism.　　ISBN 0-941483-49-5　　8.95

EDGEWISE by Camarin Grae. 372 pp. Spellbinding
adventure.　　ISBN 0-941483-19-3　　9.95

FATAL REUNION by Claire McNab. 216 pp. 2nd Det. Inspec.
Carol Ashton mystery.　　ISBN 0-941483-40-1　　8.95

KEEP TO ME STRANGER by Sarah Aldridge. 372 pp. Romance
set in a department store dynasty.　　ISBN 0-941483-38-X　　9.95

HEARTSCAPE by Sue Gambill. 204 pp. American lesbian in
Portugal.　　ISBN 0-941483-33-9　　8.95

IN THE BLOOD by Lauren Wright Douglas. 252 pp. Lesbian
science fiction adventure fantasy　　ISBN 0-941483-22-3　　8.95

THE BEE'S KISS by Shirley Verel. 216 pp. Delicate, delicious
romance.                              ISBN 0-941483-36-3        8.95

RAGING MOTHER MOUNTAIN by Pat Emmerson. 264 pp.
Furosa Firechild's adventures in Wonderland. ISBN 0-941483-35-5   8.95

IN EVERY PORT by Karin Kallmaker. 228 pp. Jessica's sexy,
adventuresome travels.               ISBN 0-941483-37-7        8.95

OF LOVE AND GLORY by Evelyn Kennedy. 192 pp. Exciting
WWII romance.                        ISBN 0-941483-32-0        8.95

CLICKING STONES by Nancy Tyler Glenn. 288 pp. Love
transcending time.                   ISBN 0-941483-31-2        8.95

SURVIVING SISTERS by Gail Pass. 252 pp. Powerful love
story.                               ISBN 0-941483-16-9        8.95

SOUTH OF THE LINE by Catherine Ennis. 216 pp. Civil War
adventure.                           ISBN 0-941483-29-0        8.95

WOMAN PLUS WOMAN by Dolores Klaich. 300 pp. Supurb
Lesbian overview.                    ISBN 0-941483-28-2        9.95

SLOW DANCING AT MISS POLLY'S by Sheila Ortiz Taylor.
96 pp. Lesbian Poetry                ISBN 0-941483-30-4        7.95

DOUBLE DAUGHTER by Vicki P. McConnell. 216 pp. A Nyla
Wade Mystery, third in the series.   ISBN 0-941483-26-6        8.95

HEAVY GILT by Delores Klaich. 192 pp. Lesbian detective/
disappearing homophobes/upper class gay society.
                                     ISBN 0-941483-25-8        8.95

THE FINER GRAIN by Denise Ohio. 216 pp. Brilliant young
college lesbian novel.               ISBN 0-941483-11-8        8.95

THE AMAZON TRAIL by Lee Lynch. 216 pp. Life, travel & lore
of famous lesbian author.            ISBN 0-941483-27-4        8.95

HIGH CONTRAST by Jessie Lattimore. 264 pp. Women of the
Crystal Palace.                      ISBN 0-941483-17-7        8.95

OCTOBER OBSESSION by Meredith More. Josie's rich, secret
Lesbian life.                        ISBN 0-941483-18-5        8.95

LESBIAN CROSSROADS by Ruth Baetz. 276 pp. Contemporary
Lesbian lives.                       ISBN 0-941483-21-5        9.95

BEFORE STONEWALL: THE MAKING OF A GAY AND
LESBIAN COMMUNITY by Andrea Weiss & Greta Schiller.
96 pp., 25 illus.                    ISBN 0-941483-20-7        7.95

WE WALK THE BACK OF THE TIGER by Patricia A. Murphy.
192 pp. Romantic Lesbian novel/beginning women's movement.
                                     ISBN 0-941483-13-4        8.95

SUNDAY'S CHILD by Joyce Bright. 216 pp. Lesbian athletics, at
last the novel about sports.         ISBN 0-941483-12-6        8.95

OSTEN'S BAY by Zenobia N. Vole. 204 pp. Sizzling adventure
romance set on Bonaire.                ISBN 0-941483-15-0       8.95

LESSONS IN MURDER by Claire McNab. 216 pp. 1st Det. Inspec.
Carol Ashton mystery — erotic tension!.      ISBN 0-941483-14-2      8.95

YELLOWTHROAT by Penny Hayes. 240 pp. Margarita, bandit,
kidnaps Julia.                         ISBN 0-941483-10-X      8.95

SAPPHISTRY: THE BOOK OF LESBIAN SEXUALITY by
Pat Califia. 3d edition, revised. 208 pp.     ISBN 0-941483-24-X      8.95

CHERISHED LOVE by Evelyn Kennedy. 192 pp. Erotic
Lesbian love story.                    ISBN 0-941483-08-8      8.95

LAST SEPTEMBER by Helen R. Hull. 208 pp. Six stories & a
glorious novella.                      ISBN 0-941483-09-6      8.95

THE SECRET IN THE BIRD by Camarin Grae. 312 pp. Striking,
psychological suspense novel.          ISBN 0-941483-05-3      8.95

TO THE LIGHTNING by Catherine Ennis. 208 pp. Romantic
Lesbian 'Robinson Crusoe' adventure.   ISBN 0-941483-06-1      8.95

THE OTHER SIDE OF VENUS by Shirley Verel. 224 pp.
Luminous, romantic love story.         ISBN 0-941483-07-X      8.95

DREAMS AND SWORDS by Katherine V. Forrest. 192 pp.
Romantic, erotic, imaginative stories.      ISBN 0-941483-03-7      8.95

MEMORY BOARD by Jane Rule. 336 pp. Memorable novel
about an aging Lesbian couple.         ISBN 0-941483-02-9      9.95

THE ALWAYS ANONYMOUS BEAST by Lauren Wright
Douglas. 224 pp. A Caitlin Reece mystery. First in a series.
                                       ISBN 0-941483-04-5      8.95

SEARCHING FOR SPRING by Patricia A. Murphy. 224 pp.
Novel about the recovery of love.      ISBN 0-941483-00-2      8.95

DUSTY'S QUEEN OF HEARTS DINER by Lee Lynch. 240 pp.
Romantic blue-collar novel.            ISBN 0-941483-01-0      8.95

PARENTS MATTER by Ann Muller. 240 pp. Parents'
relationships with Lesbian daughters and gay sons.
                                       ISBN 0-930044-91-6      9.95

THE PEARLS by Shelley Smith. 176 pp. Passion and fun in
the Caribbean sun.                     ISBN 0-930044-93-2      7.95

MAGDALENA by Sarah Aldridge. 352 pp. Epic Lesbian novel
set on three continents.               ISBN 0-930044-99-1      8.95

THE BLACK AND WHITE OF IT by Ann Allen Shockley.
144 pp. Short stories.                 ISBN 0-930044-96-7      7.95

SAY JESUS AND COME TO ME by Ann Allen Shockley. 288
pp. Contemporary romance.              ISBN 0-930044-98-3      8.95

LOVING HER by Ann Allen Shockley. 192 pp. Romantic love
story.                                 ISBN 0-930044-97-5      7.95

MURDER AT THE NIGHTWOOD BAR by Katherine V. Forrest. 240 pp. A Kate Delafield mystery. Second in a series.
ISBN 0-930044-92-4    8.95

ZOE'S BOOK by Gail Pass. 224 pp. Passionate, obsessive love story.
ISBN 0-930044-95-9    7.95

WINGED DANCER by Camarin Grae. 228 pp. Erotic Lesbian adventure story.
ISBN 0-930044-88-6    8.95

PAZ by Camarin Grae. 336 pp. Romantic Lesbian adventurer with the power to change the world.
ISBN 0-930044-89-4    8.95

SOUL SNATCHER by Camarin Grae. 224 pp. A puzzle, an adventure, a mystery — Lesbian romance.
ISBN 0-930044-90-8    8.95

THE LOVE OF GOOD WOMEN by Isabel Miller. 224 pp. Long-awaited new novel by the author of the beloved *Patience and Sarah*.
ISBN 0-930044-81-9    8.95

THE HOUSE AT PELHAM FALLS by Brenda Weathers. 240 pp. Suspenseful Lesbian ghost story.
ISBN 0-930044-79-7    7.95

HOME IN YOUR HANDS by Lee Lynch. 240 pp. More stories from the author of *Old Dyke Tales*.
ISBN 0-930044-80-0    7.95

EACH HAND A MAP by Anita Skeen. 112 pp. Real-life poems that touch us all.
ISBN 0-930044-82-7    6.95

SURPLUS by Sylvia Stevenson. 342 pp. A classic early Lesbian novel.
ISBN 0-930044-78-9    7.95

PEMBROKE PARK by Michelle Martin. 256 pp. Derring-do and daring romance in Regency England.
ISBN 0-930044-77-0    7.95

THE LONG TRAIL by Penny Hayes. 248 pp. Vivid adventures of two women in love in the old west.
ISBN 0-930044-76-2    8.95

HORIZON OF THE HEART by Shelley Smith. 192 pp. Hot romance in summertime New England.
ISBN 0-930044-75-4    7.95

AN EMERGENCE OF GREEN by Katherine V. Forrest. 288 pp. Powerful novel of sexual discovery.
ISBN 0-930044-69-X    8.95

THE LESBIAN PERIODICALS INDEX edited by Claire Potter. 432 pp. Author & subject index.
ISBN 0-930044-74-6    29.95

DESERT OF THE HEART by Jane Rule. 224 pp. A classic; basis for the movie *Desert Hearts*.
ISBN 0-930044-73-8    8.95

SPRING FORWARD/FALL BACK by Sheila Ortiz Taylor. 288 pp. Literary novel of timeless love.
ISBN 0-930044-70-3    7.95

FOR KEEPS by Elisabeth Nonas. 144 pp. Contemporary novel about losing and finding love.
ISBN 0-930044-71-1    7.95

TORCHLIGHT TO VALHALLA by Gale Wilhelm. 128 pp. Classic novel by a great Lesbian writer.
ISBN 0-930044-68-1    7.95

LESBIAN NUNS: BREAKING SILENCE edited by Rosemary
Curb and Nancy Manahan. 432 pp. Unprecedented autobiographies
of religious life.                        ISBN 0-930044-62-2     9.95

THE SWASHBUCKLER by Lee Lynch. 288 pp. Colorful novel
set in Greenwich Village in the sixties.   ISBN 0-930044-66-5     8.95

MISFORTUNE'S FRIEND by Sarah Aldridge. 320 pp. Histori-
cal Lesbian novel set on two continents.   ISBN 0-930044-67-3     7.95

A STUDIO OF ONE'S OWN by Ann Stokes. Edited by
Dolores Klaich. 128 pp. Autobiography.     ISBN 0-930044-64-9     7.95

SEX VARIANT WOMEN IN LITERATURE by Jeannette
Howard Foster. 448 pp. Literary history.   ISBN 0-930044-65-7     8.95

A HOT-EYED MODERATE by Jane Rule. 252 pp. Hard-hitting
essays on gay life; writing; art.          ISBN 0-930044-57-6     7.95

INLAND PASSAGE AND OTHER STORIES by Jane Rule.
288 pp. Wide-ranging new collection.       ISBN 0-930044-56-8     7.95

WE TOO ARE DRIFTING by Gale Wilhelm. 128 pp. Timeless
Lesbian novel, a masterpiece.              ISBN 0-930044-61-4     6.95

AMATEUR CITY by Katherine V. Forrest. 224 pp. A Kate
Delafield mystery. First in a series.      ISBN 0-930044-55-X     8.95

THE SOPHIE HOROWITZ STORY by Sarah Schulman. 176
pp. Engaging novel of madcap intrigue.     ISBN 0-930044-54-1     7.95

THE BURNTON WIDOWS by Vickie P. McConnell. 272 pp. A
Nyla Wade mystery, second in the series.   ISBN 0-930044-52-5     7.95

OLD DYKE TALES by Lee Lynch. 224 pp. Extraordinary
stories of our diverse Lesbian lives.      ISBN 0-930044-51-7     8.95

DAUGHTERS OF A CORAL DAWN by Katherine V. Forrest.
240 pp. Novel set in a Lesbian new world.  ISBN 0-930044-50-9     8.95

THE PRICE OF SALT by Claire Morgan. 288 pp. A milestone
novel, a beloved classic.                  ISBN 0-930044-49-5     8.95

AGAINST THE SEASON by Jane Rule. 224 pp. Luminous,
complex novel of interrelationships.       ISBN 0-930044-48-7     8.95

LOVERS IN THE PRESENT AFTERNOON by Kathleen
Fleming. 288 pp. A novel about recovery and growth.
                                           ISBN 0-930044-46-0     8.95

TOOTHPICK HOUSE by Lee Lynch. 264 pp. Love between
two Lesbians of different classes.         ISBN 0-930044-45-2     7.95


These are just a few of the many Naiad Press titles — we are the oldest and
largest lesbian/feminist publishing company in the world. Please request a
complete catalog. We offer personal service; we encourage and welcome
direct mail orders from individuals who have limited access to bookstores
carrying our publications.